SINGAPORE BLING

GORD HUME

SINGAPORE BLING

GORD HUME

A Samantha and the Sheriff Adventure

ST. PETERSBURG
PRESS

ST. PETERSBURG

——— PRESS

First Edition Copyright © 2020
Burnstown Publishing House
Burnstown, Ontario, Canada

Paperback ISBN: 978-1-77257-274-2
eBook ISBN: 978-1-77257-275-9

Revised Edition Copyright ©2023
Published by St. Petersburg Press
St. Petersburg, FL
www.stpetersburgpress.com

Composition by St. Petersburg Press and Isa Crosta
Cover and Interior design by W.D. Clements
The cover art is a compilation of works created by various artists who are generous to license for free usage. Images and characters used are found on vectorcharacters.com, freepik.com, all-free-download.com, www.vecteezy.com. and stock.adobe.com
Paperback ISBN: 978-1-940300-83-2

Prologue

"AND THAT'S WHAT makes you such an astute investor," Mitch O'Reilly concluded.

The lies flowed easily. He'd had two decades of practice.

"You understand the global money market is changing. The old ways of investing just don't work anymore. The future is global crypto-currencies. That's why this is such a remarkable opportunity for you," he concluded with an oily grin.

As the mark hesitated, Shannon Thorpe leaned forward, offering a generous display of deep, creamy cleavage. The mark's eyes were suddenly transfixed. "You can get in on the ground floor of the WYRT," she added. "A smart man like you knows that Bitcoin went from being worth only a dollar or two and shot up to $19,000 a coin. Huge returns." She breathed deeply. So did the mark as he wiped his suddenly moist brow.

"And *that's* your opportunity," chimed in O'Reilly smoothly as he stroked his little moustache. "The potential is there to make tremendous amounts of money with a modest investment today. This is only available for a few discerning investors. Why don't we put $75,000 in to our new fund?"

"That would be just wonderful for you," said Shannon breathily, channelling her inner Marilyn Monroe.

The mark swallowed deeply, stared once again at the wonders of her gaping blouse, and nodded.

"Excellent," said O'Reilly. "Now remember, this is an exclusive offering and it is private, so you won't hear any media buzz about it for several months. It is important that we keep this confidential. Okay?"

The mark nodded. Shannon breathed deeply again and was rewarded with a sloppy grin from the lonely sixty-eight-year-old. "You've made a wonderful decision," she smiled at him. "Gosh I like smart men who are so decisive." She leaned over just a bit more.

A few beads of sweat appeared on the man's forehead. Reluctantly he looked up from that enticing valley and finally reached for his check book.

O'Reilly swiftly slid the check into his briefcase and nodded thanks. It had taken a couple of sessions with the old fart, but Shannon's appearance had sealed the deal. That often happened with solitary older single men. She was hard to resist, with her chestnut hair, hazel eyes, and spectacular figure. She was a great closer.

"We'll be in touch with an email update from time to time," he assured the man as they gathered their things and rose from the couch. The view of the Detroit River from the high-rise condo was spectacular. Belle Isle seemed very close. "It will take a few months to put all this together because it is a global currency investment. But remember not to talk about it with other people, because we're keeping the opportunity so limited."

The old guy nodded, not really listening because Shannon had grabbed his arm and pressed it into the side of her bosom. He was transfixed by the sensation.

Shannon smiled at him as they left. "I really enjoyed meeting you," she said sweetly patting his upper arm as they drifted apart. "I hope we'll see each other soon."

It was enough to spring eternal hope in the old guy's fevered imagination.

In the car leaving the condo, Mitch grinned at his partner. "That pretty much finishes our $1.8 million target out of Michigan and Ohio."

"Good. Now let's get the hell out of town. I can't stand this cold weather." She shivered into the grey November day.

"Which do you want, Florida or Arizona?"

"Florida. There's a lot of sand but damn little ocean in Arizona," she replied tartly as she pulled the collar of her jacket around her throat.

He nodded. "We'll hit the road tomorrow. Figure out your next name. And find us a luxury condo by the beach as a base. Florida should be a good market for this great investment."

She snickered as she started the search on her tablet.

CHAPTER 1

"I, KIMBERLY DIANE SHARPE, do solemnly swear..." Samantha Summers sat in the audience, enthralled and beaming broadly as her friend swore the oath of office before taking her place as the newest member of the Port Manatee City Council.

It had been a fierce election battle. Samantha had managed the campaign, but it hadn't been until Kim destroyed her main opponent in the final debate that her election had become a reality. Lester Maddox, a relic of smoke-filled backroom party politics, had insulted Kim and her prosthetic foot, which she had lost during combat in the Middle East.

In the most memorable line in recent Florida political history, Kim had replied to his insult (that she "didn't have two legs to stand on") by telling him, "One leg is all I need to KICK. YOUR. ASS."

It swung the election.

Samantha had gleefully had bumper and windshield stickers printed with "KICK ASS" on them. They had flown out of campaign headquarters. Women voters had been universally outraged by Maddox. Kim's margin of victory was the largest in the region.

Samantha's attention refocused on the council chambers. Sonja Rodriguez was just finishing her oath of office as mayor. Ironically, it was District Court Judge Cynthia Green who administered the oath. She had presided over the recount after the vicious campaign that eventually saw Rodriguez elected mayor by a stunning five votes over the former deputy mayor.

The other members of the city council had laughingly nicknamed the mayor "Landslide Sonja."

The official ceremonies were complete. The mayor banged her gavel, welcomed the new council, thanked City Clerk Kathy James for organizing the ceremony, and declared the meeting adjourned for the reception that was to follow.

The invited audience buzzed quietly as they moved into the city hall atrium for the party. Samantha hung back, watching intently as Councillor Sharpe—she grinned to herself at Kim's new title—walked out with City Manager Roy Crawford.

It was known in the community that Kim and Roy were dating. Samantha had made a point of warning both of them about their new professional relationship that was now on display in the public forum.

They had both acknowledged the awkwardness that was possible.

Samantha didn't think either of them fully understood the dangers. She shrugged as she picked up her purse. That was for another day. Today was for celebrating.

Chapter 2

"Antoinette."

"What?"

"My new name. I want to be Antoinette. Toni for short."

"You're not a Tony."

"T O N I, you idiot. And why can't I be Antoinette?"

"It's too memorable. Nobody in the US is named 'Antoinette'."

She sighed loudly as she stared him down. He refused to look at her as he drove the rental car through the streets of Chicago. They had flown from Detroit on a United shuttle the day before. Now they were about to meet with the guy who would provide them with new identities.

He peered at a street sign that was hanging askew. The neighborhood was far from the Magnificent Mile of pricey stores and residences that flaunted Lake Michigan.

"You sure about this guy?"

"Used him before. Pricey but good. Keeps his mouth shut."

"I need to get my hair changed before the pictures."

"What this time?"

"Blonde, of course. It is Florida. Everybody's blonde. Maybe a nice, tawny ash-colored shade—hey, that's it!"

"Tawny? For God's sake..."

"No. You are so stupid. Ashley. Ashley, um, Monroe."

He grunted as he turned the big car down a back alley. "Yeah. That'll do." He paused. "Ashley. Sounds sophisticated. I like it."

He stopped the car at an unmarked, tightly closed heavy metal door. They got out. High above, a security camera studied them. At last the door squealed open.

CHAPTER 3

"FIVE MORE!" DEMANDED the physical therapist.

Sheriff LeRoy Perkins grunted in protest, but he did the five extra lat pulls the P. T. required of him. She was a killer, he thought to himself. Cute as hell, but then that mean streak in her took over. No sympathy for a poor wounded sheriff who had been shot in the line of duty by a Central American assassin.

His shoulder screamed as he finished the exercise. He was sweating. "Suck it up!" She was unrelenting in their daily series of exercises to rehab and strengthen his shoulder, neck, and upper arm.

"What happened to sympathy and warmth?" he groaned as he sat recovering. He gulped from a bottle of orange Gatorade.

"Sympathy left town crying, and I kicked Warmth's ass until he sobbed like a little baby," she told him as she glowered at her watch. "Break time is over. Time to stretch it out and massage the scar tissue area. Try not to squeal too much this time. You're scaring the other patients."

CHAPTER 4

HE LOOKED EXHAUSTED when Samantha picked him up at the hospital.

"Physio was a little rough on me today," was all he said.

She knew better than to question him further. Perk was the toughest man she'd ever known. If the therapist was pushing him so hard, it had to be for his own good. The faster the recovery, the sooner he could get back to full service as the county sheriff.

Rosie had grudgingly jumped into the back seat when Perkins opened the car door, and was now busy licking his left ear. He laughed and gave her a good petting. Rosie always assumed that the front right seat was her throne in any vehicle. It was good to be the queen.

He looked out his window as Samantha drove back to her condo at Sapphire Blue. As always, the action on the street fascinated him. Scared him sometimes. People could be really, really stupid.

The driver in the big grey pickup roared by in the far right lane and then cut over three lanes to the left turn lane, leaving angry drivers horn-blowing behind. His turn signal never blinked once.

A couple wandered down the sidewalk holding each other up. Perk was betting on marijuana affecting their better judgment as they teetered along.

A large dog, or maybe a small horse, was taking its owner for a walk. There was no doubt which of them was in charge.

A couple of tourist couples stood in the bright sunshine of their motel parking lot. The men were drinking beer out of cans. Their faces, arms and shoulders were already pink turning to angry red. They would have a very uncomfortable couple of days ahead. There is only so much aloe in the world.

A man walked down the street talking to himself. It used to be a pretty safe bet that a person like this was sort of crazy, thought the sheriff. Now, maybe he was on a Bluetooth business call to Thailand closing a million-dollar deal.

He looked at the sign in a restaurant and bar that promoted "Monkey Mondays." If you brought in a live monkey on a Monday, you got free drinks. "Just wait until the monkey gets drunk, goes crazy, and attacks some innocent family," he muttered.

Samantha glanced over at him, concern etched on her face. Monkeys? Was the physiotherapy somehow affecting his cognitive powers?

She pulled up beside the Sapphire Blue guardhouse, was waved through, and parked in her allotted space. Rosie bounded out of the car as soon as the door was open and raced for the elevator. Perk followed more slowly. Samantha resisted the impulse to offer an arm to assist him. His pride was important to him, and he wasn't one to complain about pain and suffering. Still, she knew he was hurting.

"I see you haven't taught her how to push the elevator buttons yet," he joked as they found Rosie standing impatiently at the elevator doors.

"Scared to," she laughed. "We'd never see her except for meals."

The elevator door opened. Two small kids tumbled out and shrieked in delight at Rosie. They immediately began petting her as their mother stood there.

"She's fine with kids," Perk reassured her.

"Mommy. Mommy! Can we have a puppy? Can we? Puhleeezze."

Samantha looked at the weary mother with sympathy. Good luck on that argument, she thought as she pushed Perk onto the elevator and grabbed Rosie's leash. Perk was looking very tired.

A moment later she opened the door to 606 and moved her entourage inside. She sat Perkins on the lanai, got him a cold IPA, gave Rosie a cookie, and finally poured herself a large glass of Pinot Noir.

Chapter 5

THE SHRILL SCREAM of Perkins' phone brought Samantha jerking upright as her heart pounded. She heard him groaning in pain as he reached with his bad arm to grab his cell phone. She looked at the bedside clock: 2:08 a.m.

Nothing good happens at 2:08 a.m.

Perkins listened intently and finally muttered, "Okay. I'll be right there," and punched the OFF button.

"Sorry. A family emergency. Twin sisters, four years old, have been abducted. We might need to issue an Amber Alert. The mother is hysterical. But apparently the abductor is holed up in a trailer and says she'll only negotiate with me. Not entirely sure where the kids are. It could get bad." He swung out of bed, bit back a groan and headed for the bathroom.

"Do you want coffee?"

"No, thanks. I'll get some at the scene. You stay in bed." He closed the bathroom door. She could hear water running, then listened as he fumbled his way into a shirt. He was very sensitive about performing normal functions without help, but she knew he was struggling.

Samantha got out of bed, heart still pounding just a bit from the early morning eruption. She shrugged into a robe and went out to the kitchen.

Rosie gave her a sleepy-eyed look from her doggy bed. She didn't look very happy about having her sleep disturbed either. However, she got up in case snacks were being offered, or food was dropped on the floor. That made it Rosie's; Rosie was pretty sure there was a federal law somewhere that said that.

"It's your daddy's work," Samantha explained softly. Rosie snuffled the floor hunting for cookies or dog treats. Nothing.

Perkins joined them a moment later, dressed in uniform and gun belt. "Sorry," he offered again. "The job." He shrugged, kissed her gently and headed out.

Two baby girls abducted, Samantha thought in dismay as she turned out the lights and went back to her bedroom. The mother must be frantic.

What a job the sheriff had.

It was difficult for her to get back to sleep.

<h1 style="text-align:center">Chapter 6</h1>

THE POLICE CRUISER was waiting in front of the lobby door as Perkins stepped out into the sultry night. A full moon shone down. *Naturally,* he thought as he climbed in. *Full moons always bring out the crazies.*

He gratefully sipped the hot coffee that Deputy Chad offered him.

"What's the situation?" he asked after a few restorative swallows.

"Two women in their early forties had a big domestic brawl. Twin-four-year-old daughters. Women are married to each other. One grabbed the kids and stormed out making threats and waving a knife. She's holed up in a trailer in the Palms Trailer Park. Kids are screaming. Other woman is hysterical."

Perkins grunted in dismay. Cops hate domestic violence situations. They are always ugly and often flare into ferocious outbursts. The kids get scared. And were usually scarred.

"We've surrounded the trailer," the Deputy continued. "Woman is screaming she'll hurt the kids and kill herself. Says she'll only talk to you." Chad paused as he adroitly pushed the SUV around some slower traffic and accelerated toward the trailer park. "I guess she knew your name from the Campanelli kidnapping of Samantha."

He glanced at his boss. Perkins had coolly shot the kidnapper who had abducted Samantha a few months earlier. It had gotten a lot of media play throughout the region.

Perkins grunted again. "We got a name?"

"Clarice is the mother. The, uh, other mother is DeShaundra. The twins are cute as hell. We've got a picture of them."

"Yeah." He sipped again. "Who's running the scene?"

"Captain Williams."

"That's a break," Perkins said quietly. Captain Willie Williams was a twenty-three-year veteran who had been in charge of the kidnapping scene after the sheriff had been shot. He had made the call to the sniper that took out the assassin. He was a pro. Cool under fire, well-trained and experienced.

"Sorry to drag you out," Williams said a moment later as the sheriff got out of the police vehicle. "How you feeling?"

"Not great, but I'll be okay," Perkins lied sincerely.

Williams studied him for a long moment. "Yeah," he finally said, disbelief dripping from his words.

They both turned to study the trailer. It was at one end of a row of double-wides. The park had seen better days.

"We got the next-door residents out safely, and they're in a city bus waiting," Williams reported. "So is the family behind the woman's trailer."

"What's going on?"

Williams sighed heavily. "Domestic. Big fight between the two parents. Kids trapped in the middle. Clarice grabs a butcher knife from the counter, takes the kids, threatens the other woman, and drives out here. Trailer used to be hers before the two women moved in together. Now she's locked inside threatening everybody. Kids are terrified. The other mother is back at their house. Screaming and crying. We've got a couple of officers holding her there. We don't want her here." He grimaced. "It is a mess and it could get a lot worse."

Perkins nodded. "Drugs? Alcohol?"

"Booze for sure. A lot. Maybe some weed."

"And a full moon."

Williams snorted. "Yeah. I've got a SWAT team in place, but we're afraid if we push in she'll do something to the kids or herself. She says she'll only talk to you. We tried a negotiator. Nothing."

Perkins dumped the dregs of his cooled coffee. "Any intelligence?"

"Both women work. Clarice is a hair stylist, DeShaundra a mani-pedi expert, whatever the hell that is."

Perkins smiled to himself. Williams was a big man, solid. Tough as a slab of granite. He doubted anybody had ever touched his nails but himself.

"Same salon?"

"Yeah. Over on St. Joseph. Seems to be a good business."

"Kid's names?"

"Latoya and Jillian."

Perkins took a deep breath. "You got any bright ideas, Willie?"

Williams also took a deep breath. "They've been a couple for seven years, married for five. Had the kids together. I think something sparked the fight, the booze accelerated it, and whatever blew it up."

The sheriff nodded. Sounded right. He took another deep breath. "Walk with me close to the trailer, Willie, then leave me. You got a vest on?"

"Always."

Perkins nodded to the other officers nearby. "Captain Williams and I are going to the front of the trailer. We'd both appreciate it if you wouldn't comment on how good our butts look in uniform...or shoot us."

The officers chuckled appreciatively as some of the tension broke.

Domestics were always unpredictable.

Slowly Perkins and Williams walked to the front of the trailer. They stopped about ten feet from the door.

"Clarice? Clarice? Sheriff Perkins here."

They could hear the kids crying. After a minute the light outside the steps came on. "That really you?"

"Yes, Clarice. I'm Sheriff Perkins. Would it be all right if I came in to talk?"

A pause. "Okay. No guns! No tricks!"

"Look out the window, Clarice. There. See? I'm taking out my gun very slowly and I'm going to give it to Captain Williams, here. Okay?"

Cautiously he unsnapped his service weapon, withdrew it by two fingers and made a show of giving it, barrel down, to the captain. Williams followed along by snapping open the gun and removing the magazine. He slowly put the ammunition in one hand and the gun in his other. Then he turned and walked away.

Perkins waited a long moment and then said, "May I come in now?"

The lock unsnapped. He swallowed in a suddenly dry throat and slowly stepped forward. He climbed the three grubby wooden steps. He knocked on the door, waited, and then slowly pushed it open.

The furniture was sparse. No interior decorator had ever been within a thousand yards of the mobile home. The color scheme ranged from puce to purple.

Clarice was a copper-toned, big-boned woman. She wore torn jean shorts and a once-white T-shirt. Tattoos flashed on her left shoulder and right thigh. The snake on her thigh appeared to climb into personal spaces where a gentleman would be ill-advised to peek.

Two sweet little girls were crying on the floor in the far corner. They were wearing matching cartoon pyjamas. Perkins didn't recognize the characters.

Clarice was standing, swaying just a bit, and holding a big knife. Her eyes were red and puffy.

"Hi. I'm Sheriff Perkins." He deliberately turned to the girls. "Hi. You must be Jillian, and you must be Latoya." He smiled at them. "I'm LeRoy." The crying slowed as the twins studied the man standing on the steps of their trailer. "Are you both okay?"

Two little heads finally nodded. The kids both looked exhausted. Clarice glanced over at them, then back at Perkins. Nobody seemed very sure what to do next.

Perkins finally broke the silence. He looked at the woman carefully. She wore an elaborate hairstyle that Perkins could not identify if his life depended on it...and, when he thought about it, maybe it did.

"Clarice. May I call you Clarice?" She nodded. "May I come in and sit down? I got shot in the line of duty recently, and my body is sort of hurting a lot."

The little girls sucked in their breath at the statement. They already knew about people getting shot.

Clarice's eyes flared. Pretty much everyone in the city had heard about the assassination attempt on their sheriff. She nodded. Gratefully Perkins climbed in and sat on a kitchen chair that was already in the narrow living room area.

Slowly he began to build a connection. "I'm sort of thirsty," he began while looking at the twins. "Are you? Would you like some juice or water?"

Shyly both heads nodded. Perkins looks at Clarice. "Would it be alright if we all had a juice box?"

Clarice looked at him, then the twins. "Latoya honey, get a juice box for you and your sister." And then in a voice that surprised her, "And get one for the sheriff."

Cautiously the little girl in the stained pink PJs got up and went to the refrigerator. She pulled out three juice boxes and shyly handed one to Perkins.

He looked down. "Oh, grape. My favorite. Thank you." He looked at the box for a moment trying to figure out how to open the damn thing. There didn't seem to be a front lip or funnel or anything. He peeked at the two girls who were expertly ripping off the little straw and inserting it into a covered hole on top of the box. Well, you learn something new every full moon, he thought as he followed suit.

He drank. "Actually the stuff isn't all that bad," he murmured to himself as he raised his box in a toast to the kids. They had no idea what the gesture was all about, but both waved their boxes back at him. Clarice sort of smiled at the twins.

"So, Clarice, what's going on?"

It was like tapping the corner of a piece of glass and watching it shatter into a zillion pieces. The tension, booze and anger poured out of her as she began to sob into her hands. She dropped the knife on the floor, hung her head and cried.

Perkins very cautiously leaned over and kicked the knife out of reach. After a couple of minutes the twins came over. They each grabbed a leg and stood with their mother, snuffling in sympathy.

Perkins waited for the Niagara Falls to slow. It took a while.

"De...De...Shaundra...she...she...said..."Another eruption of tears. The kids were crying with their mother. Perkins pretty much wished he could be anywhere else on earth at that moment. Like most men, he was paralyzed by women crying.

Finally the story came out. It was short and nasty. "She...said...I HAD GOTTEN FAT!" More tears. More wailing. The twins were hugging their mom and bawling their little eyes out.

That was it? Perkins wondered. There had to be more. Wait until he told the entire SWAT team they were there because of some extra pieces of cake. He looked at her more carefully. Okay, and maybe some Rocky Road on the side.

"And...and...then I said her hair style was ugly! Well, it was! And then she said my nails were re—re—repulsive! And ... and..."

Somebody turned the Falls back on.

Perkins looked around the trailer. He didn't see any other weapons. The kids were upset but fine. And DeShaundra and Clarice obviously had some domestic issues to resolve.

He stood up and went to the door. "Captain Williams," he called out before he opened it.

"Sir!"

"Stand down the squad. We're coming out."

"Sir!" Perkins could hear the orders being given. He hadn't wanted any twitchy trigger fingers when he brought out the family.

He pushed open the door. A couple of officers approached. He motioned to keep their guns holstered. "Get Children's Services" he ordered quietly. One nodded and went back to the temporary HQ. He returned with a nice older woman. Perkins waved her up.

"Everybody is fine. Emotional, but fine. I think the kids can go back home. Clarice needs a night away, and we'll take care of that. Maybe you can be there in the morning with one of my family services officers when she goes back?"

The woman nodded and followed the sheriff into the trailer. She knelt down in front of the kids and started talking softly to them. Perkins helped Clarice up.

"We're going to take the kids back to DeShaundra," he told her. "You can spend the night with us and then go home tomorrow morning if that's what you and DeShaundra want." Clarice nodded as she dried her eyes.

"Okay, let's go for a ride." He took her by her left arm and escorted her down the narrow steps of the trailer. "Captain Williams!"

"Yes, sir," he said as he loomed up.

"Would you escort Clarice to our offices downtown for the rest of the evening? I think she and her wife would like to get together tomorrow morning. Perhaps you can hold off on the paperwork?"

Williams got it. "Yes, sir." He took the woman's other arm and they walked slowly to a waiting police vehicle. The Children's Services woman had wrapped the two kids in their jackets and was helping them down the steps and into a car. Perkins sent an officer with them as they headed back to their house to be reunited with their other mother.

The full moon was waning as Perkins and Williams stood and watched the SWAT team break down their equipment. The families that had been evacuated returned to their trailers.

"Could have been a lot worse, Willie."

"Yup. Could have had a lot of blood. Ruined lives. Kids hurt," responded the old pro. "You did good in there."

CHAPTER 7

"IT WAS THE mother," the sheriff reported back to Samantha later that morning. "The other mother," he clarified. "Same sex married couple. Surrogate twins. Big fight, the one woman grabbed a knife, scooped the kids and stormed out to her trailer."

Samantha listened intently. These were all new experiences for her after what she had increasingly realized had been a very secure, sheltered upbringing in NYC. As their relationship deepened, she was slowly comprehending what a dangerous job Perkins had.

"What was the fight about?"

Perkins paused. "Ah, let's just say domestic disagreements."

She waited for more but it wasn't coming. Something didn't add up, but she let it go.

"That's pretty common in these situations," he continued. She could hear him shuffling some paperwork as he talked to her.

"We also got reminded of something as a department—not to assume. Neither of the first two responding officers asked the sex of her partner. They just assumed. 'Makes an ass of you and me' when you assume."

She got it after a quick minute.

"Everybody okay?"

"Thankfully, yes. I don't think the mother…the other…well, the first party involved…will even file charges. Thank God they didn't have any guns in the house. That's when it gets really dangerous."

Samantha grunted. She hated guns and the violence that too often resulted.

"By the way, I want you to think about taking a course in self-defence. Now wait," he said quickly as she began to splutter, "it really is for your own safety. Sometimes people get in a dangerous situation. No fault of their own. But knowing something about how to look after yourself, that's not a bad thing."

She thought. Huh. He really cared about her. And her safety.

Her answer surprised him. "If you think so, okay. Set something up. I'll do it."

"Leave it with me. Thanks." He paused. "I've got to run. I've got another physio session today, and we're hosting Wayne Cooper for a seminar on fraud investigations."

"Who's that?"

"Wayne is just about the smartest guy on the state's payroll. He is supposed to be just a forensic accountant, but he's branched into all sorts of fraud investigations. The governor really likes him. So do I, even though he thinks he's the fifth member of KISS. I'm always grateful when he shows up without the full makeup and spiky shoulder pads."

Samantha laughed at the image.

"He's about five-six, and rather, uh, rotund. Brain like a steel trap. Oh, I'll probably take the guys out for a beer after his seminar. Can you drop Rosie off at my house? I'll go home from here."

"Uh, well, sure." Samantha paused. "It's just that I don't have a key to your house."

"Huh. Well, we'll have to do something about that. Just drop her off in the backyard. She's got her own doggy door, and the kids next door will make sure she's fed and okay."

Samantha contemplated that first sentence for a moment. 'Do something about that'? Maybe their relationship really was moving forward.

"I've got to run. See you later." He hung up.

"'Bye," she said softly to the dial tone.

Well. This was going to provide some interesting girl-talk with Kim and Samira, who was the third member of the Sams Club. Samantha. Samira. And Kim, who had designated herself "Sexy and Modest—SAM" when she'd invented this unusual group.

She'd better get in a fresh case of wine.

Chapter 8

"SO, HOW MUCH does fraud cost in the U. S. A. every year?" asked Deputy Chad.

Wayne Cooper fidgeted for a moment. He had a lot of nervous mannerisms to start with, and questions without answers were a problem for him.

"Nobody truly knows," he admitted finally. "My guess is somewhere between $300 billion and one trillion dollars a year. Depending on if you include Medicare/Medicaid fraud and some other stuff. A lot of fraud never gets reported," he acknowledged in frustration. "People are too embarrassed. Especially big corporations. I've seen an estimate that businesses lose between 2 and 5% of revenue each year due to various forms of fraud and theft."

There was an audible intake of breath from the assembled law enforcement officers. Fraud is BIG. Far bigger than any of them had realized.

"And of course in Florida, with the number of older people and snowbirds, we are particularly vulnerable. And every year the crooks get smarter. Look at this," he said as he beeped his PowerPoint clicker.

A picture of a line of ticket-holders in front of a museum appeared. Seniors were being gently herded into a couple of lines. Security guards were collecting cellphones in a large basket; everyone knew most museums no longer allowed flash photography because it causes degeneration of old paintings. Food trucks and ice cream carts were doing a nice business. A couple of tour buses were parked on a side street.

Silence in the room as the law enforcement officers studied the picture. It looked normal. They studied it more closely. Typical day at the museum, wasn't it?

"A nice little old lady happened to take this picture," Cooper finally explained. He hit the clicker again. "And she also took this one a couple of minutes later."

Same scene—except for the two security guards who were now running for a black van that had suddenly appeared on the side street. One was carrying the basket of cellphones.

"Son of a moose," exclaimed a deputy. "They weren't real security guards."

"That's right! They got away with 45 really nice cellphones from these seniors. All with pictures of their grand kids. Many with no passwords or security blocks on their banking apps. All of them with lots of personal data for the crooks to mine."

Cooper snorted in anger. "Everybody just formed the line because somebody in a cheap blue blazer with a tin badge told them to. Then they politely handed over their phones to a complete stranger. Identity theft."

The cops were shaking their own heads.

"It will take some of these nice old folks years to unravel their situation. If the crooks get lucky, they'll scam 'em for thousands. Drain a couple of bank accounts. Sell their personal data to a phishing company, or maybe to another scammer who will then claim they can return the phone to grandma for a 'finder's fee'. A double scam."

Cooper shook his head in frustration. "And if you think that's bad, imagine a tweener losing her phone. Life would pretty much be over for her! She'd do anything, pay anything, to get it back."

Silence in the room, although a few parents flashed knowing grins.

"Then we've got all the 'Romance Scams'. Lonely seniors are particularly susceptible. That's when some scammer, usually on social media or a dating website, pretends to offer companionship. Even love." He snorted. "Of course they then ask for money to travel to meet the person, or for a medical problem or some other emergency."

He blew out his cheeks in frustration as he continued. "The IRS scam happens every spring. The con men phone up seniors and tell them they owe money for their taxes and must pay immediately through a credit card to avoid big penalties. These tend to be very law-abiding citizens…a lot of them get scared and pay up. The variation on that is claiming to be a foreign police official and Granny's favorite grand-child has been thrown into some foreign prison and needs money for bail."

Quiet in the room. Notes were being scribbled. Heads were being shaken. "The latest one is the Jury Duty scam. The caller claims to be working for the sheriff's department or the courts, and says the person has failed to report for jury duty and is in really big trouble. The victim often claims to never have been notified. Well, that's right. So they offer up their SIN and other personal data to confirm their identity—and of course that's exactly what the scammer wants. And now we hear the old 'Pump and Dump' is making a comeback."

He looked around the room. Several of the younger officers looked puzzled. "That's where the scammers push up the price of a stock, usually with false information and fake media reports—or whatever the hell fake news is these days—and then they bail out, leaving the investors with nada when the stock crashes."

Cooper sighed. "Look, I know this is complex stuff. That's what a good con is all about—offering a hope, a promise, usually of riches of some kind, or something that the mark really longs for. A long con keeps them dangling, often for months, waiting for the payoff. The con artist creates some kind of semi-legitimate-sounding scenario, maybe an exclusive investment deal or something, and then just keeps upping the ante. They keep draining the mark. It is a vicious crime and we're often pretty helpless. Fraud destroys families and lives."

Cooper paused and drank deeply from his water glass. "Of course, the greatest fraud in our history was the '08 collapse of the housing market. Greed led the way as big banks and insurance companies and mortgage holders ripped off the public and investors. Lives were brutally changed. Families lost everything."

He drank again. "Dreadful corporate decisions were made. Bad investments. Lies. Corporate bullshit. To this day, not one of those corporate big shots has ever gone to jail," he concluded bitterly.

There was silence in the meeting room.

Chapter 9

A SHLEY HAD BEEN a cute kid. Then she became a cute teen-ager. Then she grew some real curves. Boys discovered her. She learned about boys pretty fast, which was important because she grew even curvier and men discovered her.

She learned about men very quickly.

She was only five feet four, but that and her delectable physical assets made men want to look after her. Cuddle her. Do a little more than cuddle. Ashley—her name was Lisa in those days—learned to use her dimples, wear modest but revealing blouses, and keep her legs crossed.

She got a college degree with the help of a couple of infatuated professors. Studying was pretty boring, but she was very smart about a lot of other things. Things that were not necessarily mentioned in the curriculum outlines.

She had spent a couple of years in an Indianapolis bank, a junior public relations position. It was cold there. She hated the winters. She got bored.

Then she met Frank—she thought that was his name back then, but of course he changed it regularly—at the bank. Within a month they were working together on his latest scam.

She soon learned that she craved the excitement and the thrill of a good con. And the big money, of course. And that she was good at it.

The new partners split their take fifty-fifty. Expenses were shared equally.

They also split the bedrooms fifty-fifty. He stayed in one, she stayed in another. Nobody crossed the mid-field stripe, although he kept trying. Sometimes they had to play a married couple. He enjoyed that a lot more than she did. He would squeeze her tight. His hands would roam possessively. She would have to smile.

In their scams so far, she had netted a little over $3.8 million, most of it tax free. And most of it was carefully secured in off-shore, interest-bearing accounts. She kept some US bank accounts active, and filed an income tax return every year. It was a lovely piece of fiction.

She enjoyed the pretence of her freelance public relations job.

The flight to Tampa finally took off from O'Hare. A different airline each time they flew, Frank had taught her.. Different passports, different names with each con. Leave no pattern. Leave no trail.

Massey. That was his name this go-round. Massey Ferguson. A distinguished-sounding name without any pretense.

"You look terrific," he told her as they settled into their first class seats. Always go first class was another lesson. Fewer questions, more perks, and you meet much more interesting people. Some had become clients. So to speak.

"Thanks. The ash-blonde hair should fit right in with Florida West Coast society."

"Is that where we're going?"

"Yeah. I found this big condo complex on the Gulf Coast named Sapphire Blue. I've rented us a nice two-bedroom on the beach. We can drive over there from Tampa. Looks like a high-end complex. Should be lots of older folks. Maybe some lonely men." She smiled smugly.

"And rich widows," he grinned back. "Ah, thank you," he said as the pretty flight attendant offered them each a glass of champagne. It was actually Prosecco, but an airline had to save a little cash where it could.

"We had to have a minimum three-month rental agreement," she continued as she sipped her wine. "I took an option for two additional months."

She savored the bubbles.

"We're in something called the Blue Building. Guess the developer is real patriotic. Named the three buildings Red, White and Blue." She raised one carefully plucked eyebrow.

"Huh," he grunted as he admired the walk of the flight attendant back to her little service area.

"We're in 617. The decor is purple polka-dots and green striped wallpaper," she said slowly.

"Huh," he said again. "Sounds lovely." His eyes remained locked on the flight attendant's skirt.

"And we also get our own pet alligator."

"Great."

She finally shook her head in disgust. No wonder they'd never hooked up. Nor would they. Ever.

"Oh, did I mention the Burmese python?"

"Fine." He held up his glass for the attendant to see. She came over with the bottle and refilled his flute. She didn't offer any to Ashley. Massey's eyes followed her intently on her return to the galley.

Finally he looked at her. "Wait. A Burmese what?"

Chapter 10

TRYING TO MINIMIZE the alcoholic intake of the Wives was like cheering for the NY Mets. It was difficult, it aroused derision, and it held very little promise of reward. It was about as smart as buying takeout sushi from a gas station convenience store.

Several husbands and a couple of hangers-on still had the scars to prove the futility of pointing out to their beloveds that not every bottle of wine that was opened had to be consumed within minutes.

There was pretty much zero chance of any wine within the grasp of any of the Wives reaching its "best before date."

The Wives, a group of semi-domesticated women who ruled the Sapphire Blue complex and its complicated social structures, simply did what they wanted. They were rich, they were retired, they were brassy, and they just didn't care what anybody else thought.

It was a lethal combination, especially when fuelled by adult beverages. These started about noon as they arrived at the pool and settled in to their special corner. Sipping, glugging, and imbibing continued well into the evening.

Ashley strolled into the pool concourse, wearing a black net cover-up over her cute two-piece swimsuit, a big floppy black and white hat and black sandals. She stopped the conversation in its tracks.

The Wives studied her intently, as they did all newcomers and interlopers and assessed the three big questions: Were they dangerous to their own marriage? Were they going to infect the social structure the Wives had imposed at Sapphire Blue? Were they a threat of any kind to any of them?

This trespasser had the poor taste to be young and beautiful. Her skin was taut. Her breasts were big and tilted up. There was a good chance they were real. Her hair had a sheen that while it may not be natural was attractive.

All in all, she was quite dislikeable.

The husbands, on the other hand, had a simpler system of judging. "Geez, great rack," said one. "Cute as a bug," said another. "You kind of want to hug her and cuddle up and..." stumbled another one; the ... being left undefined.

"She could climb into my—yes, dear?" another husband abruptly corrected as his Wife beckoned.

He wandered over to get his latest marching orders. "More ice? Of course, my darling. I will be back soon." He rolled his eyes at his fellow supplicants as he shrugged on a T-shirt and flip-flops, grabbed his keys and left in search of frozen water.

Momentarily his mind wandered. Frozen water. Ice. Hard. Sharp. What if a large chunk accidentally fell onto his wife's head? Wouldn't the murder weapon be melted by the time the police...stop it. That was unworthy of their loving relationship.

Still, there wouldn't be any fingerprints on the murder weapon. Hmmm. Makes one think.

"A wife is like a grenade," muttered another husband in a low voice. "Remove the ring and BOOM! There goes your house."

One-time Vegas fringe comedian Denny B immediately perked up. He still had hopes of appearing on the *Tonight Show with Jay Leno*. His friends hadn't had the heart to tell him that Leno had been off the show for years. Denny was in bed by 9:30 every night. Still, he tried. "Wife says to her husband, 'I look fat. Give me a compliment.' Husband says, 'You've got perfect eyesight.'"

Ashley settled in a far corner of the pool concourse. She lifted her cover-up over her head and then replaced her hat. She stretched out in the warm sun as a couple of dozen pairs of eyes tracked her every move.

She had told Massey to stay away from the pool until she could get a feel for the social hierarchy at Sapphire Blue. This was their first full day in residence.

The flight had been uneventful. Their new IDs had worked perfectly. They were obviously worth the $18,000 they had each paid to the mysterious little Korean man in Chicago who had created them.

They had rented a Cadillac XT5. White. A Florida car. Florida plates. It was a shrewd choice—a luxury car but not an ostentatious statement.

That was how they'd decided to present themselves—a rich couple from Calgary specializing in personal financial investment management. They were taking the winter off to relax after Massey had had a mild heart attack from working too hard for his clients.

It was crucial to gently infiltrate the condo complex before starting to dangle the investment opportunities. They had to earn the trust and friendship of their fellow Sapphire Blueites. She paused. Blueites? Is that even a word?

She massaged sun tan lotion onto her creamy skin. She was aware of the lecherous eyes of the men in the other corner following her, so she gave them a show. Oops. Her top almost came off. Then she had to *reeeaalllly* stretch to put the SPF 50 on her back. And then bend down to get her legs covered.

Finally she lay back on the towel.

The men would remember her.

They would like meeting her.

Now, would the women be happy to do a little business with her...when the time was right? That was the more interesting question.

In the far corner of the concourse, a fat guy sat alone, unobtrusively puffing on his cigar. Watching the action quietly.

CHAPTER 11

"WHAT DO YOU think he meant?" asked Samira Al-Saadi.

The stunning Persian woman was a top-ranked orthopaedic surgeon who looked after Kim and her prosthetic foot. She was a leading member of the medical community. She reached forward to take the glass of crisp New Zealand Sauvignon Blanc from Samantha.

"I…I'm not sure," Samantha admitted. "It just kind of popped up when he asked me to take Rosie to his house and I said I didn't have a key." She took a long sip.

"Does he have a key to your condo?"

"Uh, no."

"Well, that's going to be the next decision for you. Do you exchange keys? How does that change the relationship between the two of you? What happens if you break up? No, no, don't get me wrong, I'm not suggesting that," Samira hastened to add as Samantha glared at her. "You know me. Just being practical."

Kim snickered. She enjoyed seeing Samira on her back foot for a change. It didn't happen very often.

The three friends were dissecting the relationship between Samantha and the Sheriff.

It was complicated.

It had begun tumultuously when he had nearly arrested her as the primary suspect in a murder in the hot tub at Sapphire Blue.

After Samantha had been cleared, it had quickly become a hot romance. The sex was fantastic. They were compatible together. She loved Rosie, the Sheriff's smart dog with hair similar to her own burnished-gold locks. Rosie adored her.

"But how well do you really know him?" Samira continued in a softer tone of voice. "You've never travelled together. You've never spent a long time together. And I know that you're still coming to terms with his profession."

"Well, that's true. Trying to understand the danger he faces every day. And accept it. Then his getting shot. The whole assassination plot to kill him." She paused and sipped, then sipped again. "And maybe me," she finally confessed to her two closest friends.

Samantha had had a very difficult time comprehending that a paid Central American assassin might have also been targeting her—just for being the Sheriff's girlfriend.

This was the first time she had openly admitted that dreadful truth to her friends since the terrible incident.

She closed her eyes for a moment. Kim and Samira studied her carefully, and then looked at one another.

"It is good for you to acknowledge that," Samira said finally. "It is a reality of your life with someone in law enforcement. It shouldn't change your life, but you should be more aware of what's happening around you. The dangers that lurk."

Samantha nodded. She hastily wiped her eyes and poured a little more wine into their three glasses.

"Well, heck. I think I love the big galoot. I guess that makes a difference."

The three friends laughed together and raised their glasses.

Kim and Samira looked again at each other. These were two big steps Samantha had taken tonight.

CHAPTER 12

THE FIRST FIGHT on the new City Council was bound to happen. The fact that it was in just their third meeting was ominous.

Kim was settling into her new role as councillor for Ward 3. She was learning quickly that what she said at meetings and in public was fair game for reporters and local media commentary. It still kind of amazed her that a sentence or two she spoke at a meeting could result in a headline and a week of community controversy.

She was smart enough to keep her head down, her mouth closed, and her ears open during her first few weeks in office. She was also cautiously exploring the new working relationship with City Manager Roy Crawford and how to continue their torrid personal connection.

They were both well aware of the landmines inside city hall for their relationship. They could become fodder for critics who had their own political ambitions. Or they could implode because of a public disagreement over some proposed policy or civic issue. Or they could be attacked by the trolls on social media just because—well, those scum didn't need a reason.

Mayor Rodriguez had taken over the council with a firm hand. Everyone on council except for Kim and two others had been re-elected, so it was an experienced group. But it was also one that had clung to many old conflicts and dislikes.

"Councillor March! Councillor. Please sit down."

Grudgingly he did. He angrily tossed his pencil on his pad so hard that it bounced and landed in the centre of the horseshoe-shaped council table.

A newspaper reporter clicked his cellphone with glee. The first big spat of the new council term. Terrific.

"Councillor Johnson. You have the floor."

"Thank you, Madam Mayor," replied the pugnacious community organizer who had previously served on council and was back after a two-term absence. She was a "take no prisoners" council member.

"If we are going to get this city moving again, we need to change our city budget focus to help people in the hardest-hit neighborhoods. We need to get them a guaranteed income. We need to help them get Medicare coverage, because a lot of these families can't afford to see a doctor. And we need to reinvest in their schools because for years we have seen the quality of teaching decline and the graduation rates sink. This city's record of progressive action has been abysmal!"

She sat down angrily. For a long moment no one else on council spoke. Finally Roy Crawford stood.

"I'm sure many in our community understand and sympathize with the councillor's feelings, Madam Mayor. However, we have an economic development plan that is just underway. We have a new program to ensure planning and development for housing and neighborhood improvements. And we have a budget that invests in community development and families and kids. For Port Manatee to completely change those priorities now would be…inappropriate. But certainly the administration would be happy to work with Councillor Johnson to develop a plan to enhance education, living, and social supports in those neighborhoods."

It was a smart, sensible way out for everyone. Instead, Councillor Johnson erupted. "I will not be pushed aside by some staff person! I ran to get social justice back on this city's agenda! So get used to it, folks!"

Kim found herself on her feet almost before she realized it. "I also ran on a platform of justice," she said as she smiled at her new colleague who sat two seats down on the U-shaped table. "But I also believe in the city manager's plan for the economic and planning and investment strategies that he outlined."

She paused. "I think we should be very candid with our community. The previous city council was a stain on this city. The former mayor and two elected members of that council were convicted of fraud and corruption and put in prison, and that harmed our city's image. They damaged our reputation with the people of Port Manatee. And nationally."

Kim paused and gathered her thoughts.

"I think this new council was elected to bring order from chaos, to bring prosperity from failure, and to make planning decisions that will benefit the city and improve our tax base. That's why I will support the city manager's concept for exploring new ways we can improve the lives of all our people. But this is not the moment to disrupt the core strategy that he has outlined."

"I think that is a prudent concept," agreed Mayor Rodriguez as she looked around the horseshoe. The other councillors were nodding. Except for Councillor Johnson, who was frowning angrily.

"The next item on our agenda is approval of a contract to build on the Delvecchio Bridge site. Ms. Carlson?"

The planning director rose and clicked on the big screen in the council chambers. An architect's concept of a twin-tower apartment with a large sidewalk atrium appeared.

"Staff is recommending council approve this development by Starwind Construction. The principal is Elliott Webster. He is with us tonight if council members have questions. The proposal is for a sixteen-storey tower on one side, a nineteen-storey tower on the other, and a joint community and recreation centre area that will be open to both buildings as well as to the neighborhood. There will be a playground, open access to the beach behind the new buildings, and eight apartments allocated for low-rent artists' 'live-work-play-display' spaces. There will be several rent-controlled apartments in each building. The value of the project is $187 million. It will generate $3.4 million in new taxes each year once it is finished. It has the unanimous support of your administration."

She remained standing at the podium. Council members were quick to praise the new concept of mixed-use dwellings, street-level commercial, and the integration with the existing neighborhood.

"Mr. Webster, this playground design. Isn't that kind of unusual for such a housing complex?" asked Councillor Policy.

Elliott Webster rose and approached the podium. "It is, Councillor. It will come at a cost, which we are happy to absorb. We consulted extensively with the neighborhood. We have retained the playground designer who came up with the original concept and who will continue to liaise with neighborhood leaders. We think her concept and design are quite extraordinary."

Kim was an enthusiastic supporter. After all, it was Samantha's design.

The combative Councillor Johnson spent six minutes hollering about the need for more social housing, supporting low-income families, and questioning how the disenfranchised would benefit from this project. But, at the end of the day, even she couldn't find much reason to oppose it—especially as several community leaders were in the front row to support the project.

After ten more minutes of questioning Webster on development details, Council voted unanimously to award the contract. The audience applauded.

Moments after the meeting ended and the media scrum concluded, the mayor and Roy Crawford sat down for their usual post-meeting analysis.

"It was going to happen," Sonja Rodriguez said firmly. "Maybe it is better to get it out in the open now, so we can work around it. Kim was wonderful, by the way. She's a keeper."

Crawford nodded proudly. He and Kim were careful to keep their personal relationship out of city hall. Well, except for that one night just after she was elected when they had made fierce, passionate love on his office sofa. He had been exhausted by her energy.

Thank God he didn't have to welcome every new council member that way, he grinned to himself.

CHAPTER 13

IT TOOK ASHLEY two days to figure out the social structure at Sapphire Blue. The Wives ran the place. Rebecca was their sort-of leader. The staff just did what they were told. Short-term renters and visitors were at the bottom of the totem pole.

The husbands were simply the flotsam in Sapphire Blue's sea of life.

Ashley timed her walk around the large pool carefully. Rebecca was alone for a moment. Ashley stopped. "Excuse me," she began softly, "but I couldn't help but notice your hair. It's lovely. I just moved down here and am looking for a new stylist..."

It was an opening pretty much guaranteed to win. A nice compliment to a woman about her hair. Asking for help. Sharing a confidence. A home run in relationship-building. Ashley could have taught the class.

Rebecca reflexively patted her grey-blonde do. "Oh, thanks. Good hairdressers are hard to find down here. Where are you from?"

"Calgary. We're staying here for the winter. Some friends from Toronto recommended Sapphire Blue. It is great."

"It is. I'm Rebecca."

"Hi. Ashley. It's a pleasure."

"My hairdresser is Michel at Monsieur Michel. He's about a mile down the main road. You'll need an appointment."

"Perfect, thank you."

A short, blocky woman with mousy brown hair rushed onto the concourse. She was banging a clipboard against her left thigh. Her glasses were pushed up on her forehead. Her face was the color of cheap Merlot.

Ashley waited for a long minute. "Uhh..."

"Our beloved president of the condo board. Sheila Brown. A heart-attack on two stumpy little legs."

Ashley laughed.

"A train wreck waiting to happen."

Ashley laughed harder. She wiggled her ring finger. The sun refracted the glitter of a fine diamond. Rebecca noticed.

"What do you do in Calgary?"

"Massey and I…well, it's interesting actually. We are investment advisors." She paused for a moment.

"Because of an old friend of mine in California, we got an exclusive territory to sell advance units in WYRT. It's all sold out, so we decided to take a break and enjoy the winter—in the sun. Massey had a little health issue, so…"

Ashley waited expectantly for the hook to sink in. It did.

"A what? A wirt?"

"W Y R T. Wur-tee. It is the new Asian crypto-currency that some freakin' genius in Singapore is developing. It's all based on the Korean Won, the Chinese Yuan and the Japanese Yen, the Indian Rupee and the Bangladesh Taka. The currencies of the future. W. Y. R. T. Wur-tee."

"Huh. Never heard of it."

"Gosh, I hope not. It has all been really secret until now. The information is just starting to come out before the public launch in a couple of months. We're sort of allowed to talk about it now to friends, but no media. It is going to be really big. The initial investors are going to make a killing."

She let that sink in for another moment.

"The Asian economies are booming, and the financial markets over there are bubbling. And as you know, crypto-currencies are the way of the future." She paused again. "Of course, Massey is the expert in this."

She winked and Rebecca offered a tight smile. "Hey, I've taken up too much of your time. Thank you for the hairstylist. I'll be sure to tell him you recommended him. Have a great day."

Ashley stood up, smiled broadly at Rebecca and slipped away to her own corner. She took off her cover-up and slid into the pool. The water was glorious. It was a perfect day for fishing. And she'd just thrown out a hook for the first big trout.

Chapter 14

"Samantha, it's Elliott. We got the contract!"

"Really? Hey, that's fabulous! Congratulations!"

"City Council approved it Monday night. We've been finalizing the contract with the city solicitor and just signed off this afternoon. Didn't Kim tell you?"

"No. We've agreed to not talk about anything to do with this project until it is all public and approved."

"Smart. Well, now it is! Why don't you join our management team for a celebratory drink tonight? Since you'll be working on this with us."

Samantha paused. Perkins was tied up tonight. Rosie was at his house. "Sure, I'd enjoy that. When and where?"

***

SAMANTHA WALKED INTO the rooftop bar in the fourteen-story beachfront hotel. She was wearing a pretty summer dress in turquoise and ivory, and high-heeled sandals.

It wasn't hard to pick out the management team from Starwind Construction. They had taken over the prime corner of the patio and spread out over three couches and several chairs. It was not their first round of drinks.

"There she is," exclaimed Elliott as she walked into the open-air terrace, "our design star!"

His colleagues greeted her enthusiastically and she soon found herself seated on one of the couches, a glass of chilled unoaked chardonnay in hand.

She raised her glass to the group. "Congratulations! What a great project for you! I'm happy to be on the team." They toasted her back.

"In all seriousness, the playground design was the main thing that separated us from the other proponents," the VP of marketing told her. "Your work with the neighborhood and talking to the local kids was inspired. Several city councillors mentioned that in the discussion."

"I am so happy to hear that," Samantha replied with a smile. "That neighborhood has been ignored and abused for so long. The families don't know what to believe anymore. This will be a huge boost for the community."

Drinks turned into dinner. Samantha was seated beside Elliott. They shared a seafood platter for two and some crisp Italian Pinot Grigio.

Samantha could see the fatigue setting in on his face as they finished their food. She could only imagine the pressure of signing a $187 million contract. It would guarantee employment for a hundred people for the next couple of years. For a medium-sized company like his, this was an immense responsibility.

She looked across the table at the VP construction, who had been overserved. She looked down the table and caught the eye of the VP marketing, who nodded.

"We've got a big limo waiting for us outside," she reassured Samantha. "I'll make sure we get the gang home safely."

Samantha nodded appreciatively. They got up from the table, stumbled down to the elevator, and emptied onto the sidewalk where the long limo awaited. There were handshakes and hugs. Elliott planted a big kiss on Samantha's cheek together with a warm hug. The marketing VP looked at them intently.

The limo door finally slammed and took off.

Samantha decided not to risk driving after three glasses of wine, so she called a LYFT and went home.

There was a message from Perkins on her answering machine. He had escaped his meetings early and was free and wanted to have dinner.

CHAPTER 15

KIM AND SAMANTHA were having their usual morning walk on the beach before the sun got too high and too hot.

They grinned over the snippets of random conversation they overheard as they passed other walkers...

"And she keeps putting her underwear in my husband's suitcase..."

"That's where an eight-foot bull shark killed a baby dolphin the other day..."

"My thong keeps riding up...if my butt didn't look so good in it, I wouldn't wear one..."

"I don't care: if he's fooling around with his secretary, I'm going to take him for everything he's got..."

A woman with a harsh Slavic accent was talking on her phone while storming down the beach. "I kill him!"

"Wouldn't want to be married to *that* one!" Kim muttered.

A flock of seagulls fought over the scraps of something dead. "Looks like a pack of teenage boys at the free nacho bar," Kim said.

Samantha laughed. "Gulls have no manners, do they?"

They stopped for coffee and muffins at a beach bar. The waves were rolling in from the west. The sky looked threatening. It was muggy. It was Florida.

"Did you hear that Mrs. Fuentes died the other day?"

"Ah, no. I liked her," said Kim. "She voted for me. And got her family to as well."

"I feel sorry for Mr. Fuentes. He'll be all alone now."

"Don't worry," said Kim firmly. "The trip from being single to remarried for a rich, recently widowed man in Florida can be measured in nanoseconds after the dirt hits the casket. Usually accompanied by a parade of tuna—or should I say piranha—casseroles. And carrot cakes."

Samantha tried to stifle her laugh but couldn't. She almost snorted coffee out her nose. The two of them were soon laughing helplessly.

CHAPTER 16

THE RED ELASTIC band hung from her patio railing. It had been a yellow band to start, she recalled, then green, now red. The blue one sat malevolently on the table.

The broad bands were steadily increasing resistance for the sheriff's continuing physiotherapy. She had watched from afar as he diligently did his exercises to strengthen his arm and shoulder.

He had banned her from the immediate area when he did them. From two rooms away, she had seen him sweat and suffer in pain. He had never flinched from completing his thrice-daily routine.

She also knew that he always did an extra couple of pulls for each of the six exercises. That was Perkins—do everything better, be tougher, be stronger. Be stoic.

She had seen the agony lance across his face as he struggled.

Neither one of them ever mentioned that.

She had secretly tried to pull the red band the way she'd seen him do it. She could barely stretch it out before it wanted to snap back. Doing it ten times in a row, the way he did it, was staggering.

His self-control amazed her. His strength of character thrilled her. His tenacity always impressed her.

Slowly, steadily, each week his strength and flexibility were getting better. She had realized that the other night when he easily flipped her on the bed. She smiled. That had led to some fun games.

CHAPTER 17

"WHAT IS IT with women and handbags?" Perkins asked. There was a note of wonderment in his voice.

He was standing inside the walk-in closet off the master bedroom in Samantha's condo and was surveying the racks of clothes and accessories. Many racks.

"What is it with men and watching stupid sports on TV?" she snapped back.

The sheriff was no fool. He promptly retreated to the living room to watch college basketball, hockey, and golf. Whoever invented the TV remote control should have a national holiday named after them, he thought.

Rosie remained, looking around the closet with interest. There were some delicious leather smells coming from the racks.

Samantha looked at her suspiciously. "Don't even think about chewing any of my shoes," she warned her. Rosie looked around again. She was a lady. She understood.

Whoever had designed the condo, Samantha thought happily, had been really smart. Or a woman. Most likely a really smart woman, she concluded.

The walk-in closet for the woman was huge. It had built-in racks for shoes, handbags, and other necessities of life. Lovely open shelves for sweaters. Drawers to keep lingerie. A lockable cabinet for jewelry. A marble centre island on which clothes could be laid out. And lots and lots of hangers and racks. Two full-length mirrors.

The man's closet was pretty much a piece of dowelling hung between two nails; three wire hangers, a couple of drawers and a built-in laundry basket for dirty underwear and socks. Not that the guy actually used it, but still, it was a nice thought.

Samantha sighed happily. Besides, she couldn't have more than thirty or forty handbags, and maybe only fifty pairs of shoes. Well, maybe a few more. But they were needed. Each and every one of them.

She reluctantly closed the closet door. The lights automatically went out. Rosie led her out to the living room, where the sheriff was perched happily on her couch. She glanced at the screen. Something about Kansas and UCLA. Whatever.

The screen clicked to hockey. What?

The two ladies wandered out to the lanai. Rosie peered down at the huge blue swimming pool below. She had only been allowed to go swimming in it once. Well, Rosie recalled, perhaps "allowed" was a generous interpretation of her jumping into the pool. The kids had loved it. The security guard, not so much.

Perkins came out a few minutes later. "Game finally over?" Samantha growled.

"Yeah. The Maple Leafs beat the Red Wings. Now the Knicks are playing the Celtics. Then there's more golf."

Samantha just looked at him. Perkins grabbed the red elastic and began again his elaborate series of exercises. She was soon exhausted just watching him strain.

"Want to go for a swim?" he asked after he had finished.

"Are you allowed back in the water?"

"Yes. Finally. Even the hot tub. Today is the end of my sixth week of rehab. The PT and the doctor said it was okay now. Can't wait."

"Just let me change. What about the baby?"

"I brought over a new chew toy for her. She'll be fine."

Samantha disappeared into her recently maligned closet and came out a few moments later wearing a cream bikini with black trim, black sandals, and a floppy sun hat. She posed for him.

"Maybe we could go swimming later," he suggested. His throat was suddenly hoarse.

Samantha laughed softly. "Hold that thought, big boy." She spun away deftly, and slipped on a cover-up. She grabbed keys and towels as Perkins gave Rosie her new toy.

A moment later they were at poolside. Perkins didn't hesitate to step into the water. He dove under, and came up a long moment later. "Man, I've missed this." He dunked himself again, and swam several yards underwater before surfacing like a dolphin.

Samantha didn't hesitate to join him. She was a good swimmer, and enjoyed circling around him and brushing against him in the water. She would then dart out of reach, teasing him and turning up the heat in his eyes as he grabbed for her slippery body.

He finally caught her and held her firmly. His hands dropped below the water to savor the feel of her butt. He squeezed gently and Samantha found herself squirming under the sensation. She locked her legs around his waist and he groaned softly.

They kissed, broke away, clinched again and then kissed more deeply. Her hand drifted down to his—"For Pete's sake, you two, get a room!"

They jerked apart, only to find Kim and Roy standing at the side of the pool laughing at them.

Kim jumped in to splash them both and came up giggling. Roy cannon-balled beside them, soaking everyone. It turned into a mock battle that lasted for only a moment before they were all laughing loudly.

Several teenagers sunning themselves shook their heads in dismay at the unrestrained antics of the old folks. The noise! The splashing! Didn't the fogeys understand that sending texts and taking selfies required quiet?

From the far corner of the pool concourse, Ashley watched the foursome frolic in the pool. She didn't know who they were, but they were obviously very close. The gorgeous redhead and the lean, muscled man with what looked like a recent scar on his upper arm had come out of the Blue Building. Her building.

A recent bullet scar? She had some detecting to do.

The four friends ended up back at Samantha's. They ordered in pizza, popped some chilled IPAs, and sprawled happily on the lanai. Rosie shared in the pies. She was pretty pleased about that.

Later that evening, after they'd walked Rosie, Perkins looked at the reddish-haired canine sternly. "You stay here. You can watch the Warriors-Lakers game. I've got ten bucks on the Lakers. Tell me about it in the morning."

With that he grabbed Samantha and firmly shut the door of the bedroom.

The sounds of excitement from the basketball game just barely exceeded the sounds of excitement coming from Samantha's bedroom.

Rosie ignored both and gnawed on her new bone.

CHAPTER 18

EVERY WEDNESDAY MORNING at about 11:43 a.m., the boys sidled over to Krazy Kenny's Bar and Grill. It was the weekly noon-hour special: two-buck beers, two-buck burgers, and two-buck cigars. Considering the ingredients, all of them were overpriced.

The Wives always worried about their beloved's cholesterol—and, in some cases, that of their husbands as well. Their diligent efforts six days a week at ensuring their mates ate healthy, took their appropriate prescriptions, and got some moderate exercise were almost completely counteracted by the one day of indulgence at the smoky little bar.

On the other hand, it did give the Wives an afternoon off.

The first round of chilled rosé was being poured by Mary Lou. There were seven or eight Wives sitting around the prime tables in the SW corner of the pool concourse. Palm trees waved gently. The sun burned down on the umbrellas that provided shade for their shady conversations.

Rebecca drank deeply and sighed happily. The other Wives joined her. There was quiet for a long moment. The rosé seemed to be evaporating under the hot Florida sun, so another round was required.

Some nice little snacks were circulated by Wife Three, in open defiance of the rule about no food at the pool. What, some wimpy little security guard was going to challenge the Wives? Or report them to Sapphire Blue General Manager Virginia McIntyre? So what if Condo President Sheila Brown saw them?

The Wives ruled.

It was during the ceremonial opening of the third large box of wine by Wife Seven that Rebecca spoke.

"Any of you ladies heard of Wur-Tee? WYRT."

Silence from the audience. Finally, Mary Lou spoke up. "What the hell is a wyt-ree?"

"No. Wur-tee. It is spelt W Y R T. Pronounced Wur-tee."

Two of the Wives reached for their cellphones and commenced punching buttons authoritatively. Google buzzed ostentatiously over the pool WiFi.

"Here it is," Delores finally announced. She read slowly, trying to tilt the small screen away from the noonday sun. "Found a web page. Says it is a new currency. What do they call that fake money stuff?"

"Crypto-currency?" said Luanne. "Like Bitcoin?"

"Yeah, guess so," replied Delores. "Not much info. Something about Asian money. Well, cry-uh, crypto money I guess…"

"That's what I thought," said Rebecca. "I'm told it is just emerging. It will be unveiled soon." She paused for a long moment as enquiring eyes followed her. "Seems to me that some smart people got in on that Bitcoin thing early and made a piss-pot full of money."

Nervous giggling as another round was poured. Delores went back to her cellphone. A moment later, she whistled. "Wow. That Bitcoin started at a buck or so. Then it skyrocketed to $19,000. Then it had a big fall, and then it came back strong. Sitting around $8,000 right now. What, for one coin?" she asked plaintively.

Silence around the tables. Everybody absorbed that for a long moment.

These women were pretty smart. Several of them had been in business. Most had a college degree. They kept up on current events. They had raised kids in the hectic '80s and '90s. They were survivors.

"So. Rebecca. Just what are you saying?" The question came from Sandy, the sweet-faced brunette from Illinois.

"Not sayin' nothin' right now. Just kind of pondering." A long pause. "But I can't help but think that some smart investors are going to do pretty well investing in this new Asian crypto-thingie. Hell, that's where the world's economy is headed. I read a report that by 2040 Asia will top 50 percent of the world's GDP. They're building all these new cities, investing in infrastructure. We're sitting on our asses because Washington can't get its act together and we keep electing lying idiots. Gotta impact our economy sometime…"

June Rose nervously popped the tab on the next box of rosé, which had been sitting in an ice bath. She poured herself a big glass and then handed the box around. Nobody refused the refill.

Finally Luanne spoke up. "What if we, uh, put a little house-keeping money into this thing?"

It was what they'd all been thinking. Again silence.

"What I was wonderin'," Rebecca finally said, "is if this is somethin' we should be doin' ourselves. You know, build a little slush fund just for us girls. Just for shoes and wine and a few other necessities."

Giggles. Nods. Thoughtful looks went up as the rosé level went down. A tiny bit glassy eyed, perhaps, but still thoughtful.

"Ah, Rebecca. Darlin'. Just how would we go about investing a dollar or two in this thing?"

"Not sure. I met this woman who's wintering here. Seems nice. She and her husband are financial gurus. Investment advisors from Calgary. I guess her husband had a heart procedure of some kind so they're taking the winter off. She said the thing was sold out."

A low murmur of disappointment.

"Of course, with these financial things, there's sometimes a little extra around the edges, or some investor bails out. I could talk to her..."

Enthusiastic nods. "But in the meantime, I don't think we should say anything to anybody. Like, nobody. Especially..."

She nodded in the direction of the sidewalk that led into the middle of the pool area. Their men were returning from their lunch.

Most of them were frantically chewing breath mints. However, the fried onions, greasy burgers, and whatever was in the cigars was scoring a major TKO against the mints. The candies had never been designed to counteract a lunch at Krazy Kenny's.

There were friendly welcomes and even hugs exchanged.

No one mentioned possible secret investments in Asian crypto-currencies.

CHAPTER 19

THE GROUND BREAKING ceremony for the Delvecchio Bridge development was attended by every member of the Port Manatee City Council, many city hall officials, the executive team at Starwind Construction, fifty or sixty neighborhood residents whose kids were really excited, local media, a couple of bored hangers-on, three people there just for the free snacks, one passerby, two local pastors, and Samantha.

Mayor Rodriguez and Elliott Webster sat together in the cab of the big excavator. The huge articulated bucket ceremonially dug the first scoop of dirt to begin the excavation for the foundation for the twin-tower complex. Cameras followed the action. The crowd applauded.

This development was very big news in a mid-sized city like Port Manatee. It would create local jobs, be a big boost to the economy, pay city hall huge new taxes, and change the face of the neighborhood.

It was that last part that had intrigued Samantha. She was standing with a cluster of parents and kids as she watched the big bucket dig dirt.

Two of the community leaders came over to hug Samantha. "Never thought it'd happen," said one happy mother.

"I remember meeting you that day a year ago out here. You were all by your lonesome. My little girl thought you looked like an angel, all in white with that hair o' yours." She looked at the cluster of city hall officials. "Never thought that would become this." She shook her head.

Samantha had slowly developed a deep trust with the local community. Her plans for the children's playground had been designed with the kids. It also opened up access to the beach behind the new condos so local families would still have swim-and-sun rights.

The fact that the architects and Elliott's construction design team had embraced her concepts still made her smile. This was the start of a new career for her.

The ceremonies were soon over. Everyone retreated to the big white tent where refreshments were served.

Kim immediately came over to stand with Samantha and the neighborhood families. This was part of her new ward, and she was trying hard to extend her political foundation.

Already Kim was learning the tough reality of modern politics: protect your base.

Her genuine enthusiasm for working with the community was apparent to everyone. She was already gaining popularity and support because of her commitment to her constituents.

Samantha deliberately took a couple of steps back so Kim could have the spotlight. When Roy started to come over, Samantha subtly motioned him to stay back. He got it.

The speeches were mercifully brief. The refreshments were lovely. By 11:30 the crowd was dispersing. There were a lot of smiles, and the local TV and newspaper cameras had caught that vibe. The press coverage would be great.

It was much later at the small luncheon that had included only a few invited VIPs Samantha was digging in her purse when she felt a piece of stiff, laminated cardboard stuck in a side pocket. She plucked it out. A simple piece of white card stock: P. J. Hozworm. And a local phone number.

Huh. Who could that...Um. Wait. The memory came back to her slowly. The last time she'd used this purse was at Kim's final political debate before the election. It was there Kim had used her now-famous "KICK. YOUR. ASS." line.

Samantha had a vague recollection of a small, grey man, dressed in grey, who had appeared suddenly at her side and told her that the election was over and that it would be Kim in a landslide.

He had been right. And way before Samantha or anybody else in their campaign had understood that.

She thought back. Hadn't he said to call him sometime? Something about having a nice chat?

Hozworm. Odd name. Odd little man.

She could feel her spidey senses tingle.

Chapter 20

"Rebecca, this is my partner, Massey Ferguson," Ashley said as she made the introductions.

"A pleasure, a real pleasure," Ferguson said as he held Rebecca's hand. She smiled politely.

Rebecca introduced Delores. She had wanted some support for this meeting.

Ferguson was several years older than the delectable ash-blonde. He was wearing a yellow golf shirt, white linen pants and slip-on loafers with no socks. He had a pencil moustache that made him look like a card counter in Atlantic City who had been thrown out of the last casino.

She looked around the condo as she sat down. It was a modest two-bedroom. Big TV against the living room wall. Two couches. One easy chair. The dining room table seated six. Some mid-range outside chairs on the patio. Pretty standard. Typical rental unit. There would be one big master bedroom, one smaller guest room.

The kitchen was pretty dated. The cupboards needed to be replaced and the Formica countertop was two decades out of style. The kitchen appliances weren't new, weren't old.

"Thanks for coming over. Since my heart procedure I've been keeping quiet. Doing walks every day, some light exercises. Ashley keeps me on my toes about eating better," he said, smiling at his partner.

Rebecca nodded. Pretty typical recovery pattern.

"Nice you could take some time off in the winter," she said. "Oh, thanks," she said as Ashley offered her a glass of white wine. She sipped. "Oh, very nice."

Delores nodded agreement. She was studying Ashley intently.

"Yes. We've done quite nicely with our investment company. We decided we'd earned a break after the WY—oops, sorry."

"It's fine, dear," Ashley interjected quickly. "I told Rebecca about the WYRT. She's so smart she figured it out real fast."

Ferguson nodded and turned back to Rebecca. "No problem, then. We just have to keep it on the down-low until the formal announcement of the IPO is made. That's probably in a month or two." He waved his hands with a little irritation in his voice. "This is all being run by some kazillionaire in Asia, so we don't have much clout." He sipped ice water and then chuckled. "To be honest, we've got no clout at all. Nobody does."

Rebecca sipped again. Really nice wine.

"Ah, I hadn't heard about it until Ashley and I were chatting."

"No, you would not have heard anything. It has all been private sales and advance orders so far, so that when the public IPO is finally released there will be this huge base of investors already committed. They are getting in at a really good initial price, so none of them are doing anything to screw it up. That pre-sold base will really drive up the price quickly."

Rebecca sipped again. Ashley smiled decorously and passed a plate of small brie and caramelized onion tarts.

"Uh, how did you and Ashley get…you know, chosen?"

"The Asian genius picked a few people in each country to do the prelim sale. The guy for California and the Western US happened to be a friend of Ashley's. They met at some investor conference two years ago. He recommended us to handle all of Western Canada. It didn't take long for us to agree!"

Rebecca thought some more. "Is that market big enough to…"?

Massey looked irritated. "All we got was a lousy $100 million to sell," he said. "It went like…well, you know what through a goose." He laughed in a coarse way.

Rebecca smiled. Ashley looked a bit appalled. Delores seemed unmoved. Everyone had another sip. Ashley refilled everyone's glass from the open bottle. Rebecca glanced at the label. A Muscadet from the Loire Valley district. VERY nice.

"I didn't think there was that kind of money up there."

"Oh heck, between the Hong Kong money flooding into Vancouver, the oil money in Calgary, the big agricultural money in the prairies, and a surprising number of innovative companies doing interesting things in R&D, we could have sold what, honey, twice that?"

Ashley nodded. "At least. It was really easy. People saw it was such a great opportunity." There was a pause in the conversation. "So, how do you like the weather these days?" she asked brightly. "It is sure a lot warmer than Calgary. They just had another blizzard yesterday."

Blizzard. What a terrible word.

"What does your company do?" Rebecca asked finally.

"We are a small, boutique, private investment firm," Ashley responded. "We only take on a certain number of clients. We don't advertise. We both hate social media, so we have no personal stuff online." She shuddered demurely. "People don't understand how much of their privacy they are losing out there."

"Uh huh. Um, a friend of mine said she found an item on the Internet about this new crypto-currency—"

"Ah, I guess they finally decided to release the basic fact sheet," Ferguson responded smoothly. "We've been expecting it. Their tech centre is in Mumbai. I guess they are starting the introductory information campaign before the IPO. I suppose they figure by quietly allowing the public to learn about it, it will make the global sales push easier when that campaign launches formally on the Singapore Stock Exchange."

"We're not sure what the final target will be," Ashley said confidentially as she leaned toward Rebecca and lowered her voice, "but we're guessing at a valuation of 5 or 6 billion for the launch. It's going to make those early investors a lot of...well, you know."

She turned to look out the window. There was silence in the living room.

Rebecca finished her wine and reluctantly put down her glass. "It has been lovely, thank you. I've got to run. Maybe we can do it again sometime."

She got up and they all shook hands. Ashley and Massey saw them out. Rebecca was very thoughtful on the elevator ride down.

Delores wasn't. "Did you see the bling she was sporting? Holy Cow, the ring had to be two carats. And the sapphire earrings were spectacular. I know a bit about jewelry." She paused thoughtfully. "They looked real to me."

Rebecca looked at her friend. Delores did know her bling. If she said it was real, then she'd bet that the jewelry Ashley was sporting was authentic. And expensive.

Chapter 21

SAMANTHA WAS SEATED in the lobby of the Sheriff's Department, waiting for Perkins to finish up. They were joining Samira and her latest boyfriend for a soft-shell crab dinner. Kim and Roy were tied up at city hall with meetings.

Seven very pretty young women burst through the main doors of the Sheriff's Department. They were giggling and talking to one another. A tall blonde went to reception.

"Hi," she said with a grin. "We're here to meet with Deputy Chad. It's about that thing at the Bonga-Bonga Room last night." They giggled a bit more.

The receptionist looked at the sergeant behind her, who shrugged. She dialed a number, spoke briefly, and then looked at the ladies. "He'll be right out," she reported. "Please have a seat."

The group swarmed onto the hard chairs in the lobby. They looked at Samantha with interest. Their chattering paused as they assessed her briefly, and then went back to talking.

"I can't believe those three old men started fightin' last night," said a brunette, shaking her head. She had long, long legs, and a short, short skirt.

"It was over me," confessed a tiny Japanese girl with an exquisite figure.

"What you mean, girl! It was over me!" insisted another one. She was a platinum blonde with green highlights, and a bosom that the good lord had not given to her.

"Um, ladies. Please," said Deputy Chad as he arrived in the reception area. He looked nervously at the gaggle of strippers.

"Oooh, aren't you just the cutest thing," said the tall blonde as she got up, went over to him, and started rubbing his shoulder and arm. Chad flinched and the girls chortled.

"Tha...thank you for coming in to give your statements," he began. The blonde kept patting him.

"I'm Brandi. That's Candi. She's Kandi with a K. She's Mandi. That's Randi. She's Sandi. And she's Wanda. Don't ask." The ladies all waved.

"Where's that good-looking Sheriff?" demanded Kandi.

"Yeah. If we're really naughty, will he spank us?" giggled Randi.

That got Samantha's attention.

Chad was quickly going underwater. "Uh, no, ladies, please, we are—"

"What, honey. Are you going to in-terr-o-gate us? Any handcuffs needed?" Sandi laughed as she got up and jiggled Chad's service belt that included a pair of handcuffs. "I sorta like handcuffs..."

"Awright, ladies, that's enough." The gravelly voice of the desk sergeant cut through the chatter in the reception area.

The girls retreated. Chad wiped his forehead. He glanced at Samantha with near-panic still in his eyes. He'd out-toughed some nasty hombres on the streets and back alleys of Port Manatee, but this was much harder.

"We'll start with you and her," he said, pointing at two of the septet.

"Candi," said one. "Kandi," said the other. Dismay flashed across the deputy's face.

"Down here, ladies," he gestured as he walked to the door leading into the office area. They preceded him, hips swinging.

The remaining women sat down and chatted for a moment. Their attention was soon focused on Samantha.

"Hey, honey. You a working girl too?"

Samantha looked up from her tablet. "Uh, well, yes, I guess I am." She paused and enjoyed the looks on the faces of the five women. She flashed a well-toned thigh as she made a little show of re-crossing her legs. "I design children's playgrounds," she finally told them.

A mixture of relief and disbelief blazed across their faces as the quintet sat back in their seats, looking hard at her.

"Geez, honey, thank god you're not in the business. With your looks, we'd all go broke."

"Ah, thank you. I guess."

Perkins burst through the interior doors and immediately went to Samantha. She rose, took his arm and they headed out the main doors. As she walked by the gaping women, she smiled and tossed her reddish-golden hair at them.

"Of course, sometimes I am quite naughty."

Jaws dropped as Samantha waltzed out. She made sure her hips were gyrating at them.

"What was that all about," demanded Perkins as they headed for her car.

"Nothing, sweetie. Just some working girls discussing discipline in the workplace."

CHAPTER 22

"I'D LIKE TO get a little piece of the pre-sale of this WYRT thing," admitted Rebecca to the other Wives. It was the day following her meeting with Ashley and Massey.

Heads were nodded and Moscow Mules were sipped.

"Delores and I had a glass of wine with Ashley and Massey yesterday," she explained. "Pretty good wine, by the way." That was a good sign to the Wives. "Didn't warm up to Massey very much. Hate his little moustache. But he seems pretty clever and they have this exclusive territory for the pre-IPO run-up. Says it's sold out, though."

Disappointed silence.

"Uh, any chance we could still get a little chunk? Say if we combined our household savings, maybe we go together as a consortium?"

Rebecca looked thoughtful as she pondered Luanne's question. "When you're dealing with such big numbers potentially, you'd think there'd be a little wiggle room. You know, a bit of stuff that fell off the truck."

A flicker of hope around the tables. They had kept their voices low, so their husbands in the surrounding tables couldn't hear them. Of course, between the men's hearing aids being pulled out and sitting on the table before they swam, and their attention fixed on the nubile Ashley's assets as she stretched out on a pool-side lounge chair, the Wives were as secure as the Joint Chiefs of Staff in their briefing room.

"What, uh, do you think it might take to, uh, buy us a little piece?" finally offered Sylvia. Several Wives nodded. Now it was getting interesting.

Rebecca took a long time to respond. "Don't know." She paused. "But if we did try, I'm guessing they wouldn't even look at anything under half a million."

A couple of indrawn breaths. One gasp. Several nods. Wife Four patted her hair, and Wife Eight sat back in her chair.

"That's actually not that bad," ventured Mary Lou. She was a brittle blonde who had run her own small business for years.

The other ladies looked at her. "Think about what Rebecca said. What if we put together our own consortium? I don't know, maybe ten of us at fifty grand each? That's the half mil right there."

Several husbands rose, sucked in their stomachs and discovered they needed to walk to the pool. Their path just happened to take them beside Ashley's lounge chair.

The women waited. Soon the area around them was clear.

Each woman had obviously taken the intermission to think about raising her share of the investment. No one wanted to be the first to plunge in, however.

The silence lengthened. Rebecca finally put down her mug and leaned forward.

"I think this is a really unusual opportunity. Risk? Sure. Hell, waking up every day is a risk. I'd be prepared to pony up if anybody else wants to come in."

No one spoke for a long moment.

The first one to offer was a surprise. Sandy was a sweet-faced northerner from Wisconsin. She and her husband lived in a modest two-bedroom condo that they had astutely bought after the crash in 2009. They were frugal, and proud of it. The other Wives had always assumed they were just thrifty. Really thrifty.

"I can put together the fifty," she said. "I'd go in."

Surprised looks around the tables. A few raised eyebrows. "I've been saving a little money from the household budget," she admitted with a little smile. "The fifty won't be a problem." More surprised looks, but that sparked more commitments.

"I still think we should talk to our husbands," confessed Wife Eight. A couple of nods. Several head shakes.

"Respect that," Rebecca finally said. "But, I think we need to keep a really tight lid on this thing until the IPO comes out. That's if we can even get a piece of the pre-sale. They might want an NDA from us. So the fewer the better." She grinned mischievously. "Besides, wouldn't it be great to build our little nest eggs by ourselves?"

That drew nods of the heads and smiles from the Wives.

"What's an NDA?" asked Wife Four.

"Non-Disclosure Agreement," replied Stephanie. She had driven her husband to grow their company and had pushed her three kids through college. She had never gone herself, but she had acquired a lot of street smarts over the years.

"It means you can't tell anybody about an imminent business deal or any insider information. If you do you can be sued or have to pay a penalty or something."

That quieted the group. Suddenly this idea was getting very real. There were consequences to their actions. Second thoughts were shooting across their faces.

"Look, nobody has to do anything right now," concluded Rebecca. "Let's take a night to think it through. Maybe talk a little more tomorrow? See if there's serious interest."

Relief and nods around the table.

"Besides," she concluded, "we may never be able to actually buy into this new crypto-currency." She paused again. "Wurt-tee," she pronounced carefully. "Helluva name." She paused again. "Course, what the hell is a Bitcoin?"

Thoughtful nods. The Wives would have a long night ahead.

CHAPTER 23

THE BOYS HEADED for their weekly grease-fest at Krazy Kenny's the next morning. That triggered a swift resumption of the investment discussion around the Wives' corner of the pool.

Two of the Wives immediately bailed. Wife Five and Wife Nine obviously weren't on board. They said so. There were shrugs of understanding and a rapid excommunication to the rear pews.

"We've checked the web page announcing the WYRT. Rebecca has met with the two investment people, Ashley and what's his name with the ugly moustache. I Googled them, but didn't get any hits. Rebecca tells me neither one is on social media, which sorta makes sense if you're running a very exclusive investment company," reported Luanne.

"They're renting here for the winter, so that's what, twenty-five, thirty grand. Car is a newish Caddy. She's got nice clothes. Expensive jewelry. Rebecca tells us they've got good taste in wine. Seems legit to me. I'm in."

"I just like the idea of beating the pants off my husband on an investment deal," laughed Mary Lou.

"I like that too," confessed Wife Seven, a relative newcomer to the clan. "And I also like building my own little nest egg. You know, in case something happens."

Knowing nods. There were lots of pre-nups in the group. But, there were also lots of smart lawyers on tap to break them.

At the end of the day, a wife had to look after herself. They all believed in their original secret wedding vows: What's mine is mine, what's ours is mine.

Suzanne spoke up, which was a bit of a rarity. She was tolerated by the group but hardly embraced. She had been a beauty queen a few years back. Her talent had been packing a suitcase. She hadn't climbed very far up the academic scale in the years since.

She had, however, been smart enough to marry well. Very well.

"Can't I just ask Jackie-poo for the money?"

"No. We don't tell the men anything. This is our deal."

"Oh. Okay. I guess I can cash in some of those what do you call 'ems? The paper things."

A brief pause while the ladies tried to follow.

"You mean bonds?" asked Rebecca.

"Yeah. Those papers with pretty pictures on them. Or are those stocks?"

"Those would be stocks. Dear. You have your broker sell some and she'll send you the money. But you have to do this, not...Jackie-poo," she concluded with distaste.

"Okey-dokey. I'm in." Suzanne smiled beatifically.

"All right. Let me get this straight now." Rebecca had been scribbling on a pad. "I've got nine of us committed right now. That's $450,000." She looked unhappy as she double-checked her notes. "Sure like to get to that half mil figure. I'd think that would be more of an attention-getter."

Everybody thought for a minute.

"What about Kim? You know, our new city councillor."

"Don't think she's got the money. Besides, she's really into her new role at city hall. Doin' good so far," Rebecca opined.

"Samantha? She sort of owes us for bailing out Kim's election campaign last year."

"Hmmm. I like her. She's with that good-lookin' Sheriff all the time. Not sure she'd be a joiner with us on somethin' like this, though."

The group stared out at the pool. They watched a young man excavate his left nostril. He then wiped the residue on his thigh. There was a group eye-roll. Men.

A small plane flew slowly over the beach. It was towing a sign for an insurance company that made promises to consumers that the company would never keep.

Rebecca sighed loudly. Not having the half-mil felt like finishing fourth in the Olympic downhill.

"Aw, shoot, I'll take the last piece." Delores had been married to George for more than forty-five years. "This'll be the first time I've ever kept anything big from him," she announced. "Guess it's about time I had a little fling as well." She paused. "After all, he did buy that damn 'Vette last year."

She was still bitter about that. He hadn't consulted her. It took a crane and about five minutes to lever himself out of the low-slung car. Two hip replacements.

"Whoopee! Ladies, that does it. We've got the 500K!" Rebecca confirmed the numbers on her pad.

Congratulatory murmurs from around the tables.

Glasses were raised in a toast.

"Now we just have to see if we can actually get in on this WYRT thing!"

CHAPTER 24

L IKE MOST GENTLEMEN of a certain generation, the husbands and hangers-on of the Wives were pretty oblivious to domestic stress.

"You, uh, noticed anything peculiar about the ladies lately?" ventured George after the second drafts had been poured at KKs.

"Nope." "Un-uh." "Heck no." "What? How would you tell?" "Uh, don't think so." "Who?" "About what?"

The answers from the assembled males were clearer than the last presidential debate.

Except for one.

"Er...why do you ask?"

George paused before answering. "I dunno. It just seems... peculiar at the condo these last couple of days. Like there's some big secret that I know nothing about."

"If you knew about it, George, it wouldn't be a secret!" came the laughing response from Husband Five. Chortles around the tables. Cold drafts were swigged.

Responses from the rest of the group were as slow in coming as a bacon double cheeseburger coursing through the plaque-filled arteries of a fat man.

"You know," said Roger after a while, "now that you mention it, the wife has been a little odd. Odder." He drank from the icy mug. "Sometimes hard to tell the difference."

Heads nodded. Somebody waved to the barkeep for one more round.

"When I think about it," ventured one more husband, nose wrinkled in concentration, "she has been pretty secretive about something. Phone conversations end when I come in the room. Who knows?" he concluded with a shrug.

That seemed to be the popular position in the polling numbers. Talk turned to the glories of days gone by, as it often does in a huddle of men at the bar.

"I was one of the top three sales reps in the entire SW USA!"

"Wow. How many reps in the territory?"

"Two."

"You know you're getting old when all your doctors are younger than you are," grumbled Cedric. Grumpy nods all around.

A final round appeared at the tables. Burps were burped; farts were farted.

"There are certain immutable facts of life," pondered the closest thing the group had to Socrates in his best days. "One size does not fit all." Groans and laughs.

"Never play cards with a man named Doc." Rueful nods of agreement.

"There are no fat prima ballerinas, and no skinny middle linebackers." A chorus of "Uh-huhs" rang out.

"Governments will always find a way to screw it up." Angry nods. A lot of them. For quite a while. Most of the boys had been in business. They had learned you are not in business *with* the government; you are in business *despite* the government.

The tables eventually quieted to wait for the latest philosophical treatise to continue.

"Why are there three pieces of dim sum on a plate when there are usually two or four people at the table?" Mutters of dismay. Apparently restaurateurs had been screwing with customers for many centuries.

"Tell us, oh great sage, seer and swami, oh great mystic," asked a chortling husband who had been slightly overserved,"provider of male wisdom—tell us, what is the greatest threat to marriage today?"

That stopped the conversation short. Ears waggled. The response was quick in coming.

"Oh that's easy, my son. HGTV."

Roars of laughter from the multitudes. "Geez, the wife's addicted to that thing," confirmed a couple of the boys. "They watch a couple of shows. They get all excited about redesigning the bathroom. Next thing you know, you can't take a crap in your own bathroom for six months because of the reno! And you're out fifty grand!"

The bar quieted as the lunch ran down to its inevitable conclusion.

"One final thought," offered the modern Carnak. "Suckers aren't born every minute…they're born every second."

Cheers and applause ended the lesson for the day.

The acolytes put down their empty mugs, carefully stretched their knee and hip replacements, and slowly pushed themselves up from their chairs.

CHAPTER 25

ROSIE KNEW SHE was special. She wasn't exactly sure of her realm, but she was pretty sure she was the queen of it.

She assumed the two-legged people around her were there to pat her, pet her, say nice things about her, and give her treats. She responded with enthusiastic tail-wagging, tongue-lapping, and doggie kisses.

People loved her. She loved people. They were her playmates.

She pranced down the hall of Samantha's condo, looking back once to make sure that Sheriff and pretty lady were coming. They were. Rosie got to the elevator doors first and waited patiently. She didn't really understand the funny box that moved, but it seemed to work fine for getting her out to the grass and trees and fire hydrants of the world.

The cluster of three waited. The elevator finally dinged softly and the doors opened. Rosie was ready to charge in, but two people stepped out.

"Oh, hi. Rosie, come here," Samantha said. "Wait, you must be my new neighbors. Hi, I'm Samantha. This is LeRoy. Sheriff Perkins. I'm down in 606."

The adorable little tawnyhaired blonde immediately stepped forward to shake hands. "Hi. Thanks. I'm Ashley. This is Massey."

The scent emanating from the young woman was a strong lily-of-the-valley with a sweet vanilla overtone and a flowery base. Samantha tried not to wriggle her nose. It was a very distinctive aroma.

"And this is Rosie," announced Samantha. Rosie came forward with a bound to say hello to Ashley, who petted her for a long moment. Then Rosie turned to the man standing behind her. She immediately stiffened. She stood looking at him for a long moment.

Massey made a half-hearted effort. "Nice doggie."

Rosie was too much of a lady to growl. Instead she stalked back to stand between Samantha and the Sheriff.

Ashley made a little joke about how Massey was more of a cat person and then said goodbye. They walked down the hall to their condo.

Rosie stared after them, still stiff-legged. No tail wagged.

Perkins finally pushed the elevator button. The elevator was still on 6, so the door slid open immediately. They got in and Perkins hit L.

He reached down to pat Rosie's head. She licked his hand.

As the door opened to the lobby, he looked at Samantha. "That was weird. I've never seen her react like that before."

Samantha just looked down at Rosie and waved her hands. It *had* been very weird.

Six floors above, Massey fumbled with the lock to 617. "Just frickin' great. We've got the damn sheriff shacking up with the broad who lives on our floor. And now a damn dog." He shook his head as he finally got the door open. He pushed in to the hallway. Ashley followed. She was shaking her head as well, but not about the dog.

CHAPTER 26

SAMANTHA SPENT THE morning working with the neighborhood on the Delvecchio Bridge development project. After just a few days she could already see what the big equipment from Elliott's construction company had accomplished. The pit was big and deep.

There was real excitement from the community now that the long-debated and much-delayed project was underway.

Part of her job with Starwind was to coordinate with the neighborhood leaders and make sure they were kept up to date and happy. Webster and his father had learned early in the expansion of their construction company that local issues can fester and explode quickly. And local governments usually sided with local voters.

"I just think the playground is going to be so special," said one mother as she patted Samantha on the arm. "My kids are really excited."

"Just make sure they stay away from the construction site," Samantha warned. "It is really dangerous for them."

The ladies thought about that for a moment. "Maybe we should do our own Neighborhood Watch program around the site," ventured one.

"That is a really smart idea," Samantha responded quickly. "I'll make sure to tell Elliott. And the fencing around the site will protect the kids. Please make sure the kids understand not to try to go past the fence, especially when there is equipment working."

She was proud of herself for learning about the construction process.

"Can you post signs in Spanish as well?" questioned a Latina mother. Her two babies squirmed on her lap.

"Yes, of course. Another good idea. Thank you for reminding me." Samantha looked around the coffee party. "Anything else? No? Okay, you've all got my email and phone number. Contact me anytime."

Goodbyes were shared and hugs were given. It was a diverse neighborhood, and one that Samantha had adopted—and the ladies of the community had as quickly adopted her.

Despite her protests, she left with a homemade coffee cake, half a dozen muffins, and the remnants of an iced carrot cake.

"You need to get a little more meat on those pretty bones," said one lady with a laugh. "And give the sheriff our best!"

More laughs. Samantha gathered her gifts and headed for her car. Thinking about the sheriff gave her an idea. She swung by HQ and carried the baked goods in to give to Mary, Perkins' assistant.

The home-baked treats were welcomed. Perkins was in a meeting, but Mary promised to save a slice of the carrot cake for him.

Rushing back to Sapphire Blue, Samantha barely made it in time to greet Samira. The surgeon had a rare half-day off, so she was coming over to spend it at the beach.

"We don't see each other as much," Samira complained as they settled into the warm sand. They had stuck an umbrella deep into the ground. The waves lapped gently against the shore.

Samantha poured each of them a gin and tonic. She used plain red plastic glasses. The sheriff's department patrolled the beach for underage drinkers and people causing problems. Technically there was no drinking on the beach. Samantha didn't want to cause any of Perkins's deputies any problems. Like having to arrest his girlfriend.

"No, that's right. I miss our Sams Club sessions," Samantha responded. "But with your surgical schedule, Kim's city hall meetings, and now my work on the condo complex, it's just... hectic."

Samira sipped appreciatively at the tart, refreshing drink. "Yeah, I guess. Still..."

They relaxed as the afternoon sun dwindled. The Gulf called them after an hour of sunshine. The water was refreshing...or pretty cool, depending on one's perspective.

They retreated back to their little umbrella, towels swirling, to reapply suntan lotion.

"Hi," came a tentative voice. Samantha and Samira turned.

"Oh, hi. Uh, Ashley, right?"

"Yes. Hi," she said turning to Samira.

"I'm Samira. Friend of Samantha's. User of her free beach and drinker of her expensive booze."

Ashley joined in Samantha's laughter.

"Would you like a now-watery G&T?"

Ashley nodded at Samantha's query. The last drops from the thermos were distributed amongst the three women.

"I love walking on the beach," admitted Ashley. "So peaceful."

After a thoughtful moment, Samira asked, "What do you do?"

"I'm a financial planner. Investment advisor. And you?"

"I cut up people for a living."

"So, a stand-up comic?"

"Not usually," Samira replied laughing. "Surgeon. Mostly knees and hips. Or whatever else our veterans need."

"That's terrific. Do you do private as well?"

"Yes, some. I consult for a private surgical practice in Tampa. But I'm based at the St. Petersburg VA Hospital."

"Gosh, I've driven by there. It's huge."

"Yes, big campus. Sad that our country needs those kinds of huge hospitals, but I'm proud to serve."

Ashley saluted her with her cup. She drank the last few drops and rose lithely. "I've got to go and get showered and changed. Thanks for the drink, Samantha. Samira, a great pleasure and honor to meet you. I hope I'll see you again."

Goodbyes were exchanged. Ashley walked back to the condo grounds, thinking. One of her first lessons in money management was that there were two kinds of investors—smart money, and doctor money.

She thought hard as she strolled back to the Blue Building. Now she faced a real ethical dilemma—should she tell her partner?

Chapter 27

THE STEALTH ATTACK on Port Manatee city hall started at 12:01 a.m.

It didn't take long.

When the first staff arrived early the next morning and tried to open up their computers, they all got the same stark message flashing in red:

WARNING! WARNING! YOUR COMPUTER SYSTEM HAS BEEN FROZEN! DO NOT ATTEMPT TO FIX IT OR YOUR ENTIRE STORED DATA WILL BE ERASED!

TO GET YOUR DATA RELEASED CONTACT US IMMEDIATELY AND PAY 100 BITCOINS.

When City Manager Roy Crawford arrived at his usual 7:30 a.m. start time, the early shift staff were in full panic mode.

The IT people soon confirmed it. The city hall computer system had been hacked. It was being held for ransom.

City taxpayers couldn't do business online. City hall couldn't do its normal business. Pretty much all municipal operations were at a standstill.

Crawford promptly tracked down computer genius Wayne Cooper through the governor's office.

"Not you too!" Cooper exclaimed. "Shit. You're the eighth Florida city to get it, plus three state government departments and a hospital."

"You have any bright ideas, Wayne?"

"You've got three choices. Pay them. Hope they are honorable thieves and scoundrels and they will then release your data. Second, don't pay them and hope your IT people have full backup off-site. You'll then need to dump most of your existing system and rebuild it. That'll take some time. In the meantime, dig out some pencils and paper and hope enough of your staff remember how to write in cursive and use carbon paper. Or, third, you can try to negotiate with them to get the ransom down and have your files released."

Crawford thought hard. He was angry with his IT manager because one of his first jobs when he had taken over as city manager months ago had been to inquire about the city's tech security. Crawford had been assured that the IT department had it under control and it was secure.

Apparently not so much.

Recriminations, however, would have to wait. The city's day-to-day functions were in jeopardy. They still needed to take tax payments, process applications, issue permits, and do the rest of the critical activities of all local governments.

"What's the demand?" Cooper asked.

"One hundred Bitcoins."

"Shitshitshit. That's what, over eight hundred grand at to-day's quote?"

Crawford grunted agreement.

"Anything you can do?" Crawford finally asked again.

"Dammit, Roy, I'd like to say yes but that'd be a lie. Over time we might be able to trace them, but the odds are pretty good that they're based in one of the 'Stans, or Asia, or Russia. Good luck getting at them there."

Crawford grunted again. "Okay, thanks. I'll keep you informed. This'll hit the local media any minute. There'll be hell to pay here."

"Best option might be to try to negotiate with the bastards," concluded Cooper. "Try to get the ransom down and get your info released." He paused. "You insured for this?"

"Yeah. The city wasn't when I arrived. I insisted to the last city council that we add that coverage. Couple of 'em didn't want to pay the bill, but I forced it through. Still," he continued bitterly, "this will cost us. Time. Money. Confidence of the community. Staff work." He sighed. "It is a mess."

"Yeah, it is." Cooper was not noted for sentimentality.

"Okay, got to run," said Crawford. "The staff is lined up at my door, and I've got to tell the mayor."

Crawford made that call four minutes later. It did not go well.

"How could this have happened?" demanded Sonja Rodriguez. She was clearly not pleased. Crawford could hear the mayor's cellphone pinging as they spoke on her home phone. He suspected the news was now exploding in the city. He clicked on his own cell service.

Exploding was too small a word.

"I will find that out," replied Crawford grimly. "But right now, we've got to make a decision about what to do. I've talked with Wayne Cooper at the capital. You remember him from last year and the investigation into, uh, your predecessor."

Rodriguez began to calm a bit. "Yeah, I remember him. Super smart."

"He is. We're the eighth Florida city to be hacked. He says either shut down and start again, pay the ransom, or try to negotiate. The demand is over eight hundred thousand dollars."

Rodriguez sucked in her breath. Nobody was going to come out of this looking good.

"What is your recommendation?"

Crawford paused. There was no right answer, but there were sure a lot of wrong ones.

"Trying to rebuild our entire system will take weeks, if not longer. That assumes we've got a complete backup to midnight last night. In the interim, we'd be back to paperwork and some rigged-up new computer systems. If we pay 'em, there's no guarantee we'll get the files reopened, although usually that does happen." He paused and took a deep breath. "Or, you could tell me to try to negotiate with them and see what happens. No guarantee, of course."

Rodriguez paused for a long moment. She clearly now understood the implications for her new administration. Community outrage could be devastating to the cohesiveness and effectiveness of the new council.

She threw it back to Crawford. "And?"

He took a deep breath. "I would be willing to try to negotiate with the hackers, Your Honor."

Another pause. "All right. Good luck. I'm on my way in. I'm going to want answers. Fast." She set the phone down in its cradle with considerable vigor.

Crawford winced as he hung up his own phone.

Well, this had suddenly turned into a career-threatening day. And it was only 7:58 a.m.

Next was the call to the insurance company. That was sure to be a fun-packed conversation.

Then a local press conference. That would be even more delightful.

He sighed and picked up the telephone.

CHAPTER 28

"WHOSE FAULT IS this? Who's to blame?" demanded a brittle blonde TV reporter. Channel 7.

"About the same as their ratings," muttered Crawford snarkily to himself.

The mayor looked at Crawford. He stepped forward to the podium as she retreated.

"Ultimately, I am responsible for the operations of this city hall and for the people who work here."

"What do you have to say to the people of Port Manatee?" came from a long-time reporter for the *Port Manatee Observer*.

"We understand there will be some short-term disruption in their dealings with city hall," continued Crawford. "We apologize for that. Our staff will do everything we possibly can to assist our residents. Any late fees or penalties because of this disruption will be waived. Our staff will assist residents in filling out forms manually. We will try to conduct business as usual but we hope our residents will understand this unusual situation."

"What will all this cost the taxpayers?" came the follow-up.

Ah, that was a nasty one. "We are still in the process of determining that as we work to resolve the situation."

"Will the final bill be reported in public?"

"Yes. The mayor has insisted on that." Might as well throw her some political cover, Crawford thought.

"What is the time frame to resume full operations?" The brittler and blonder reporter from Channel 2. Why were they all brittle blondes? Crawford wondered as he willed his forehead not to sweat on camera.

"We are working on that now. We hope very soon. And with that, we're going to get back to work."

Crawford stepped back from the podium and off the raised dais. The mayor hesitated for a moment and then followed.

There were a couple more shouted questions from the media. They both ignored them and exited to an anteroom.

"Where are you on negotiations?" Rodriguez snapped as soon as the door shut.

"In progress. I have made contact. I have attempted to bring down the ransom. I am waiting to hear now."

The mayor nodded curtly and pushed open the door to her office. Crawford stood there for a minute. He and the mayor had always had a close relationship. Of course, political instincts for self-preservation kicked in very quickly for most politicians in a time of crisis.

Crawford rushed back to his own office. Kim was waiting for him.

"You did well," she told him as they headed into his private office.

"Thanks. It is not an easy situation. We can't tell the public everything. But hopefully soon." He stared at his computer with yearning.

"I'd better run," Kim said as she kissed him briefly on the cheek. "I don't want to be accused of special treatment from our city manager."

He smiled wanly as she left. He suspected that was going to happen regardless of—

His computer dinged. He rushed over. Finally, a reply from the ransom demanders.

"YOUR SOB STORY IS PATHETIC! TYPICAL AMERICAN BULLSHIT! MAKE ANOTHER OFFER!"

So, the one Bitcoin wasn't enough. It had been an opening gambit. At least it sounded as if they were prepared to negotiate.

Crawford thought for a long minute before typing back his counter-offer.

The reply didn't take long.

"BULLSHIT BULLSHIT BULLSHIT! WE DO NOT CARE ABOUT YOUR POOR CITY. YOU ARE BORING LITTLE MAN. SEND 5 BITCOINS IMMEDIATELY OR YOU LOSE EVERYTHING!"

Crawford thought for a brief moment before replying his acquiescence.

"AGREED! YOU ARE NOT WORTH OUR TIME. PAY NOW!"

His Treasurer had been standing by and the insurance company had agreed to pay up to ten Bitcoins. Minus the deductible, of course. Crawford thought it was a pretty good settlement, all things considered. The alternative was a lot worse.

The e-deal was completed within seconds. Then they waited.

And waited.

And waited.

Crawford paced around his office nervously. If he had just paid $41,000 to accomplish nothing, then his career in Port Manatee would be measured in nanoseconds and not—

His computer pinged. The message about the ransom disappeared. A moment later what looked like the normal business function of city hall appeared.

Crawford rushed to the door of his office. He looked out. His staff was high-fiving as their screens returned to life.

He sagged in relief and staggered back to an office chair. The stress of the situation had drained him. He sat slumped in the chair until the mayor, Kim, and another council member rushed in.

His IT manager rushed up and stopped in the doorway. "We're back on line!" he shouted enthusiastically. "Good to go!" He rushed out.

The planning director rushed in. "We've got everything back! All our files are good!" She rushed out.

The mayor looked at him. "What did you do? And what did it cost us?"

Crawford looked at her. "I negotiated, as you asked. I explained our situation. They seemed to prefer quick cash to prolonged negotiations. We settled on five Bitcoins." He paused. "About $41,000, depending on the price this morning."

"Well. That's certainly better than I had been bracing for. And insurance will cover most of that?"

Crawford nodded.

"Huh," said Her Honor as she departed suddenly. "I need to update the media about what I've accomplished." She rushed out.

Kim stared after her. "What *she* has accomplished?" she spat out bitterly. Even the other councillor looked a little taken aback at the naked political ambition.

They rushed out.

Everybody was rushing, thought Crawford as he moved to sit behind his desk. Any smell of victory seemed to energize politicians.

He prodded his keyboard. Everything seemed normal to him.

Whew.

An hour later, the mayor announced that the IT crisis in Port Manatee was over. She explained that negotiations with the hackers had been successful. The cost to the taxpayers would be very modest. Full operations on the city's website were up and running.

She stumbled a bit when asked about the next steps to make their IT system impregnable.

Crawford hadn't been invited to share the podium with Her Honor, so he couldn't provide that answer.

Politicians.

Kim clenched her fists as she stood at the back of the room and watched.

Crawford shrugged.

Better one should step in front of a slavering tiger that was charging you while you were holding a juicy T-bone steak than get between a politician with good news and the TV cameras.

(HAPTER 29

"MR. HOZWORM?"

"Good morning, Ms. Summers. How lovely to hear from you."

"I wasn't sure you would remember me."

"Of course I do. And I've been waiting for your call."

Samantha could barely remember the small grey man who had appeared at her side at Kim's final debate and slipped her his card.

"I wonder if you would care to join me for tea this afternoon?"

Tea? It wasn't wine. But perhaps her liver would enjoy the respite.

"Uh, yes, that would be fine. Where?"

"How nice. There is a very small, very private boutique hotel located on Princeton Street, just off Adelaide. La Casa Adrianna. They do a lovely afternoon tea. Shall we say four p.m.?"

"Fine. I look forward to seeing you then."

Six hours later, Samantha pulled up to a charming old inn that she had not known existed. It was a former hacienda that had been converted. She parked for free—free!—in their lot and walked through beautifully landscaped grounds into the foyer.

Samantha was dressed in a demure summer cocktail dress, heels and for some reason had dug out her mother's pearls. Her hair was in a French twist.

She looked around as she entered. Dark wood, oiled and polished. Comfortable upholstered chairs, a discreet reception desk, and two ceiling fans gently blowing a cooling breeze. Elegant. Sophisticated. Private.

Off to the left she saw what looked like a small restaurant. She peeked in the door and was greeted by a motherly Latina wearing a black dress. She smiled. "Ms. Summers? Welcome. Mr. Hozworm is waiting for you. Please follow me."

They walked to a quiet corner table where Hozworm rose to shake hands. "Thank you so much for coming. It is lovely to see you again."

Samantha smiled as she sat down and crossed her legs. She barely remembered his face. He was again dressed in an elegant grey suit, white shirt and a black tie with a small pattern in it. He shot his cufflinks as he sat down after her and gold flashed.

To be honest, he was quite forgettable in appearance, she thought. A perfect spy.

"I much prefer this hotel to a noisy bar," he explained. "No one knows about it except for a very loyal and very, uh, judicious, clientele. I have been coming here for many years. Ah, thank you, Rosita."

The plump and happy woman in black quickly served them a silver pot of tea with lemon, sugar, and milk on the side. "I chose Earl Grey. I hope you don't mind," Hozworm announced as he let the pot steep.

"That will be very nice," Samantha replied as she began to relax. She looked around the intimate dining room. "This place is utterly charming. I've never even heard of it."

"No, most people haven't. I don't drink, and I don't like loud. This has been my…hangout, although that's not a very elegant word…for a long time. I think I'm the only unelected person in the political game they've ever allowed in," he said with a chuckle.

A moment later Rosita returned to the table with a classic, highly polished, three-tiered silver cake stand. It displayed crustless cucumber and smoked salmon sandwiches, scones with clotted cream and strawberry jam, and some tiny, delicious-looking pastries.

A small group of people arrived quietly and was escorted to a round table in the other corner. Samantha looked at them casually. She started. She thought she recognized the man with the short grey beard as the chief justice of the Florida Supreme Court.

"Shall I pour?" Hozworm enquired politely as he reached for the teapot.

"Yes, thank you." Samantha looked up as another group arrived. Good heavens, it looked like, oh heck, what was her name? She was a highly respected Broadway actress. Golly, she was gorgeous. Her entourage was small and quiet. Hadn't she been nominated for a couple of Tonys?

Samantha added a bit of sugar and lemon, stirred and then sipped. "Exquisite." She helped herself to a quarter smoked salmon sandwich. Her eyes opened a bit. "This is terrific. Scottish?"

"Nova Scotian, I believe. They are very close in flavor. I am so glad you are enjoying it." He paused as he nibbled a cucumber sandwich. "The English do some things rather well, don't they?"

"Indeed. The scones look—oh, what the heck, I'll exercise a little longer tomorrow. Oh, they are still warm," Samantha said as she helped herself. She slathered a bit of cream and jam on a piece and popped it in. "Wow. Great."

"They bake them here, the old fashioned way," Hozworm assured her. He scooped one up himself and devoured it with pleasure.

He poured a second cup for each of them and settled back. "This is very pleasant. I am so glad you were free to join me. I have been looking forward to our little chat."

Samantha studied him. "You were right when you predicted Kim in a landslide," she said.

"Yes. She is smart and talented. I'm sorry I wasted so much money on Lester Maddox." He shrugged. "A party stalwart who wanted a shot. No big loss." He casually dismissed the recent election result. "Frankly, Ms. Sharpe is smarter and a better choice."

Samantha listened intently. She had perused the list of donors for both Maddox and the other competitors for Kim's Ward 3 seat. The name Hozworm had never appeared.

"Forgive me," she began tentatively. "I'm not sure exactly what it is that you, uh, do."

"Yes. Well, I don't do a lot, really." He smiled politely. "I sort of look after some political things in this region of Florida. You know, provide a bit of financing to candidates, do a little fundraising, and help to get the right people in the right spot. Take care of any problems that might pop up. Just sort of help out here and there. All behind the scenes, of course."

Samantha looked at him steadily as he sipped from his cup. Her father, who had been deeply involved with local politics, had taught her about political fixers. They were the quiet men— and a few women—who ran the party machine. The smart ones stayed well back in the shadows. She eyed her tablemate. He seemed to be very clever.

"So basically, you control the money, the candidates and the elections," she said.

He laughed lightly. "Oh my dear, you are just delightful. No, you give me much too much credit. I'm just a simple man trying to assist a few worthy people in public life." He delicately reached over and chose a small apricot tart from the top shelf of the serving dish.

Samantha smiled wickedly at him. "Uh huh." She took a sip of her cooling tea and replaced the cup on the saucer. She eyed the shortbread cookie. "So, why would I possibly be of interest to such an unobtrusive man who doesn't do anything?"

He smiled back. "Please. Call me PJ. I think we are going to get along famously." He paused and also contemplated the shortbread cookie. "Are you going to eat that, or just stare at it?"

Samantha snatched it with a smile before he could take it. She practically moaned with pleasure as the buttery, sugary cookie melted in her mouth. It would be a long walk on the beach tomorrow.

"Again, PJ. As delightful as this tea has been, and it has been truly lovely, why am I here?"

"Simple, really, Samantha. May I call you that?" She nodded. "Thank you. And it really is quite simple. I'm also sort of a talent hunter. Like a baseball scout—you keep an eye on the kids playing in the minor leagues, Class A ball, to see who might become a major leaguer. Some make it to the big time, most don't. Those are the odds. But every so often you find somebody who has real talent and real potential. I think Kim has both of those."

Samantha sat back and absorbed his words. She had never really thought past getting Kim elected to the Ward 3 seat on Port Manatee City Council. Kim had never said a word about any other office.

Of course, it had been Samantha's idea for Kim to run in the election after the scandals of the previous council. The campaign had been fierce and exhausting. Was there a next for Kim?

She absently squeezed more lemon into the teacup that PJ had refilled.

"There is nothing specific today that we need to talk about," he continued. "I just thought it would be appropriate for us to get to know each other."

"Yes. This has been eye-opening. And thoroughly enjoyable," Samantha said.

"One thing. No. Two things, if you will permit a little friendly advice from an old man who has seen a few things." Samantha shook her head at the old man reference and smiled at him.

"First, I think Kim has the smarts and the personal history to go into national office at some point. A decorated war hero. Wounded in battle. Smart as heck. Doesn't speak great in public yet, but that will come. Wants to serve for all the right reasons. But it will be up to you to provide her with that safe home base that all political people need."

He paused to sip his own tea.

"Being elected to public office today is very stressful. Kim doesn't understand yet that she will become controversial. Some issues will jump up and bite her. There will be surprises. She is already a public figure. Everything she does will be judged. It will be difficult for her. She needs to toughen-up politically. She will need you and a few others to be her 'kitchen cabinet'—people who will give her the unvarnished truth. People who will care for her and protect her. She will need a safe harbor because she will make enemies."

He sipped his tea again. He looked Samantha in the eye. "Some enemies she will know." He dropped his eyes and contemplated the remaining amber liquid in his cup before raising his eyes to look squarely at Samantha. "Most she will not."

Samantha nodded slowly. Politics today was too often nasty and brutish. Neither she nor Kim was properly prepared for those realities.

He paused again, sipped again, and looked a little uncomfortable as he eyed her over the tea service.

Finally he ventured one last comment. "And please forgive me for this, but be warned—her relationship with Roy Crawford is a real danger zone for her as long as she is on city council and he is city manager."

Samantha absorbed his words. He had no reason to lie to her, other than he was a veteran of dozens of political battles and had spent his life doing things in political circles. Did he lie for a living? Did he have an ulterior motive?

He seemed genuine to her.

Hozworm waited a long moment until she refocused on him. "Second, I would suggest that you start building a war chest early. Do some tactical fundraising. I think women are a critical part of her base. They should be a good target for unique fundraising events. Then start expanding her base. And get her social media credentials extended."

Samantha nodded.

"It will be fairly easy right now to do some innovative fund-raising for her. We're still in that dead-zone period when everybody is still recovering after the local elections. There won't be much competition for dollars. If you can pull off some fun new ideas and raise some good money for her, and do it as a kind of Political Action Committee, then you don't have to declare the money and Kim can use it for whatever campaign might come in the future. Nobody in local politics ever thinks that far ahead."

He paused. "Just in case new opportunities come around, you would be very well-positioned with some money in the bank," he concluded with a smile.

Samantha continued to think about what he had said to her. It all made perfect sense. Even if Kim wanted to stay on city council, campaigns still cost a lot of money. And when everybody else was mining for donations once a campaign started, if they had money in the bank already...

She shook her head. "Forgive me," she said with a sweet smile, "my mind was running around thinking about all that you have said. It makes sense. I appreciate your advice. And candor."

He nodded approvingly. "You have my card and my phone number," he questioned. Samantha nodded. "Good. Keep that. It is my private number. I have an office downtown, but you don't want to be seen there. People are always watching." He shuddered slightly. "It is a curse of my life. There is no reason for you to suffer from that as well."

Samantha rose gracefully from the table and shook his hand. "I feel honored to have been invited here. The tea was wonderful. Thank you. I appreciate our conversation. It was... enlightening. And will, of course, remain private."

"I am so glad that you found it interesting. I am just an old man on the fringes of a few little political things. I take great pleasure in helping good people understand some of the things I've learned over the years."

He smiled once again. "Call me anytime on my private line. And perhaps you and Kim would be my guests here sometime in the future."

"We would love that. Thank you." She gathered her purse and turned from the table.

He escorted her to the door, where Rosita was waiting. "Rosita will show you out," he told her. "Forgive me. I need to pay my respects to the chief justice."

With that, he gave a slight bow. She left the elegant little room with Rosita and they walked into the lobby.

"This was delightful," she said. "May I come back here on my own?" Samantha questioned tentatively.

"Oh yes, Señorita. Now that we know you, you are most welcome." Rosita smiled warmly at her.

"Thank you. I will look forward to the next occasion," Samantha dug into her purse for her car keys. "It was lovely."

Chapter 30

"WE'VE JUST HAD confirmation from Dubai," said Ashley breathlessly. "We've been okayed to accept your $500,000 for the WYRT pre-sale investment!"

Rebecca softly clapped her hands. "Great! The ladies will be so happy. Thank you."

Massey Ferguson sat back on the sofa and watched his partner reel in the big fish. It was always a pleasure to watch her at work.

Finally he leaned forward. "We're setting up a special US bank account just to handle your investment," he said confidentially. "We didn't want to get into the mess of transferring funds into our Canadian accounts and exposing you to any potential problems for cross-border currency transfers or tax issues." He sighed. "Governments. All their silly regulations over a simple financial transaction."

Rebecca nodded her thanks.

"Now, you understand that this will take a little time before the launch, and then it will take a little time to build the excitement of this new e-currency?"

"Yes. Although we think the return will be great."

"Very smart. When the first dividends come out, shall we make payment directly into your account?"

"Yes. We're also setting up a new checking account at the bank. We're consolidating our investments in that account and we can then transfer proceeds directly to the ladies. So yes, you can deposit directly."

Rebecca flushed with pride at the expectation of a strong dividend stream coming into their account. The Wives were going to be pretty excited when that cash started to flow. That might even be a good time to tell their idiot husbands about their marvellous new investment.

"And you understand why we have to keep the details of this secret until the new IPO is confirmed and announced," repeated Ashley.

"Yes, of course." Rebecca sipped her wine. "It is really quite exciting being in on the ground floor, isn't it? Well, probably not for you two because that's your business and you do it all the time, but for us…"

Her voice trailed off as she stared out the window. This international finance stuff was pretty stimulating. Hubby was going to get lucky tonight.

A few moments later Rebecca walked straight to the corner where the Wives dominated. Conversation stopped as she approached.

She gave a short, tight-lipped nod to the women assembled beneath the umbrellas. There were efforts to keep a straight face but most weren't very successful. They immediately started whispering amongst themselves.

Their male entourage looked on, puzzled. Then somebody said something about the hockey playoffs, and their attention refocused on much more important issues.

The ladies poured Bloody Marys all around. A toast was made to riches and prosperity. Big grins.

The guys talked golf.

CHAPTER 31

"I ALWAYS TAKE OFF my shoes when getting weighed at the doctor's office," Ashley confided to Samira.

"Heck, I take off my earrings," Samira confided back.

Ashley laughed. They were sitting around the pool at Sapphire Blue. Kim was off in the corner on her cellphone. Some constituent with a complaint about garbage collection.

After a moment, Samira looked at her new friend. "You look worried about something."

"Do I? Oh darn. It's such a nice day, and here I've got to figure out the advance marketing for the new digital currency that—oh, sorry, I shouldn't be boring you with this."

"No, I'm interested. My family has always had a keen eye for international finance."

"Well, you are so smart. That is really the next huge investment opportunity. Digital currency is going to take over so many aspects of the financial transactions around the world. Let's face it, there are trillions of dollars sent around the world every day. Many of them are legal. The system needs faster, easier and more secure ways to deal with multi-national currency and business needs."

Samira nodded. "Makes sense to me. How are you involved?"

Ashley paused, looked around and then leaned closer to Samira. "Don't tell anyone, but I've got some exclusive investment opportunities before the IPO for a new Asian e-currency comes out. Pre-sell, they call it. It is a start-up investment opportunity."

"Like Bitcoin?"

"Exactly! You got it precisely. And you know how much money some really smart people made by investing early in that!"

Samira sat back thoughtfully. She sipped her ice water. Her dark eyes peered into the future.

Ashley sat there in the sun. Her big sun hat covered her head and shoulders. She waited patiently.

One of the hardest lessons she had had to learn in the con game was to shut up. Silence was a really powerful tool, be it for police interrogations or letting other people's minds play with possibilities.

Whoever spoke first usually lost.

"What kinds of investments are being accepted?" Samira finally asked.

"I've only got a hundred million," Ashley pouted. "Chump change in the global marketplace." She drank some water. "Still, it's a pretty unique opportunity." She drank again and sat back. "My allotment was almost sold out in a flash."

Samira continued to stare past Kim, who was still arguing over the urgent garbage issue. Ashley swore she could see the computations going on in that very smart brain.

Ashley could also see Samantha, that handsome sheriff, and that damn dog coming out of the Blue Building. That was going to change the mood pretty fast.

Samira finally blinked, hunched forward, and said quietly, "What if my family wanted to put a few bucks into this thing? What is it again?"

"WYRT. Wur-tee. Named after the big Asian currencies."

Samira nodded again.

Samantha and an excited Rosie were getting closer.

"Can you expedite the process to make an investment in this...Wurt-thing?"

Ashley paused as if thinking hard. Finally she nodded just as Rosie came panting up to kiss Samira. "I think that can be arranged. Just don't tell anybody else. One?"

Samira looked at her through the red-gold hair of the dog. She nodded.

Ashley fought to keep a triumphant smile off her lips as she leaned over to pet Rosie.

Oh darn, there went the top of her bikini again, her boobs practically falling out as she bent over.

Perkins flushed. Ashley peeked up at him with a tiny triumphant grin.

She has a warm smile, he thought. But hard eyes.

Chapter 32

"I WANT TO SEND a little dividend check to each of our Michigan and Ohio investors," Ferguson told Ashley a few days later. "Let's face it, the winter is slipping away, our lease will be over soon here in Florida, and we need to consolidate our money, get it out of the country and then we need to split."

"All right," she agreed. "Giving them a little dividend will keep them happy and away from any nasty law enforcement agencies for several more months." He nodded. "I guess the question is, when do we wrap up here? I think I can get the half mil from the ladies in the next couple of days. I think we should get out of here next week."

Ferguson nodded. He looked at her for a long moment.

"We've done okay together. Are we going to keep the partnership going?"

Ashley paused before replying. "I don't know, Massey. I'm getting a little tired of the cons. Moving every few months. Pressing my boobs into lonely old men so they will write a check. Worrying about some hot-shot cop catching a sniff of us."

Ferguson watched her carefully. Conners conning conners. It was a hard equation to figure out.

"With the $1.8 mil from our latest 'investors' in the north, the $500K here at Sapphire Blue, that's 2.3 less expenses. Say 300 grand, give or take some small change. That's going to be about a million each for the Asian currency caper."

She nodded. She had never really trusted him. And of course, he had never really trusted her.

It was the reality of living a life of dubious character.

It was also why both of them needed to sign off on any bank transfers.

They each used their own security code. It was a bit cumbersome, but in this era of electronic banking and instantaneous global currency transfers, a girl couldn't be too careful, Ashley thought.

Besides, she really, really didn't like his moustache.

And she was tired of the handsy crap. The dopes just seemed to love pinching her bum. She sometimes felt she'd had more hands patting her butt than an NFL wide receiver who had just caught a Hail Mary pass to win the Super Bowl.

She looked at him steadily. "Yeah, I think it might be time. We've done well. Made a lot of money. This WYRT scam is a very nice little retirement fund. Time to move on."

He nodded slowly. He had figured she was getting restless. And she was certainly getting harder to deal with. And obviously he wasn't going to get into her pants, despite several earnest attempts.

Time for a younger, prettier, more acquiescent protégé.

"Fine. Let's finish the deal here, then get the funds transferred, close the account, get to Singapore and divide the money."

Singapore had become his overseas home base. A great city: English banking traditions, Asian flexibility. A city that respected you for having money and wasn't too squeamish about how you got it. Most of all, it was safe and secure for his own investments. And as a nice bonus, it was far, far away from any angry investors in the States who might pop up. They would never find him hidden deep in mysterious Asia.

He would eventually reinvent himself once again and reappear with a different assistant and a new scam. He liked the game. He liked the rush. He liked winning. And it was very lucrative.

And more often than not, the scammed were too embarrassed to complain or tell the cops.

Ashley nodded agreement. She grabbed her laptop and started researching flights. It was a long trip. First-class tickets beckoned.

Chapter 33

REBECCA WAS ACCOMPANIED by two of the Wives when they presented Ashley with a thin envelope. It had one check for $500,000 from the ladies' new investment account. They were calling it "The HoneyMoney Fund."

Ashley made a show of signing a corporate receipt for the investment. Everyone felt very good about the transaction. Everyone had a glass of Dom Pérignon to celebrate.

Ashley's ruby pendant attracted the eyes of the women.

Massey hung in the background. This was Ashley's deal to close. Smart kid. He'd taught her well.

Still, he'd miss having that cute, curvy little butt of hers to pat.

He mentally shrugged. A quarter of a mil from this one, and another three quarters of a million from the work in Michigan and Ohio would be ample compensation. It would add nicely to his nest egg. If he recalled correctly, this would get him over the six million mark. Tax free. Retirement would be comfortable.

Someplace warm without any of those pesky extradition treaties.

The thought still lingered a couple of hours later when he and Ashley returned to Sapphire Blue from finalizing the local banking deposits and transfers. It had all gone swimmingly.

Then the damn sheriff had appeared in the lobby. Obviously he was going to visit that red-headed bimbo on their floor. At least he didn't have that stuck-up dog with him this time.

Still, one had to be civil. Especially to law enforcement.

"How are you, Sheriff?" Ashley began.

"Fine. Fine. And you?"

"Great, actually. We just finished a business transaction that took some time, but all is good."

Perkins nodded. "Say," he spoke as the elevator finally arrived, "You're from Calgary, right?" They nodded. He punched the button for 6. "I remember a Canadian Football League game on ESPN a few months ago. Wow. Exciting game! I think it was the Edmonton Eskimos versus the Calgary Cowboys. That must have been your team?"

Massey nodded curtly. Football. Who gave a shit. Ashley was cooler. "Yes, we often went to games there. It was lots of fun."

Perkins grunted. The elevator door opened. He graciously waved the couple out first. They walked down the hall toward their condo. He paused and watched them carefully before turning toward Samantha's condo unit.

CHAPTER 34

"MARY, IS CHAD in this morning?"

"I'll see. You want him?"

"Yeah, if he's got a minute. Oh, I'd love a coffee."

"So would I. Cream, no sugar."

Perkins sighed. He and his assistant had never quite sorted out who was really in charge of running the Sheriff's Office.

She came in a moment later. "He's on his way. Are you still doing your physical therapy?"

"Yes." He rolled his shoulder. "The arm feels a lot better. Still a bit stiff, and my strength isn't quite back yet, but it's improving." He tried to look a little pathetic and in pain, hoping for coffee. Mary just stared through him.

"Morning, Sheriff. How are you?"

Chad was relentlessly cheerful. He was an up and coming deputy and Perkins was trying to give him some different assignments to see how he would respond.

"Good, thanks. Sit down. You want a coffee? Great. Grab me one while you're up, will you?" He smiled triumphantly at his assistant as she sniffed and left his office.

"I want you to run a quiet little probe into a couple of people. Nothing obtrusive. They're residents of Sapphire Blue. A Massey Ferguson. And Ashley something. They are in 617 of the Blue Building. Renters."

Chad nodded as he made notes.

Perkins sipped his coffee. "Apparently they are from Calgary. Not sure I believe that."

Chad nodded again. He waited, and then grabbed his own mug.

Perkins thought some more. "I can contact my friend at the RCMP if you need a Canadian connection." He shrugged. "Lemme know."

Chad nodded again, closed his notebook, grabbed the dregs of his coffee and left. He loved these special assignments, and he loved the confidence the sheriff kept placing in him. He was aiming to become a detective in the next couple of years.

Perkins worked through the stack of paperwork that Mary had piled on his desk. Lord, the number of government forms was astonishing. No wonder it was so inefficient most of the time.

CHAPTER 35

IT WAS TWO days later when Deputy Chad reported back. It wasn't very good news.

"I talked to the GM at the condo, Virginia McIntyre. She doesn't know them. She said the rental of units is a private matter between the owner of that unit and the renters, as long as they meet the condo rules for a minimum three-month rental. That's to eliminate the short-term partiers and college kids who want to come down, get drunk, and chase girls on the beach. Or boys, I guess."

Perkins nodded. Spring Break week was always hell on the Sheriff's Department. And it now seemed to go on for a month as various colleges and universities celebrated the break at different times.

"She's met them," Chad continued. "Says they are quiet people. Some kind of financial advisors in Canada. He isn't seen around much, something about recovering from a heart thing. She's often at the pool. Pretty cute from what I hear."

Perkins nodded again.

"Nobody can quite figure out their relationship. He's a lot older but I guess that happens." Chad ran his fingers through his long brown hair. "She's made some casual friends around the pool. Oh, her last name is Monroe. Like Marilyn. Now that was one sexy lady."

Perkins finished the cinnamon bun that had somehow appeared on his desk. It was good.

"But here's the thing, Sheriff." The deputy paused, clearly uncomfortable with the next part of his report. "I can't get a real handle on 'em. You would think social media, well these days, with the lack of privacy, pretty much anybody and everybody are listed somewhere. On somebody's website. Or chat line or whatever." He swallowed. "But I've got nothing."

Perkins straightened up as he brushed the residue of the bun off his left hand.

"You said keep it quiet, so I didn't go around interviewing people or anything," Chad concluded. "But they didn't show up in the national crime computer, and Homeland Security has nothing on either one. Nor any other national search engine I could access. Without their passport number or birth date or SSNs, I can't go deeper into the government computers. Still…"

"Somehow I'm not surprised," the sheriff told his deputy. "I never had a good feeling about them. The guy in particular. Even Rosie didn't like him, and she likes everybody." He thought some more. "I suppose that was my first clue. Samantha noticed it as well when Rosie went all stiff-legged and wouldn't say hello to him."

He finished his coffee. "And he has this ridiculous little pencil moustache. Looks like a row of mouse turds on a kitchen floor. Disgusting."

Perkins took Chad's notes and nodded. "You did well," he said. "Thanks."

Chad nodded gratefully and started to return to the deputy's bullpen. He paused. "One last thing. Nobody at the condo has seen them for a couple of days. Maybe they've gone on a little trip. Maybe binge-watching Netflix. Don't know."

A tiny warning bell went off in Perkins' head as he thought some more. No crime had been committed, so why waste time and resources on this mysterious couple? Was a horrid little moustache enough to pursue his hunch?

Finally he decided. "Mary," he hollered. "See if you can track down Jean-Luc Nadeau at RCMP headquarters in Ottawa, will you?"

CHAPTER 36

"*LEROY, MON AMI, comment ça va?*"
The boisterous RCMP inspector's voice boomed over the speakerphone in Perkins' office.

The two law enforcement officers had met at an FBI training session on international terrorism at Quantico, Virginia, a couple of years before. The beer-drinking, English-speaking sheriff and the wine-sipping, French-speaking inspector had somehow connected immediately. They had remained friends.

"Je swees, uh, bon? Bien? Ah shit, Jean-Luc, I'm good."

Nadeau's laugh echoed across the office.

"Come visit me and I'll have you talking *en francais* in a couple of weeks," he boasted. "And bring that gorgeous girl of yours! I still don't understand how you won the lottery and got her!" He laughed again. Perkins joined in.

"Neither does anybody else. I just keep hoping that Samantha doesn't ever stop and try to figure it out."

The news of the romance between the sizzling New York divorcee and the stalwart Florida sheriff had buzzed across the private blue telegraph that connects all law enforcement.

So had the shooting of Perkins the previous year. "How is the arm?" Nadeau inquired carefully.

"Coming along. Hurt like hell for a long time," Perkins hadn't even told Samantha how much pain he had been in. He had refused to take any opioids. It had been a hard rehabilitation.

Nadeau grunted in sympathy.

"And your family?" Perkins asked politely.

"Good. Both kids in university. Marie is at home doing her painting. She had a show at a gallery in Montreal last month. Sold four."

"Wow. Give her my love." Perkins cleared his throat. "Listen, Jean-Luc, I'm quietly looking into a couple of people down here. They haven't committed any crimes that I know of. But I also have a feeling that they are as phony as a three-dollar bill."

Nadeau instantly turned serious. He respected the instincts of smart cops.

"What's the story?"

Perkins paused. "Look, this may sound crazy. But they claim to be investment advisors from Calgary. Said the guy had some heart surgery so they came to Florida for the winter to rest and recuperate."

Nadeau grunted. Perkins could hear him scratching notes on a pad.

"So the other day I happened to meet them in the elevator. I was wary of them because Rosie reacted really negatively to the guy. That's not like her."

"I want to meet this wonder-dog," Nadeau chortled. "Everything you've told me about her...*elle est merveilleux.*"

"Yes, she *is* marvellous. Anyway, I asked them about living in Calgary. I said I'd seen a CFL game on ESPN between the Edmonton Eskimos and the Calgary Cowboys. She said they used to go to some of those games, and—"

"But, *mon ami!* Stop! *Sacre bleu!* The name of the Calgary football team is not the Cowboys. It is the Stampeders!"

"I know that. They didn't."

They both thought that through.

"What is the name of—well, what names are these two con men using?"

It was the first time anybody had said out loud what Perkins feared. He grabbed Chad's notes as the deputy continued to sit and listen to the conversation.

"Here. A woman. Ashley Monroe. And the man. Massey Ferguson."

Nadeau's laugh again boomed out. "Really? Massey Ferguson? I can tell you, that isn't a real name. Nobody in Canada would name their kid Massey Ferguson. It was a big tractor manufacturer once based in Canada. A family in Alberta naming a son Massey Ferguson? No chance!"

Perkins looked at Chad.

"Besides, the story doesn't hold up," continued the inspector. "The cost of travel medical insurance for somebody in Canada who just had heart surgery and then wanted to spend a few months in the States would be astronomical. No, *mon ami,* I think you've got a problem."

Perkins exhaled forcefully. "Yeah, Jean-Luc. I think you are right. I just don't know what we can do when there is no crime."

"Don't worry, my friend...con men can't stop conning. You know that. If not now, later." He paused. "Listen, LeRoy, I can run those names for you. I also know a couple of senior people in the Calgary police. But I'm betting you a dinner with your lovely lady and my wife that there are no such people in Calgary."

"I'll decline that bet, but I'll look forward to the dinner. And yes, I'm paying." He waited for a moment. "They just smelled phony to me from the start. Rosie was right."

Nadeau barked a laugh over the phone. "I've got to run. A meeting with the commissioner. Something about security for the prime minister's trip to Kyiv. Let me know what is happening, LeRoy. Call me if I can be of more help. *Adieu, mon ami.*"

They hung up. Perkins leaned back in his chair. "Well. Now what?"

His deputy looked back. He was smart enough to know when to talk and when to listen.

"Maybe I'll talk to Samantha. See if she's heard of anything strange going on around the pool. But we don't know of any crime that's been committed. We've had no complaints. Can't get a search warrant because there's no probable cause. Can't arrest them for anything. Can't even bring them in for an interview because we don't even know who they are. It is no crime to change your name." He pondered the problem. No solutions arrived.

Finally he stood. He flexed his arm and shoulder. Time for his physical therapy.

"Thanks, Chad. Now we need to try to find out who they really are." He thought some more. "Maybe Samantha can get a fingerprint off a bottle of tanning lotion or something."

He remembered the incident last year when Kim and Samantha had secretly gotten a coffee mug and cigarette butt from the person who had eventually been charged with the murder in the hot tub. Perkins had given them holy hell for that stunt. But it had worked out.

This was a more complex case. Or not yet a case. Maybe never would be a case.

Still, Rosie was usually right.

Chapter 37

"THE COUNCIL MEETING was pretty brutal," confided Kim. The Sams Club was assembled at Kim's condo. The remains of two pizzas and two bottles of red were strewn across the table. Samantha and Samira had insisted Kim order in instead of cooking. Their past experiences with Kim's culinary expertise had solidified that demand.

"The mayor was really pissed about the whole hacking and ransom thing. Roy was under the gun half the night. I had to be really careful about what I said. I wanted to defend him but he kept fighting back. It was awful," she concluded with a shudder.

Samira and Samantha glanced at one another. Like an old mortar shell lying around, this issue was doomed to explode at some time. The personal relationship between the city manager and the new city councillor was unprecedented. It was a powder keg. It was going to go BOOM.

"I think Roy was protecting his head of IT," continued Kim, "but he wouldn't say that. He sees part of his role as defending his management team from political attacks or interference. It was nasty. A couple of the other councillors piled on to Roy. I didn't know what to do or how far I should go." She twisted her wine glass in frustration.

"Councillor Johnson was really aggressive. I don't think she likes me." Kim had the stem of her goblet spinning so fast it practically shot sparks. "'Course, I dunno know if she likes anybody."

"What did the council finally resolve to do?"

Kim turned toward Samira. "They ended up congratulating Roy for negotiating a great settlement and for keeping the cost to the taxpayers to almost nothing. The insurance company paid most of the ransom. We had to upgrade our security and switch some email access codes and so on, but overall we escaped pretty easily."

Her face twisted in emotion. "The council meeting turned out to be just political theatre. Politicians chasing headlines," she said in disgust.

Samira thought for a moment. "So, likely this was more about the new political dynamics on the council than it really was about Roy or this hacking situation?"

Kim pondered for a long moment. She poured the dregs of the second bottle into her glass. There wasn't much.

"I guess that's right." She brightened a bit. "Hey, maybe that is true. The mayor has had a bit of a rough time getting the council to really pull together since the election. I think she's frustrated. Mikayla Johnson is proving to be a handful. She seems really angry about...everything."

Samantha had been thinking about Kim's situation ever since her elegant tea party with PJ Hozworm.

"I've got a suggestion, sweetie." She cleared her throat. "I know this is a bit out of the box." She paused. "Okay, a lot out of the box. But we all knew that your relationship with Roy was going to be an issue. It is sort-of known around town, but you've never really confronted the situation. It is really, uh, unique."

She peered into the bottom of her wineglass. A thin film of purple glazed the bottom. Damn. Nothing for a poor girl to drink.

"Does the city have any specific policies about relationships inside city hall?"

"Uh, a general policy. Sorta says, don't do it."

"What I'm suggesting is that you and Roy come out together and openly admit your personal relationship. You both sign, I don't know, some kind of full disclosure agreement or conflict of interest declaration or something. File it with HR or the city clerk or somebody. You promise to recuse yourself from any council discussions on compensation or a contract or anything personal like that between Roy and the city as his employer. And you both pledge not to discuss city business except at city hall in the normal course of business." She paused again and checked her wine glass. Hmmm. Still no miracles.

"I think it would be a one-day story for most people," she continued, "but it gets it out in the open and clears the air for both of you. Roy would have to think it through from his management perspective, but maybe it would be good for him as well. At least there is no direct-report relationship. You are elected and on the political side. He heads the administrative side. He has a contract with the corporation of the city. You have a contract for four years with the people of Port Manatee."

Samantha threw up her hands. "I don't know if it's a good idea or not but I thought you might want to consider it."

Samira nodded a couple of times but didn't say anything. Kim was deep in thought.

"The last thing I want to do is smudge my reputation," she began flatly. "Or Roy's. We've talked about this a bit, but never really...well, you know. It's hard. Damn it."

She banged her wine glass on the glass coffee table. No cracks in either. "I just hate the loss of privacy, of having to talk about my personal life..."

Samantha waited a long moment before saying gently, "I understand. But this is not going away. All I'm saying is, right now you can control the narrative. You can get in front of this. Then hopefully it goes away so you and Mikayla can become bosom buddies!"

Kim joined the laughter. But it took her a moment.

"Okay. Maybe. I'll think about it." She looked at her two closest friends. "I want to, to, *nourish* my relationship with Roy. For the first time in my life I really see a future with a man. I won't jeopardize that."

Samira and Samantha waited again, sensing intuitively that Kim's deeply personal revelation was not yet over.

"I think I would step down before seeing him hurt or his position threatened. But I don't want to do that either, because I am really starting to enjoy my elected role. I love helping constituents. I love helping to shape the future of our city. But..."

Quiet on the condo's terrace. A distant honking of some geese flying a night flight to somewhere. The waves from the Gulf lapped softly against the shore.

Finally, Kim looked up again. "Maybe you're right, Samantha. I'll talk to Roy. Maybe to the city solicitor or the clerk. I'll see." She suddenly yawned. It had become an exhausting evening.

She smiled at her two friends. "What I don't want to lose is the...lusty...relationship that Roy and I have together." She had a lascivious grin on her face. "That is non-negotiable."

Samantha and Samira laughed, both in envy and in admiration. During these complex, tumultuous times, when any relationship finally clicked it was to be treasured.

Samantha was edging into that territory with Perk.

Samira, on the other hand, continued her rejection of all eligible males between twenty-two and sixty-six in the state of Florida, usually after one date. Few could come up to the beautiful surgeon's standards, although many aspired. Kim and Samantha both worried about their friend's status.

Samira seemed unconcerned.

The evening broke up quickly. The three hugged and kissed goodbye. Samantha groaned just a bit when Samira patted her upper arm. Her self-defence tutoring sometimes had side effects.

Chapter 38

"Hey, anybody seen that really cute little girl with the great rack?"

Headshakes from the boys sitting on the edge of the pool at Sapphire Blue as they dangled their wrinkled ankles into the eighty-six-degree water.

Husband #5 didn't have to elaborate. The luscious little cutie had been the talk of the guys at the pool for months.

A size M T-shirt was stretched tautly over the XL stomach of Husband #2. "She is a hot little thing," he agreed.

The happy sound of tabs opening on beer cans popped around their corner of the pool as another round began. It was always interesting to try to account for the volume of liquid being taken in and the volume of liquid being released by visits to the pool-side bathroom—or other, closer locations.

Ralph eventually got up on creaky knees to hit the can. His much younger and much prettier wife was sunning on a chaise. He was in trouble financially because of her spending.

"Man, he's gotten so cheap he's reusing paper napkins," chortled Ricky as Ralph disappeared.

Ralph was loud and obnoxious. He was a former CEO who had driven the company into five straight quarters of losses before the board mercifully fired him and agreed to a $9.4 million settlement. His imminent demise would not cause tears to be shed.

And besides, that well-stacked young wife of his might—

"Everything come out all right, Ralph?"

He grunted and popped another brewskie. "I tell you what I found the other day in the condo?" Head-shakes all around. "We've lived there three, nearly four years since I married her." He drank deeply. "Opened the oven door. The original plastic was still stretched across the bottom floor of the oven."

The guys whooped a little. Not many of the Wives used their kitchen appliances all that much. Except for the ice maker. And the wine cooler.

Two cute tourists from Illinois arrived at the pool. Their white skin gleamed icily in the hot sun as they took off their cover-ups. It was possible SPF 200 might save them.

The Wives were huddled under their umbrellas. They were asking the same question about their investment guru although without the same references as their gentlemen about her bountiful anatomical details.

"Where is Ashley?" was the theme of the week.

"Let's just go knock on her door," said Delores. The other Wives twitched. Sometimes the simplest ideas are the best.

Two of the residents of Building Blue were promptly dispatched to visit 617.

They were back within seven minutes, shaking their heads. "Nothing. No answer."

A few palms began to sweat just a tiny bit. It seemed odd. Rebecca thought back to the little check-handing-over ceremony they had had last week. Neither Ashley nor Massey had said anything about going on a trip or leaving.

"What, uh, do you think that means?" enquired Wife #8. Tentatively. None of them were very anxious to draw the wrath of Rebecca.

Still, wasn't it Rebecca who had first raised this WYRT idea?

A couple of the ladies began to convince themselves that it really was Rebecca who had...well, forced might be a strong word, but certainly neither of them would have had anything to do with such a risky scheme if Rebecca hadn't...

"I think I'll wander over and see Virginia McIntyre," Rebecca ventured. The Sapphire Blue General Manager ran a tight ship, including keeping track of the short-term renters.

Virginia had quickly figured out the pecking order at the condo complex. She knew who the de facto social leaders were, and it certainly wasn't her weird little chair of the board, Sheila Brown.

Sheila's hair always looked as if she'd just French-kissed a light socket.

Virginia privately thought that Sheila had a face that only a hatchet could love.

Sheila spent most of her day rushing around the condo complex, banging her clipboard on her thigh and trying to convince anyone she ran into how busy she was. As a result, she lived a very lonely life.

"I have not seen Ashley in maybe a week," the GM reported to Rebecca. "One of the workers said he saw them with a couple of suitcases each getting in an Uber early one morning. Their Caddy is still in its parking spot."

Rebecca thought carefully. "I'm just concerned for their, uh, health. We know that he had some heart problems. I wonder if they are okay."

Virginia thought that one through. She suspected there was a lot more to this story than Rebecca's sudden and unprecedented concern for someone else's health.

Still, permanent residents were the ones who ponied up those lovely monthly condo fees. It was only prudent for a hired GM in her first year of governing this large den of iniquity to keep the condo community leaders happy.

"I suppose," she began diffidently, "that with the health concerns you mention, I could call the unit owner. See if she would like me to check on them." She paused. "Probably be all right if you came as a witness. Just to make sure everything's okay."

Rebecca understood. She nodded, got up and left. "See you at three," she tossed over her shoulder.

Virginia nodded back.

Chapter 39

NUMBER 617 BLUE was empty.

Rebecca could feel it in the air as soon as Virginia opened the door with her emergency key.

The cheap furniture was still there, but there were no signs of human habitation. Closets were empty. There were minimal food supplies in the pantry, mainly canned tuna, crackers, cereal, and a partially filled jar of mixed nuts. The refrigerator had a few used condiments on the shelves in the door. The remnants of a quart of half-and-half was about to go rancid. There were two Coors sitting in lonely splendor on the second shelf.

Rebecca gulped hard. She tried to not let Virginia see any weakness.

They re-locked the door and headed to the elevator. Samantha was coming out of her condo and they met at the elevator. Samantha looked at them curiously. No one said anything.

It was a slow ride down.

CHAPTER 40

"I DON'T KNOW," REBECCA said in a low voice. The Wives huddled around her. The husbands were back in the pool enjoying the antics of the two women from Illinois as they writhed under their reddening skin. Aloe was flying madly.

The late afternoon sun drooped behind the palm trees.

"Their clothes were gone. The car is still there. Not much food in the fridge or pantry. Place feels empty."

Winces on several faces. This didn't feel right. It didn't smell right. It couldn't be right.

And most important, of course, was the rather urgent matter of half a million dollars of their own hard-earned money that just may have disappeared.

Really.

Half a million.

Two of the ladies promptly searched their devices for any news of WYRT, new Asian crypto-currencies, Ashley Monroe, or Massey Ferguson.

They were spectacularly unsuccessful.

This caused a considerable flurry of angst and anxiety. The Wives were used to summoning information and answers about anything through the ingenious World Wide Web.

This time, nothing.

Really.

There was a sombre pause. Rebecca finally took a deep breath and exhaled loudly.

"I think we've got to figure we might have been flimflammed." There was a collective intake of breath. "Not certain, but I sure don't like the vibes I'm getting."

"Do we tell our husbands?" came the timid question.

"Hell no!" Rebecca was firm. "This was all our money. We're supposed to be pretty smart. I think it's time we pull on our big girl panties and figure this thing out." She paused. "And if it means pulling every dyed hair from the head of that bitch Ashley to get our money back, well, so be it!"

The boys were stirring at the pool. They'd be back in their corral soon, wanting drinks and dinner.

The Wives quickly agreed that drinks would be a good thing for the boys tonight. Lots of drinks.

"So what do we do tomorrow?"

Rebecca thought hard for a long moment. She looked over her shoulder. The boys were heading for the tables to rejoin them. She really didn't want them involved in this mess.

Really.

Suddenly she looked up. "Got it. We'll go see Samantha tomorrow morning. She's sorta our friend now, after the election campaign. But mostly she's got that good-looking sheriff wrapped around her little finger. He's the one we need. And she's the conduit."

CHAPTER 41

"I'M MAKING YOU shrimp and asparagus risotto," Perkins announced.

Samantha blinked. She was busy petting Rosie, who was demanding a long tummy rub and then Samantha scratching that special spot just behind her ears.

Rosie squirmed in delight. Yes, it was always good when Sheriff and Pretty Lady focused on her. After all, she was the queen of the realm.

Perkins busied himself in her kitchen. He came out a moment later to hand Samantha a glass of a well-chilled white Burgundy. The kid in the liquor store had practically demanded he take it. The kid had figured out who he was and who Samantha was. He was determined to become their private sommelier.

Perkins figured the kid was ga-ga over the stunning woman in his life. Hopefully he wouldn't have to shoot the little brat.

On the other hand, the last four bottles that the kid had selected for their special dinners had been a spectacular success. Samantha had been eyes-wide-open impressed. She had thanked Perkins suitably and profusely later in the evening. Three times on one memorable night. He'd been exhausted.

Rosie's ears had been buzzing with the noise coming from their bedroom.

He presented the glass of delicate straw-colored wine. She smiled, swirled, inhaled, sipped, and then swallowed.

"I think you just might have earned yourself a special little reward tonight," she said throatily.

His stomach lurched for an excited moment. He grinned back. "Well, ma'am, I'm nothing but a humble county sheriff trying to keep you city folks happy."

She slowly ran her finger around the rim of the wineglass. She lifted that finger and then put it to her lips. "Well, big boy, I'm just a little ol' city girl who just happens to have some chaps and boots I need to try on. Sort of model them for somebody.

See if I could wear them." She dropped her gaze. "Do you know of anyone who could help me?"

Perkins licked his own lips as he thought that through. "Well, ma'am, I'd need to know a bit more. What, uh, else would you be wearing with those, um, chaps?"

Samantha gave him a long look through her eyelashes. The tip of her tongue peeked out for a moment. "Oh, well…" she said seductively, "just the boots."

Perkins gulped. "I could start cooking dinner right now," he proclaimed.

Samantha smiled softly. "Why don't you just do that?"

She sipped again. She stroked Rosie. She glanced at Perkins.

"Yes, ma'am." He returned to the kitchen with a feverish grin and renewed urgency. *Let's see, the risotto usually takes about twenty-one minutes to cook…*Tonight he was betting he could do it in twenty.

He was wrong. He managed to cook it in nineteen minutes and forty-seven seconds.

Chapter 42

THE LATE MORNING sun was shining softly on Sapphire Blue's huge central pool. Residents with a variety of hangovers were gradually assembling. The wise ones sought out shady corners.

Perkins groaned softly as he bent over the lounge chair. "Thank heavens the surgeon and the physio cleared me for active duty. Practically pulled a hamstring last night," he muttered.

"Oh, really? I wonder how that happened," said Samantha with a smug smile. "Were last night's gymnastics part of your recommended therapy?"

"Don't recall you complaining about it."

She smiled again. "No, I don't recall that either. Especially the second time. Wouldn't have thought you could get your leg in that position." She paused. "Good for you."

He grinned proudly. Hammies would heal.

Rosie was resting up in the condo. She had been a little snappy this morning about having had her sleep disturbed by the noises coming from Samantha's bedroom the night before.

The queen of the manor expected a lot more peace and quiet at night. There would be retribution. Rosie just hadn't figured out the appropriate response yet.

Chew up a couple of Samantha's expensive shoes? No, no lady would do that to another woman.

Up-chuck on the sheriff's kitchen floor? Always an option.

It would come to her. In the meantime she'd just rest in the cool condo on the sofa where she wasn't supposed to be lying. Her eyes closed.

Samira arrived to join them at the pool. Kim was meeting with constituents. Roy was at city hall cleaning up the week's paperwork. They would join the group after lunch. The five friends were going to dinner at a seafood restaurant up the coast that specialized in soft-shell crab. Samira's latest boy toy would meet them at the restaurant.

A lazy Saturday unfolded. A restorative lite beer was popped for each of them. It was important to stay hydrated. The palm fronds provided pleasant shelter from the sun as it climbed to its zenith.

Two female tourists from Illinois, with very red shoulders and backs, and considerable regret, sat huddled in the shade.

A few kids paddled in the shallow end. Their floaties flashed orange as their little arms wind-milled energetically. A couple of teenage girls preened for a couple of teenage boys. A baby wearing a large diaper was dipped into the water by a doting grandmother. An old man who should have been wearing a large diaper stepped carefully into the pool.

Somehow Samantha's hand slipped into the Sheriff's as he lay on the chaise next to her. His police radio sat next to them. He was always on duty. Samira was reading a medical journal as she sipped her beer.

It was so peaceful. Samantha sighed happily. Nothing could disrupt the—

"Samantha!"

"Urgh. What?" Samantha struggled to open her eyes and prop herself up on one elbow. Perkins immediately abandoned her hand and sat up. Samira dropped the journal.

"Hi! Look! Uh, can we talk?"

It was very hard to say no to Rebecca. Ever. And it seemed especially urgent now.

Samantha struggled to sit up. "Uh, yeah, sure. Sit down." She waved at an adjacent chair.

Rebecca grunted as she sat down. She nodded at Samira. Then she focused on the sheriff.

"Is this private? You want me to go for a walk?" he asked.

"No. Good you're here. Saves time."

He glanced at Samantha who gave him a tiny shrug.

Rebecca sat for a long moment staring at her toenails. They were painted aquamarine.

"This might be nothin'," she began slowly, "but it might be a problem. A big problem."

They waited. Rebecca took a deep breath.

"Thing is, a bunch of us ladies here at the pool made a little investment in our future with Ashley Monroe. You know, that cute little thing here for the winter with her asshole husband?"

Samantha could feel Samira straightening up and staring at Rebecca.

"So we invested some money into this new Asian cryptocurrency. Something called a WYRT. Supposed to be the hot new thing after Bitcoin. She said they were the exclusive Western Canadian representatives for the pre-sale before the IPO. Seemed a bit curious to me, but the girls checked it out on the web and there was a big page about this new e-currency."

She paused again. Samantha handed her a cold beer from the ice chest. She nodded gratefully and popped the top. She took a long drink.

"Here's the thing, Sheriff. We haven't seen her since the day after we all gave her our checks for the investment. We had a little signing party at their condo after she said she got permission to let us in. We got receipts, the whole nine yards. Now they're gone. Their condo is empty. Car's still here, but…"

Samira was now staring intently as the woman's story flowed out.

"How do you know their condo is empty?" Perkins asked.

"Oh. The condo GM got permission from the owners to do a site-visit. I happened to be there at the same time. Trust me, it was empty."

Perkins looked at her oddly for a long moment. "You just happened to be on the 6th floor of a different building just as the GM was inserting her key for a spot inspection. Have I got that right?"

Rebecca had the good grace to flush. "Yeah, pretty much."

Perkins nodded. "Okay. Then what?"

"Well, here's where it all gets sorta messy and ugly. Couple of the ladies searched for the WYRT website we found before. It doesn't appear any more. Now with these two gone, Sheriff, I gotta be honest, it just doesn't ring true to me." She paused again. She was obviously in some pain. "And here's the thing. I was the one who sorta pushed the other ladies into buying into this thing. By our own selves."

She pulled on the can of beer so hard she almost sucked the aluminum off the bottom.

"This was all our money, mind you. Some of the ladies saved up from the household budgets that they control." Even Rebecca couldn't help snorting. "Some of us have our own little savings or investment accounts. You know, sorta separate from the husband's." She held out her hands in an oddly pleading gesture.

"Look, Sheriff. We're not dumb. Several of us have been in business, worked corporately, got degrees from great schools. We decided we wanted to get in on this private opportunity, let it pay off big, and THEN tell our husbands. Bitcoin went from a buck or two to as high as $39,000. We figured if this only did a tenth as well, we'd all make a killing. The Asian markets are flourishing. That's where the big global growth is. It all made sense."

Samantha glanced at Samira. She was nodding. Her eyes were locked on Rebecca's. Why would she be so focused on somebody else's problem? Samantha wondered to herself. She was sorry to hear of the apparent scam and that some of her friends might be losing money, but still…

"Did you check out Ashley and what's-his-name? Massey something?"

"Massey Ferguson," Rebecca replied. "I never cared much for the man. We dealt exclusively with Ashley. And yeah, we did the usual Google stuff. Nothing on them. Ashley explained they were not on social media for security reasons for their clients. Besides, she said they had an exclusive clientele and didn't care about walk-in customers or anything. Kinda made sense to us, what with all the scams on the Internet and such…"

She stopped abruptly as the incongruity of her statement rang out. She covered her mouth with both hands. "Oh my God! We really have been scammed!"

It was obviously the first time that Rebecca had ever admitted this possibility out loud. It struck her like a heavyweight's knockout punch. It was a devastating thing to watch.

Samira sat in slack-jawed dismay.

Perkins let a long moment go by to allow Rebecca to recover. "I think it is likely that yes, you've been taken. By an expert con man. Woman. Team. Whatever. You shouldn't be embarrassed. They are professionals. This is their job. They are experts."

Rebecca slowly looked up at him. Her eyes had tears that slowly rolled down the sides of her cheeks.

"I feel like such an idiot. A fool. Me! Getting conned! Shit."

"Don't. It happens a lot more than you think or people realize. Billions of dollars every year. All around the world. Good people, nice people, who get taken."

Rebecca wiped away the tears. Samantha could see her mood changing from contrition to anger.

"I want to get that little bitch!" she spat out. "I want our money back. And I want to tear that disgusting little moustache off that putrid upper lip of the asshole she's with, hair by ugly hair!"

Perkins couldn't help but smile at the imagery. He fixed his gaze on her once more. "I know this is painful, but I need to know. How much money are we talking about?

"Fifty K. Each of us. Ten ladies. Half a million total investment."

Samantha couldn't help but suck in some air. This was big, bigger than she'd imagined.

Perkins nodded calmly. "Okay. Now we know. $500,000. It's a big number. Now we need to figure out what to do."

"Wait." Samira's voice croaked. She looked hard at Rebecca, then at Perkins. "There's another part to this." She swallowed hard. "I made the same investment with some of my family's money." She swallowed again. She looked Perkins in the eye. "What Rebecca said is correct. I went through much the same process. Ashley and I met privately twice. She presented a very attractive investment opportunity to diversify our family's portfolio. It was totally convincing. She befriends you, and then takes you. Vicious." She drew a very deep breath. "Only you should know...the total amount of the scam down here isn't 500,000. It is 1.5 million."

CHAPTER 43

"NOW IT'S PERSONAL!" stormed Samantha as she paced around the condo. Rosie was trailing her, concerned about whatever was going on.

"Some little bitch from Canada with big boobs thinks she can come down here and con my friends and steal their money! I don't think so!" She was gesturing with her right arm as her left hand held a glass of wine. It wasn't her first.

Perkins sat on a chair on her lanai and waited. Kim was sitting on the couch with Roy Crawford. Samira was inside still using the bathroom. Perkins suspected she needed time to pull herself together after her devastating admission.

"Bad enough for the ladies to get taken for fifty thousand each. They are now my friends. They helped get Kim elected. But Samira! A million dollars of her family's investment fund sunk into this scheming little fraudster! Cute! She's about as cute and cuddly as a rattlesnake with hemorrhoids!"

She stopped abruptly in front of Perkins. "I want her ass! I want to get the money back for my friends! And then I want you to send her to the deepest, darkest dungeon in the history of dungeons!"

Samantha flung herself down on the love seat as Perkins, Kim, and Roy fought to keep grins off their faces at Samantha's graphic imagery.

Rosie cautiously wandered over to Samantha and nuzzled her. She wanted the pretty lady who smelled of lemons and sunshine to know that Rosie was with her. Rosie didn't understand what was going on but she'd be there for Samantha and her friends. She gave Samantha a moist doggy kiss of support.

Samira returned quietly to the group. She waved off more wine and sipped Perrier.

Perkins finally spoke. "You know, I remember the first time Rosie met those two," he began. Rosie perked up at her name and trotted over to the sheriff. He ruffled her fur affectionately.

"She didn't react very well to the woman, and she refused to have anything to do with the man. Remember, Samantha? She just stood there, all stiff-legged."

Perkins gave Rosie a big hug as she put her two front paws on him. "You are such a clever dog. Yes, you are, you're a very smart girl," he crooned.

Rosie bestowed another kiss. She pranced around the lanai. It was a nice party, she thought, although there was a noticeable absence of doggy treats.

"I do remember that," Samantha said after a moment. "Wish she'd bitten the bastard on the ass."

Even Samira managed a wan smile at that.

"What can we do now?" Samira's question was tentative.

Perkins sighed. "Actually, I've already very quietly begun looking at them. They seemed phony to me. I asked them about their Calgary football team. They didn't know its name."

Crawford sat up. "The Stampeders? Everybody knows about them in Canada."

"Yeah, well, they didn't. So I'm questioning if they are even Canadian. The problem is," he confessed, "we don't know who they are. We can't identify them. I can tell you that Ashley Monroe and Massey what's-his-face are not their real names."

He finished his beer and put down the glass. This was going to be the hard part. "The other problem is: We don't yet know if there has been a crime committed. Now," he added hastily as Samantha bared her teeth ready for battle and Samira half-rose in protest. "I think there has been. But no formal complaint has been filed. The investment was made by intelligent people not under any duress. The investment happened only a few days ago. These people could be on a trip; they could be exploring other currencies for other investors; they could have the guy back in the hospital for tests or something on his heart."

"He would actually have to have a heart," mumbled Kim. Snorts of agreement.

"Yeah, I get it," Perkins continued. "What I want to do is get Samira to file a formal complaint. We'll keep it quiet but it will give us authority to begin an investigation. We'll talk to the feds, see if they've got any similar scams. We can then probably get a court order to search the condo and the car. Maybe we get lucky and get some prints or hairs or other DNA evidence to identify them. Assuming they are in the system. Once we do that, then we're on our way."

"But in the meantime, they're out there gawd knows where in the world, spending the ladies' money. Samira's family's money. Why can't you issue a world-wide shoot 'em-on-sight warrant or something?"

Samantha clearly favored taking the nuclear option.

"Sorry, honey, we're not quite there. Let's try to find out who they are first. Then where they're from. Then search for any web presence. Then try to link them to other crimes. Then try to track them down."

Samantha fumed for a moment. Then her eyes got big and she looked directly at Kim. "Yeah, you boys go and do what you've gotta do. Do it the long, hard way. Give them more time to eat the caviar and fly first class to wherever." She sniffed. "Do get back to us on that."

Perkins flinched a bit. "Samantha," he said flatly. "This is dangerous stuff. Don't you go doing anything silly."

"No, dear. Of course not. Not me."

CHAPTER 44

"WE CAN ASK Radar," Samantha whispered conspiratorially to Kim the next morning. Perkins was finishing dressing. Coffee was needed by all. Rosie was impatient for her morning walk.

Kim's eyes widened at the thought of the two of them playing detective once again.

"On my way," Perkins announced as he came into the kitchen. He finished the last two swallows of his coffee, kissed Samantha, flapped a hand at Kim, grabbed Rosie's leash and left.

"But you heard what Perk said last night. He warned you not to get involved."

"Uh huh. So? We've sort of solved a couple of big crimes around here before. I'm sure what he really meant to say was, 'Honey, we could use your help but I can't formally say that to you but please we really need your assistance'." She sipped her coffee. Kim looked askance. "I'm pretty sure that's what he intended."

She sipped again. Kim still looked dubious. In the past Samantha's ideas had led them down some weird roads. "Besides, he's got to follow all those rules and regulations. That'll take forever. We don't have to do that." She gnawed on a raisin bran muffin. "Besides, what's he going to do? Spank me?"

Kim couldn't help but giggle. "Aw, you'd both enjoy that." Samantha exploded, spraying muffin crumbs across the granite counter.

She dabbed her eyes and refocused. "Listen, Kim, I think those two are out there with our friends' money. Livin' large. We owe it to them to get it back. Radar is the fastest way to track them down. He can do things that not even law enforcement can do."

Kim nodded slowly. "Besides, he adores you. He would do anything for you." Kim didn't deny it.

She'd nick-named him Radar after the beloved *M*A*S*H* character. He had been a highly skilled military tech in the field. He now ran some mysterious private counter-Intel unit from somewhere in the world. She wasn't sure where. Of course, it didn't matter where he was located as long as he had his computer and Internet access. He was a computer savant.

"Okay, let's call him. Maybe he can do something."

Samantha nodded and grabbed her phone. Kim dialed a number of digits. It seemed to Samantha to be more than the usual eleven or twelve for international calls.

A moment later, Radar answered. "Captain? That really you?"

"Hi, Radar. Yes, it's Kim. Not "Captain" anymore. Kim. How are you?"

"Great. Having fun. Making a ton of money. Fighting the bad guys. I've got a team of eight working with me plus some free-lancers. All good." The audio crackled briefly. "Hey, congrats again on your election win!"

"Thank you. The website you designed was a big help. People liked it. Ah, listen, Radar, I'm here with Samantha..."

"Hey, Samantha. How are you?"

"Good, Radar, thank you. I really enjoyed working with you on Kim's campaign."

"Our pleasure. Now, what can I do to help?"

Kim outlined the problem. It took some time. "We don't think these two scammers used their real names," she concluded. "We don't know where in the world they are now. We don't know if they are still using their real—no, their latest phony names. Whatever their real names might be. No clue."

"Sounds like fun for us. It'll be a good exercise for a couple of rookies I'm trying out. A test for 'em. Besides, I don't like con artists. They suck a lot of money out of nice people. My grandmother lost some money to one years ago. She couldn't afford it. Maybe this'll help her rest in peace."

Everyone was silent for a moment.

Radar cleared his throat. "Okay. Let's do it. This phone line is secure but I've got a new email address for you. It routes through Guatemala, Peru, Myanmar and New Zealand, so it's really secure. We can communicate freely on it. Now tell me more about these two bums."

As Samantha described the two of them, she and Kim suddenly realized just how thin their information on them truly was. A fake name for each. They might make some modest changes in appearance—hair color and style for the bitch, the moustache and maybe hair dye for the asshole.

Nobody would willingly grow a moustache as ugly as he had.

Well, a couple of Albanian grandmothers perhaps, but other than that...

"They left their car here," Samantha concluded. "But it is a rental so the plates don't mean anything. The Sheriff is hoping to get a warrant to search it, maybe pull off some prints or DNA."

"That's a smart sheriff you've got there," Radar commented. Samantha beamed proudly. "You two are a great couple."

Her head jerked just a bit. She'd never met Radar. They had worked together by long distance on Kim's campaign web site. But still. She sighed. Privacy just didn't exist in the modern world, and especially so if you were a computer genius who can dig up anything on anybody.

"Um, thanks. I like him. Listen, Radar...our budget for this is pretty tight. What..."

"I never work for nothing," he responded. "Company policy." Samantha looked at Kim and they both braced themselves. "For this project, my bill will be one dollar. American." The two ladies let out a breath of relief.

Radar continued, "Listen. Captain Sharpe saved my life the day we hit that IED and got ambushed in the Middle East. Literally. She ever wants anything, anytime, anywhere, I'm here for her. No questions asked. Oh, and the one dollar charge will be deferred until 2075."

Kim swiped at her eyes as she listened. "Thank you, Radar. You are the greatest."

Samantha let the moment linger before continuing. "Thank you from me as well. I hope we'll meet sometime."

No response. Well.

"Uh, Radar, I just had another thought. Would it be any use to you to have pictures of these two? Can you use Artificial Intelligence or Facial Recognition software or something to get a true identity? I don't know if we've got pictures, but maybe we can get a police sketch artist to do something."

"Hey, yeah. Good idea. Email them to me when you've got them done. On the new secure link I just gave you. In the meantime, I'll start the team working on tracking them. See if we can locate these two bums. Be fun. Got to run. There's a call coming in from a Duke in some European country. Britain? Really? Wonder what he's screwed up this time? Or who. Thanks, guys, talk soon."

And with that the secure line was disconnected. Kim and Samantha looked at one another is amazement.

"If anybody can find these two, I'd bet on Radar."

Samantha just nodded.

Chapter 45

"She is exceedingly secure in her own view of civic affairs," conceded the mayor. "Reality be damned," she added ruefully.

Councillor Mikayla Johnson was becoming a problem for the city council of Port Manatee.

She was loud, she was brash, she was angry, she was impetuous, she was imprudent about confidential items on the Council agenda, and she didn't seem to give a damn.

She had been elected in a tough battle in a tough ward. Kim had tried to make friends with her, as they were both newly elected council members. And women.

It hadn't worked.

Most recently, Councillor Johnson had blurted out to the media information about a proposed business development that was confidential. Then she had compounded that by screaming at a reporter for using the information, and then threatening a libel suit.

The media had closed ranks. It was getting nasty. City hall was the loser.

"About the only time she stops shooting herself in the foot is to reload her gun," Kim said.

The mayor grinned painfully. She and Kim were at lunch at a charming little Italian restaurant. It was quiet and the owner had tucked them into a private corner.

Kim broke off a piece of warm focaccia and dipped it in a bit of olive oil. The sensation was delectable.

"I thought Councillor March was actually going to take a position on that development," continued the mayor. "But then he continued his policy of being firmly on the fence about everything. I hope he gets splinters up his..."

The mayor sipped her iced sparkling water as the waiter approached.

She and Kim had developed a habit of having lunch together every few weeks to talk about city hall. They both understood it was strictly off the record and absolutely confidential. They could update one another on various civic projects, and alert the other to a potential problem or crisis.

"I was by the Delvecchio Bridge condo project the other day," offered Kim. "It is really coming along nicely. Samantha's design for the playground and park is getting roughed-out. It's going to be great for the neighborhood. The families there just love her."

"She is a winner, that's for sure. Nice to see her and the sheriff together. He's a good man. Love the dog." The waiter served them lunch. Spaghetti with meat balls for the mayor and homemade lasagne for Kim.

Kim waited until they had both finished eating. "Sonja, listen. There is something I need to discuss. It's personal." She paused for a moment. The mayor wiped her lips, put down her napkin and focused intently on her new councillor.

"You know that Roy and I have a consensual adult relationship. We were dating before I ran for office. We are still dating. It is a good—no, great—relationship." She swallowed more water. "I am increasingly concerned that someone on Council or some busybody out in the community is going to try to make that an issue for me, or, worse, for Roy. Neither one of us wants to put the city in a bad position."

"Roy has been a superb city manager," agreed the mayor. "And I think you're going to be a terrific city councillor."

"Thanks. I'm trying. I'm learning. It's not an easy position." She twisted her napkin. "What I'm thinking of doing is filing an open declaration with the city clerk about our relationship. I've talked to Kathy James, and she thinks it would be a good idea. It gets it in the open, it protects the city, and it takes away a potential spear in the hands of somebody who might try to harm one of us."

"Like Councillor Johnson?" mused the mayor. She was highly attuned to what went on in the councillor's office.

"Well, yeah. Or anybody. Roy would file his own document with Kathy or HR. We're just trying to get ahead of a potential issue. It would lay out our consensual relationship and commit to not discussing city business outside of city hall. And I would declare a conflict of interest on any HR issues involving Roy, or on the conditions of his employment."

Mayor Rodriguez didn't hesitate. "I think that's very smart, Kim. Get it out there and deal with it before it is an issue. I'll support that with the media. Make sure Kathy—well, she'll know what to do."

The mayor waved for the bill. "My turn this time, I think. You got it last time."

Kim pushed back her chair. "Yeah, I've got to get back to city hall as well. I need to clean out a closet."

The mayor paid the bill and then looked up curiously. "Whatever for?"

"Councillor Johnson needs a place to store her brooms."

Chapter 46

"KIM. SAMANTHA. WE'VE got 'em!"

The two looked at one another with surprise. Then glee.

"How come it took almost thirty-two hours, soldier?" Kim demanded in mock anger. Radar laughed.

"It was a good exercise for us. Tested two of my new wannabes. One made it; the other didn't."

"So. Great. Thank you. Now, where is the little bitch?" Samantha still seethed with anger over how her friends had been conned. She was laser-focused on the woman. She wanted her. Bad.

"They flew from Tampa to Atlanta. Then to London England. Then the overnight flight to Singapore. First class. That cost 'em a pile of money." He thought for a moment. "Well, apparently not their money. The ladies'." He paused again. "You know. The stolen money."

"Are they still there?"

"Yes, as far as we know. They travelled using passports under Ashley Monroe and Massey Ferguson. No problems. They must have been really good fakes. Those would cost them about twenty grand apiece."

"Do you think they will again change names and get new fake IDs?"

"Oh, I would bet on that. They know their IDs will only last so long. There are some very good counterfeiters in Asia. Don't know of any in Singapore but there are sure to be. There have been rumors of a Chinese triad that has infiltrated some of Singapore's criminal gangs. Maybe these two have a contact. It will take them at least a couple of weeks to change their appearances and get new documentation."

Radar shuffled some papers. "We think the guy has got an apartment or condo in Singapore. We're still hunting that. The woman has got a very nice suite at the Primrose Hotel. It's a five-star hotel."

Samantha seethed at the hussy blowing through her friends' money.

Radar coughed. He paused, and Kim and Samantha could hear him swallow something. "Sorry, it's still early here." He didn't offer where "here" was. He swallowed again and continued. "Singapore is an interesting city. Very strict laws. Really clean, safe city. Very cosmopolitan."

"Why would they go there?" Kim wondered.

They could practically see Radar's shrug. "Singapore has a good, safe banking system. No disruptions by radicals or protestors like in Hong Kong and some other Asian cities. Hot and humid as hell in Singapore, but otherwise really nice. Fabulous airport and lots of flights to anywhere in the world. And it is far, far away from the USA, so they'd figure it is completely safe. Not likely anybody is going to find them or follow them to Singapore."

Samantha looked at Kim. She cleared her throat. "Well," she said slowly to the phone speaker, "this time they have figured wrong."

CHAPTER 47

IT TOOK SAMANTHA two and a half days to plan the first phase of her campaign.

She invited the sheriff and Rosie over for Saturday night dinner. She teased him about how she'd just discovered her old college cheerleader's outfit in a box in her storage unit. She wondered if she could still fit into it. She wondered if the top would be too tight and the shorts too short. She wondered if he'd be interested in seeing her in it.

He was.

Very interested.

Intensely interested.

He volunteered to come over right then to help with the assessment.

She laughed and declined. She told him to wait. Saturday night would be just fine.

He growled a bit on the phone.

She laughed some more. And promised him a memorable evening.

And she delivered.

Perkins was taking the night off, or at least as much as any sheriff can. He and Rosie arrived at 5:30. Rosie was always excited to see Samantha and it took them a few minutes to exchange hugs and kisses and petting.

Perkins stood by, a little jealous. Samantha finally rose to greet him. She made up for the wait with a long, intense, deep kiss that made his heart swell, along with another part of his anatomy.

They finally came up for air. He squeezed her tightly. His hands wandered down to caress that beautiful round bottom of hers. She wriggled a bit. They kissed again.

Rosie finally had had enough. She pushed herself between them and they finally broke apart, laughing.

Drinks were poured. Beef was removed from the fridge to bring to room temperature. Dog biscuits were gobbled.

A second round of drinks. Samantha rose sinuously from where she and Perkins had been cuddling. He came as close to pouting as a tough sheriff could come.

She patted him and then turned on the TV so he could watch the March Madness semi-finals. Whatever that was.

Rosie followed her into the kitchen. Rosie was a smart dog. She knew where the food was kept.

Samantha prepared the Caesar salad. She added extra anchovies, knowing that Perkins liked them. She decanted a beautiful bottle of a California cabernet blend. She took the baked potatoes out of the oven.

Samantha did a simple salt and pepper rub on the beef, seared it and put it into the oven. She soon called Perk to the table. She broke a house rule and let him keep the TV on for the overtime. North Carolina and Duke? Who would possibly care about that?

She served the salad. "Wonderful," he exclaimed. He forked up another large piece of anchovy and devoured it with relish.

She poured the wine after the salad was finished. She removed the beef from the oven to let it rest. She put in the rolls to warm. She quickly sautéed the green beans that she had blanched earlier. She added some crumbled bacon and slivered toasted almonds. Rosie was a very enthusiastic supporter of the bacon.

She called him to help bring the food to the candle-lit table. She carried in the platter. "Chateaubriand," she announced proudly. "Would you carve?"

"Man, it's been years since I shared a chateaubriand." He grabbed the sharp blade and carved the beef into large slices. "Perfect. Beautiful red inside. So tender. Great sear. I should find you a job as a chef somewhere."

She smiled back as she split the baked potatoes. "S and P? Butter? Sour cream? Chives? Bacon bits?"

He passed on the butter but took everything else. So did she.

Plates loaded and wine glasses filled, the lovers sat looking at one another. Samantha was wearing a long, tightly-fitting dress in forest green. It had a deep slit that went to the top of her right thigh and revealed flashes of her long legs.

"I'm not sure what I've done to deserve this dinner," he said as he raised his glass in a toast, "but I'm certainly glad that I did it! Thank you."

They clinked, sipped, and wowed. The wine was succulent, with a soft aftertaste of blackberries and the aroma of fine leather.

They ate slowly, savoring the food, the wine, and the company. Soft, easy rock flowed from the speakers once the game was over. Samantha subtly slipped Rosie a few morsels of beef.

They cleared the table together. The candles were burning down as Samantha brought out the dessert. A chocolate mousse cake, light and satisfying.

Rosie sniffed at the end of the beef. She grumpily went into the kitchen and inhaled the rest of the dry dog food in her bowl. She did find a couple of bonus bacon pieces in the bowl. She lapped some water. She returned to the living room where her two people were sitting close together on the couch.

She flopped on the floor beside them. They seemed to be tangled up like some complicated modernist sculpture. She sighed.

A while later, Sheriff came up for air. "I guess I'd better take Rosie for her walk."

Samantha stretched provocatively. "Gosh, whatever should I do when you're gone?" The slit in her skirt gaped open a little more.

Perkins licked his lips. "Uh, that outfit you mentioned..."

She laughed softly. "Oh you remembered? How nice. Do you really want to see it on me? It is so old it probably doesn't fit very well."

"No, no, I'm sure it'll be fine. It doesn't matter to me, but it will be fun for you to try it on again," he choked out.

She giggled at the lie. "Well, if you're sure..."

Perkins grabbed Rosie's leash. "We won't be long," he promised fervently.

He looked down at the dog as they rode the elevator. "If you've ever done something nice for me, take a quick whiz tonight, would you? Please?"

Rosie looked up at him with adoring eyes. She then proceeded to cavort around the grounds for fifteen minutes, carefully selecting just the right spots for her bathroom breaks.

Perkins glared at her in the dark. It didn't help. He glanced at his watch anxiously. "Come on, Rosie. Let's do this! You won't believe what I've got waiting upstairs!"

Finally everything was completed. They rode up the elevator and returned to Samantha's condo. The bedroom door was closed. Rosie wandered out to the lanai to enjoy the warm spring air.

Perkins finally chose a big armchair. It faced the bedroom door. He settled down and waited.

A couple of moments later the door opened. Nothing. Then Samantha came bounding out.

She was dressed in a tight blouse that tied just below her breasts. It was blue with white piping. There was a lot of cleavage. Her midriff was bare. The tiny shorts were a royal blue with white trim and stars stuck at strategic locations. They ended very high up on her thighs. He gasped at the vision. Her hair was loose around her head. She wore white boots to complete the ensemble.

She looked incredible.

Sexy as hell. Stunning as usual. Beautiful. And now this fantasy buried deep inside American males was coming true: the gorgeous head cheerleader, performing only for him.

Samantha strutted around the living room. She bent toward him once, and he realized with a flush that there was nothing between her blouse and her skin. It was breathtaking.

She pivoted on her boots so that her back was to him. He enjoyed the view immensely. He started to rise, but she waved him back into his seat. She stopped five feet in front of his chair, produced a couple of pom-poms from a table, and did a little cheer just for him. She kicked her legs in the air, her boots flashing. She didn't end with the splits, but she folded one leg on the floor and extended one elegant leg. She finally looked up at him, flushed and nervous.

"You are incredible," he stuttered. "You are so beautiful. And sexy. And gorgeous." He rose from the chair and helped her up from the floor. "And you're mine."

He kissed her fiercely. She responded immediately. She was as aroused as he was. They clung to each other as they stumbled into her bedroom. Perkins kicked the door shut. Rosie was a little hurt. Why couldn't she join in the game?

She couldn't see what was happening, but she could hear some feverish activity going on inside the bedroom.

Rosie wondered what "SIS BOOM BAH" meant. Both the sheriff and Samantha seemed to be saying it loudly.

Humans.

CHAPTER 48

SAMANTHA HAD A big smile on her face as she eased her way down to the pool. She needed some R&R after last night with Perk. She was exhausted. Exhilarated, but exhausted. It had been a memorable night of lovemaking.

She tossed her bag on one lounger, draped her towel over the back of another, and gratefully sagged onto the chaise. She adjusted her sunglasses and glanced at the pool.

It was crowded. There were lots of kids hollering as their parents and grandparents tried to corral them.

Two pudgy twenty-year-olds were sitting on the side of the pool. One was in an orange swimsuit with an unfortunate diamond-shaped cut-out over her stomach. The other was in a small, flowered two-piece. In both cases there was too much tummy for too little fabric.

Samantha was glowing. Her little cheerleader outfit had been a big hit with the sheriff. He had delighted in slowly peeling the parts of it off. He had spent a lot of time kissing what was revealed. It had been glorious.

Samantha and the Sheriff.

It was only after the second intense round that she had slowly broached the subject of her plan for chasing Ashley and the Asshole.

Samantha had decided that she just plain didn't like Ashley. She didn't like that distinctive flowery perfume she wore. She didn't like the way she kept shoving her boobs at men—especially Perk. She didn't like how she flaunted her jewelry. And she really didn't like the way the bimbo had treated her friends.

Samantha thought back to how she and Perkins had lain together, satiated: She finally stirred. She kissed him. She went to get two bottles of cold water. They both drank greedily. She returned to nestle in his arms.

"I really think we have to do something about this scam," she had begun quietly. She could feel him stiffening just a bit. And not in the right place.

"Yeah. Well. Maybe," he murmured.

She'd snuggled deeper into his shoulder. His arm was around her. She'd felt the scars from the bullet wound where he'd been shot. She had shivered at the recollection that she'd almost lost her lover.

"The reality is, my darling, that these two interlopers came into our home, stole from our friends, and then took off. You know they're gone, right?"

He nodded. "Yeah, everything points to that. I think you have to assume they've fled Sapphire Blue. Probably the country as well."

She caressed his chest with her right palm. "Uh, sweetie. What if I told you that I think they might be in…Asia." She cleared her throat a bit. She could feel him stiffening a little more. Still not in the right spot.

"And just how would you know that?"

She paused. This is where it was going to get awkward. "Well…Kim and I got talking about this whole problem. So we called Radar. You know, that computer expert who was in her Army company. Smart guy."

He waited.

"He tracked them flying from Tampa to Atlanta to London to Singapore. He says they are there right now." She waited a beat. "I think we should go and get them. Or you should just shoot them, after we get the money back. Whichever you prefer," she added sweetly.

Perkins came surging up from the bed. Her head bounced off his arm as he loomed over her.

"I can't shoot them! Don't even kid about it." She nodded, cowed by his tone of voice. "Besides," he went on after a long stare, "I don't have any jurisdiction in Singapore. Where the hell is Singapore anyway? And I don't have any budget to pay to send somebody on that trip. And why would you go behind my back to get intelligence from some former Army computer genius before we get our own tracing done. So no. I'm not going anywhere. Singapore. Sheesh."

He dropped down on the pillow. She waited a long moment. "Yes, I see all that. You're right."

He rolled his head to look at her suspiciously. It wasn't like her to give up a battle this easily.

She offered him another sip of water from her bottle. The silence continued for another long moment. Her palm gently stroked his chest.

"Of course," she finally began slowly, "it must sort of wound you that this scam went down in your jurisdiction. On a bunch of your friends." She rubbed his stomach. His breathing was getting a little more rapid. "I'd like to help them. Kim figures Radar can get a location in Singapore. Besides, Singapore is just a city. Not even a big country. Can't be that hard to find somebody there."

He grunted at that.

"And it wouldn't be as if you'd have to arrest them or anything. Maybe just help the local police force to round 'em up." She paused again. "Maybe they will shoot them," she said bitterly.

"Look, I know you're really angry about this. I am, too. But nobody's shooting anybody!"

"Yeah. Whatever. We'll see." She was like Rosie with a T-bone. Good luck on getting her to drop it.

He filed that thought away.

"Besides, there is no way that my department would authorize funding for me to go on a trip to Shanghai or wherever."

"Singapore." She sat up. Her breasts gleamed in the moonlight. Thinking back on it, he decided much later, that this was when his concentration on their conversation wavered.

"I have solved that one," she told him with some excitement. "When I divorced my idiot former husband, my very smart lawyer got me half of his airline points. Last time I looked, I had something like 946,000 points. That would get us to Singapore and back. And a nice hotel there. I'll pay for the taxi from the airport," she added generously.

"No, no, no. It can't—wait, what do you mean, *us?*"

"Well, if I'm bankrolling this thing, it is only appropriate that I go to superv—to help you."

"I can't go. I don't have the time."

"Nonsense. You were saying just last week that you haven't had a vacation in nearly three years. Your HR people must be screaming at you to use the time. Or maybe you'll lose it."

Perkins waved that aside. He and vacations didn't mix very well.

Still, it was departmental policy that unused vacation time did get rescinded after three years.

He could feel himself weakening. Damn it, how could he say no to this bewitching woman?

He struggled to be firm with her. It was just a crazy idea.

"I have no jurisdiction there. None. No status. No right to do anything from a police point of view. I'd get in big trouble even trying."

Samantha had prepared well. "Of course you're right." He relaxed for a moment. "Although," she continued; he stiffened again. "If you were to chat with that nice FBI district supervisor you got to know last year when you were chasing down the crazy Campanelli brothers…what was his name?"

"Robertson. James Robertson." Perkins gave up the name grudgingly.

"Yeah. You like him. I bet that he could get you a contact at the Singapore Police Department. That would give you some status there. A courtesy visit. To talk about law enforcement. International scam artists. Doesn't the FBI care about those things? And I can't imagine that Singapore wants to protect lawbreakers. They are a pretty squeaky clean city."

"Maybe they'll shoot them for me," she concluded relentlessly.

"No shooting. There won't be any shooting," he repeated. Man, she did hold a grudge.

He filed that thought away as well. If they ever broke up, which he fervently did not want to happen, he'd do it long-distance. Perhaps from Rangoon. By text.

He rallied for one last attempt. "What if they aren't there any longer? What if they've changed their names again and fled? We still don't even know their real names."

"But you've got your people working on finding that out. Getting DNA and fingerprints and hair fibres and all that other very clever stuff you do so well. By the time we arrive in Singapore, you'll probably know their identities. Then you just give it to the local police, they go arrest them, we get the money back, and we come home. Sounds pretty easy to me."

"It won't be easy. It is never easy. It will be hard. Something will go wrong. Something always goes wrong. We probably won't even find them. You know, optimism is a rare commodity in police circles. Too much real-life experience."

Samantha patted him affectionately. Her other hand continued to caress his torso. "I think you'll do great. And besides, we need to protect our friends. We need to look after them. What's your department's motto? To Serve and Protect? Well, this is serving and protecting them."

And shooting the bad guys—well, bad guy, worse girl.

Samantha was really angry with them.

"Still...I suppose I could call Robertson. Give him the story. Maybe get FBI backing on this wild goose chase you want me to do."

"Us."

"Well, that's a whole other matter. What if it gets dangerous? I don't want you put in harm's way," he said firmly. Putting his foot down. With authority.

"That is so sweet. Thank you. And of course you're right." He tensed up again, not believing she was giving way so easily. He was right.

"Mind you...oh, wait. Do you have a passport?"

He thought. "Yeah. Don't know when it expires, though. I'll have to check." Damn, he realized instantly. He'd just about nearly almost committed to going.

"Good. That's something else I can do to help. Along with packing for you. And making sure Rosie is looked after."

Rosie. He'd forgotten all about her. Another reason not to go.

"That's another reason not to go," he told her.

"Pish. Auntie Kim will be delighted to babysit for a week."

"Why can't Rosie stay here?"

"Nonsense. I'll be in Singapore with you. Looking after your travel plans. Hotel bookings. Taking care of the little details so you can catch those two. I'll be your assistant. Just in the background."

Somehow Samantha and being in the background didn't compute.

Perkins suddenly realized that she had effectively knocked down every argument he had advanced. He had nothing left in his arsenal. He was going to Singapore. So was she.

He wasn't quite sure how, but she had won.

A last thought before he went to sleep with Samantha in his arms...doesn't Singapore get typhoons?

Well, they weren't prepared for the gorgeous, angry, red-headed typhoon that was headed their way.

Not his problem. He slept.

YES, REMEMBERED SAMANTHA fondly as she relaxed beside the pool the next morning recalling their night that had been so memorable, they were heading for Singapore.

She was going to find the two con artist scoundrels, get the money back that they stole from her friends, and with any luck somebody would shoot them. Or at least throw them into a

Singaporean dungeon. With spiders and snakes. Many spiders. Nasty, mean, slithering, disgusting snakes.

Let's see how Ashley's big boobs and fancy jewelry will help her deep in that dungeon.

Convincing Perkins to go to Singapore had been the hard part. Still, Samantha thought with a grin, renting that cheerleader's outfit had been a pretty smart use of $175. The clerk has said something about the Dallas Cowboys cheerleaders and how popular the blue and white costume was.

Samantha shrugged. Her school colors had been red, black and white. And she'd never been a cheerleader in her life.

Still, Perk had really liked it. Maybe she'd buy the outfit. His birthday was coming up. Ah, well. Men.

She grabbed her pad and pencil. Time to start making lists for their trip.

CHAPTER 49

"JAMES? LEROY PERKINS here."

"Perk, my friend! How very lovely to hear from you."

The FBI Regional Supervisor was now based in Atlanta. He had been the Miami SAC when the idiot Campanelli brothers had kidnapped Samantha and tried to sell a ton of opioids around Port Manatee.

Neither of the two brothers had survived their ill-conceived business venture.

Perkins and Robertson had bonded in the extreme circumstances.

"And how is that lovely lady of yours? Has she recovered from her ordeal?" There was genuine concern in his voice.

"She is good, thank you for asking. Once in a while she gets a flash-back. But she is moving forward. I'm there for her."

"That is good. She's a keeper. What she sees in a battered old wreck like you no one can understand, but whatever..."

Perkins snorted. Samantha and Robertson had never met but they knew all about each other.

"Listen, James...I need a little help."

It took Perkins nearly ten minutes to lay out the scenario in Florida for the FBI supervisor.

"So. We've got fraud. Theft. Interstate transport. Most likely tax evasion. Wire fraud. We could probably come up with a couple more if the lawyers work on it."

"Yeah. And we've also got the two primary suspects who have fled, probably for Singapore."

"We've got an extradition treaty with them. But it's a lot of paperwork." Robertson sighed. "I hate international paper-work." He grunted. "It takes so much time." He thought for a moment. "Why don't you just go there, get the money back, and shoot them?" he said brightly.

"That's Samantha's solution; I said no."

"Wimp. So, what can the outstanding women and men of the Federal Bureau of Investigation do for you this morning, Sheriff?"

Perkins laughed. "Here's the thing, James. Obviously neither one of us has any jurisdiction in a foreign country. But Samantha's determined to chase them. Somehow I agreed. What would be really helpful is to have a contact in Singapore, some liaison person with the local police. Can you help me?"

Robertson didn't hesitate. "I can. A couple of years ago I was on a training mission with INTERPOL in Lyon, France, with some other high-ranking law enforcement officials." He paused and Perkins waited for the jab. It didn't take long. "Don't believe you were invited." Perkins grinned but didn't give him the satisfaction of responding.

Robertson continued with mirth in his voice. "I met a really sharp Superintendent with the Singapore Police Force. Zhang Keong. Great guy. I'll email him, get you two connected. The SPF is a very smart organization. They're responsible for all the security for the city. Airport, national defence, policing, everything. Really well equipped. Well trained. Top notch."

He paused again, obviously ready to throw another dart. "Try not to drag them down too much and embarrass American law enforcement." Again Perkins wouldn't bite. "Anyway, you'll enjoy meeting him. You'll probably learn a thing or two. I'll send him an email right now."

"That would be great. Thank you. I'll need somebody local there to help guide me. You know, language and everything."

Robertson laughed. "Oh hell, Perk. They speak better English than we do. A lot of British heritage and tradition in Singapore and its police force. You'll be just fine. Oh, and remember, no gum chewing."

"What?"

"I'm serious. Don't chew gum. And no spitting on the sidewalks. You'll have to behave yourself for a change." He sounded rather happy at the thought. "It's a good thing Samantha is going to keep you on the straight and narrow." He chuckled at the thought, and then turned serious again.

"Oh, and in the meantime, if you need help with any forensic stuff to try to identify these two, just let my office know. I'll get it expedited for you."

"That's great, James. Thank you. See you soon."

Less than an hour later, Perkins had an email from a Z. Keong at SPF.

We would be honored to meet Sheriff Perkins and Samantha Summers upon their arrival in Singapore. Please advise travel details when completed. Also please summarize the information concerning the possible fraud investigation. I have assigned Inspector C. Y. Holmes as your liaison officer throughout your visit to Singapore.

Superintendent Zhang Keong, SPF.

CHAPTER 50

ROSIE WAS MIFFED. She knew what those big boxes on the bed meant, and she wasn't seeing any of them with her toys or, more important, bags of food, being packed.

Her mommy and daddy were going away. Without her.

She lay in the corner of the bedroom as Samantha bustled about, putting clothes and accessories into Perkins' suitcase.

Rosie managed to look pathetic, sad, and sick.

Perkins was having none of it. "You're not sick," he said firmly. "Don't even try it."

Rosie looked even more woebegone. Samantha finally cracked. She went over to kneel beside the poor puppy. She stroked her softly. "We're just going away for a few days," she reassured her. "It is a very, very long ride on the airplane. It would not be good for you." She petted her more. "And you're going to stay with Auntie Kim for a few days. Won't that be fun? You like her."

Rosie let her eyes droop a little more. She let out a long sigh.

"We're going over there to help some of your friends you've met at the pool. Some bad people hurt them. You would want us to help them, wouldn't you?"

Rosie let out another long, deep, gloomy sigh. She sunk her head even deeper into the carpet. Her mournful eyes were fixed on the suitcases.

"Why do I need a suit?" demanded Perkins.

Samantha rose. "Because they are a bit of a formal society, as I understand it. You may need it to meet Inspector Holmes. You don't know what he's like. He might be very stiff upper lip, traditional, British-influenced. Probably has a grey moustache that curls up at the ends. And you certainly can't wear your own uniform over there."

Perkins grunted. Rosie watched, her head buried deep between her front paws, eyes peering out sadly. Samantha carefully folded dress shirts, linen shirts, and matching pants into the suitcase. She checked her list.

"It will be hot over there," she observed. "And humid. Even in late March." She added more T-shirts, a pair of shorts and a bathing suit.

"Did you know there are only three city states in the world?"

Perkins shook his head as he tossed in a couple more pairs of underwear. Samantha promptly took them out, rolled them and tucked them into the corner of the suitcase.

"Singapore, obviously. Monaco, you know from movies. Monte Carlo, the Prince, Princess Grace. Guess what the third one is."

Perkins thought for a moment as he tossed socks and a couple of golf shirts into the bag. Samantha took them out, rolled the socks into a small ball and tucked them into the deepest corner of the bag. She refolded the shirts and laid them flat.

"Uh. No. Oh, I've got it. The Vatican. Rome."

"Correct." She checked her list, looked at the suitcase one more time, and said, "You just put your toiletries in that corner of the bag. You'll want to carry the files and everything with you, of course. Good. That's it."

She swung the upper side of the suitcase closed, half-zipped it, and lifted the heavy bag and put it on the floor. Perkins looked on with a certain degree of awe. His own packing tended to be grabbing a handful of clothes from his closet and flinging them into a suitcase. This was an interesting change.

"Okay, let's go," Samantha commanded. She looked at Rosie. "You too."

Both of them responded, Rosie a bit reluctantly. Samantha was in full General-of-the-Army mode.

"We leave tomorrow at 3:55 p.m. from Tampa. We're flying Delta to New York; we've got a two-hour layover, then Delta to London overnight. We land at Heathrow, we've got another two hours to transfer, and then we go direct to Singapore. We arrive there at 11:30 the next morning. Or the next, next morning…I can never keep the International Dateline changes straight." She paused. "It will be a long day of travel."

Perkins grimaced. His experience with flying so far consisted of being jammed into Economy on smelly, sticky planes. Government agencies always tried for the cheapest airfares. His last flight was to Washington a few years ago for an FBI seminar. He had been given a window seat. 37A. Any farther back and he would have been holding on to the tail of the plane.

His seatmates had been a hefty couple. She had on a lot of perfume. Perkins had been trapped. As the jolly man in 37C had said to him as he was pushed deeper into his tiny, hard seat:

"Remember this airline's motto—'*We're not happy until you're not happy.*'"

The airline had lived up to that motto on that flight.

He was not looking forward to twenty-four hours with his knees around his ears.

Then he looked at her and finally confessed. "Uh, honey, I, uh, I've never travelled outside the United States before."

She looked a little surprised. "Really? Well, you and most other Americans. You'll enjoy it. I love Asia. I've never been to Singapore, so I'm looking forward to that experience. I've booked us into a one-bedroom suite at the Wainwright Hotel. It is supposed to be a lovely, traditional hotel right downtown."

Perkins grunted. "Long as they've got cheeseburgers."

"Oh, Perk. We're going to be able to try some fabulous new flavors and dishes. Singapore cuisine is a blend of Malaysian, Chinese, Indonesian, and Indian. Remember it was originally an important seaport that attracted shipping from all over the world. I think the local food will be divine. And I'm sure they'll have local beer."

He brightened at that.

Rosie checked her food bowl. Nothing. Just another disappointment in her poor puppy life. She gave out an unhappy snurkle. She was probably the most pathetic and unloved dog in the entire world. She sank onto the floor. Perkins eyed her.

"Don't even try it," he warned. She shifted her downtrodden gaze to Samantha. The pretty lady came over to pat her once again.

"We've got to try the Long Bar at the Raffles Hotel," Samantha announced. "That's where the Singapore Sling was invented. A lot of famous people have stayed at Raffles: Elizabeth Taylor, Charlie Chaplin, Rudyard Kipling, Ava Gardner, Michael Jackson. King Edward VIII. King Faisal. Wow. Royalty."

Perkins at least looked a little interested in the list of celebrities. He fussed through his briefcase, double-checking his notes and files.

"Okay. I think you're ready," announced Samantha as she took one last look around the sheriff's house. "Remember your passport. Really. Now I've got to run to finish my own packing. Kim is picking me up at one p.m. at my condo, and then we'll drive here to get you two and then on to the airport. She'll keep Rosie with her after that. Remember to pack a box with Rosie's food and toys."

With that she absently kissed him, patted Rosie, and hurried out the door.

She left behind two doleful souls.

She couldn't be moved by them. The general had to make sure all the logistics were in place for the invasion of Singapore. She stormed on.

Chapter 51

PERKINS WAS STUNNED. He had had no idea that airplane travel could be so nice. He stretched out in his large, reclining, very comfortable seat. A cold Heineken had been poured for him by a pretty blonde flight attendant as soon as he had boarded. How good was this?

Samantha had kept this little surprise to herself. With her zillions of points, she'd been able to book first-class seats for the entire trip. He played with some of the buttons on the side of his seat. Up. Down. Back. Recline. Private TV screen. Another cold Heineken. Ohhh, and a nice snack basket? And another pillow? Well, thank you, ma'am.

Samantha was in her own comfy seat right beside him. She couldn't help but smile at his obvious surprise and delight at discovering the joys of Delta's First Class.

She had flown long distances enough times that she realized comfort was critical to surviving twenty-four hours on a plane. She enjoyed Perkins's delight as she sipped her Mimosa.

A ground agent whisked them into the Delta Lounge in New York. Perkins again was stunned. He had no idea such luxury existed inside grubby airports.

He surveyed the trays of canapés and snacks. The bar was extensive. The food was elaborate. The beer was cold. The chairs were soft. The hockey game was on one of the big-screen TVs. The Leafs beating the Lightning? What was wrong with that?

Yes, air travel is great, he thought to himself. He handed Samantha her glass of Pinot. Somehow their hands linked. Fortunately he was an ambidextrous beer drinker.

A discreet agent reminded them that it was time to head for their gate. They were ushered directly into the First Class cabin. There was a long line of people waiting to board the back of the plane. A red-faced woman snarled at them.

A smartly attired flight attendant hung up his jacket and made sure Samantha was comfortably seated in her pod. They were offered welcome drinks. Perkins settled back into his private pod.

For possibly the first time in the history of airline travel, a passenger hoped it would be a slow trip across the Atlantic.

Delta One, huh? He felt he was the only person on the flight and the number one priority of the cabin crew.

Three hours later, he was finishing his second warm cookie. The dregs of his chocolate ice cream sundae were melting. The steak had been really good, and the meal tasty. He passed on the cheese and port. A man has to show some restraint.

Another pillow. A blanket. A toiletry kit with all the basic necessities. He stretched out and napped peacefully.

Their arrival at Heathrow was chaotic. It always is, Samantha told him. Massive numbers of travellers from all over the world. Perkins eyed the security guards and the machine-gun-toting military.

They cleared British Customs and Immigration and found their way to the departure area for the mid-Eastern airline to Singapore. There wasn't much time before boarding, so they remained near the desk. Samantha wandered into a nearby duty-free shop. She quickly bought a cashmere sweater and stuffed it into her carry-on.

They watched the cabin crew board. They wore distinctive sand-colored uniforms, cream scarves, and pert red hats. They were all very attractive, Perkins noted. Merely an observation by a trained professional, of course. He cleared his throat. Samantha watched with amusement and made a mental note to add "sexy stewardess" to her growing wardrobe of special costumes that Perkins liked.

Men.

Again they were the first to board. The plane they were in was a different configuration than that of their London flight. It was bigger, wider, and to Perkins' amazement, had a small stand-up bar in the middle of the first class cabin.

He peered around. There was a circular staircase leading to another floor. He clambered up for a look before boarding was complete, and came back with a stunned look on his face.

"They have little cabins up there," he whispered to her. "Like your own little hotel room. The attendant told me they convert to a queen bed at night." He shook his head. "And there's a shower spa. And something about moisturizing lounge wear. What's that all about?"

"They should, for what they charge for those cabins," she whispered back. "You need oil money for those!"

Samantha and Perkins stood at the bar, chatting casually with some of the other guests. A skilled mixologist served drinks. Conversation was light and pleasant. A sumptuous dinner was served.

The attendants fixed their pods for the night and they each sank back in comfort. The plane flew on, across mountains and oceans.

Pinkish light inside the cabin eventually wakened the sleeping guests. There was a rush for the well-equipped bathrooms. Breakfast was served.

Perkins shaved with the complimentary toiletry kit and spruced himself up as best he could. Samantha took a little longer but emerged refreshed and lovely. She patted his shoulder as she passed his pod.

"Let's just go to the hotel first," she suggested. "We can get settled, cleaned up, and then contact the Singapore Police. Inspector…who is it?"

"Holmes. Not sure what he looks like. I'm still grinning about your description of his grey handle-bar moustache. Probably in tweeds. Maybe a pipe in one hand?"

They smiled at one another. As Samantha turned to go to her pod, Perkins reached up and grabbed her arm. "Hey. Honey. Thank you for doing this, arranging this flight. Without you to organize everything…"

She bent down to kiss him softly. "You are very welcome. Now we just have to find those two thieves, get the money back, and what was it? Oh yeah, throw them in the dungeon."

She slipped back into her seat as the seat belt light chimed. The attendants came through handing out the Singapore Customs and Immigration forms.

Perkins read his carefully. In a box in the middle of the card was a very stark warning: IF YOU ARE BRINGING IN DRUGS YOU WILL BE EXECUTED.

Well.

That was pretty clear.

He glanced at the magazine in his seat pocket while he was waiting for the landing. Changi Airport was the best in the world, an article reported. It had everything from butterfly gardens to art galleries to live flora and fauna to great food outlets. He was amazed. Sculptures. A crystal garden.

He had been in only a few airports in the US and now in London…he didn't recall any gardens or galleries in any of them.

The landing was smooth, the goodbyes from the attendants warm, and the walk to the Immigration area easy. They were quickly stamped and waved through. They handed in their Customs cards without incident and stepped through the arrivals lounge into a huge, high, skylighted concourse.

Friends and family were waiting to greet loved ones. Porters bustled about. Money exchanges hummed.

Samantha looked around for the taxi stand.

Perkins stood there, absorbing the scene. It was very different from his usual world. He liked it.

He was looking avidly at the variety of colors and spectacles in the airport when a beautiful young woman approached him. Samantha studied her.

She was wearing a high-end designer black silk pant suit. An ivory blouse. Some expensive jade jewelry at her throat and left wrist. Shiny black heels, not too high. She had the most gorgeous blue-black hair that was shimmering in the sunlight; it hung to her shoulder blades. She had a pretty face and a tentative smile.

"Sheriff Perkins? LeRoy Perkins?"

Puzzled, Perkins nodded. "That's right. And you would be…?"

She smiled at him and extended her right hand. "I am delighted to welcome you to Singapore. I am Inspector C. Y. Holmes."

No bushy grey handlebar moustache or tweed jacket in sight, observed Samantha with slightly narrowed eyes.

Or any sign of a briar pipe.

Chapter 52

"So that's the summary," Perkins concluded as he poked a desultory chopstick at the remains of the spicy orange chicken and the double-fried pork on his plate.

Inspector Holmes had taken them to a high-end restaurant in a part of Singapore that was obviously a predominantly Chinese neighborhood. The dinner had been superb. It had started with Peking Duck, one of Samantha's all-time favorite dishes.

"In other words," Inspector Holmes summarized stiffly, "you have no crime, you have no grounds for extradition, and you have no chance of winning a court case right now because you have no evidence. Is that accurate?"

Samantha was beginning to really dislike the beautiful woman who was wearing a red-and-gold traditional *Cheongsam* dress. It fit tightly at the neck, bodice and waist. The slit up her thigh revealed an elegantly contoured leg.

Perkins flushed a bit at he ran the tip of one chopstick through the remaining sauce on his plate. "We're not here to extradite anyone at this time, but we strongly believe a major fraud has occurred."

Inspector Holmes shrugged and sipped her tea. No one said anything.

Samantha waited a long minute and then decided that since this woman was the only person in the entire city that might possibly help them, maybe she'd better bury her jealousy and make friendly noises.

"That is a gorgeous dress you're wearing," she began. "I love the intricate embroidery."

"Oh, thank you. My mother and grandmother made this for me."

"They are very talented. It is exquisite." Samantha paused. "Holmes is an interesting name…"

Inspector Holmes laughed. Even her laugh was beautiful, Samantha noted, aware she was being just a little bitchy.

"My grandfather was British. He came to Singapore more than fifty years ago and set up an import-export business. He married my grandmother, who is Chinese and still a great beauty. They had one son, my father, who also married a Chinese woman. And they had me and my brother. He's a chef. This is his restaurant. Neither of us followed in the family business. My grandmother is quite upset about that."

"Dinner has been amazing," Samantha said with enthusiasm. She paused again. "And what does the C. Y. stand for?"

"Two very traditional Chinese names, both too hard to pronounce. That's why I go by my initials. But my friends call me Cindy." She poured more tea for Samantha and the Sheriff.

"You would be surprised by the number of people who see my name and think I'm some stuffy old British detective in tweeds smoking a pipe," she continued. Samantha glanced quickly at Perkins; they both flushed a bit. "Then they meet me. I'm not what they expected." She paused. "Sometimes it is useful to have people underestimate you in police work."

Perkins nodded.

He put his chopsticks on the rest beside his plate. He looked at Samantha unhappily.

"Cindy. May we call you that?" Inspector Holmes nodded. "I'm Samantha. He's Perk," Samantha continued. Holmes nodded again and offered a gleaming smile. Damn, Samantha thought in passing, she probably also takes warm meals to the poor and teaches orphans how to write computer code.

"We realize this is a highly unusual case. We're pursuing this because some very good friends of mine were suckered by these two con artists. They lost a lot of money. The lives of their families have been…disrupted. That's why we are here. To help them."

Cindy's expression softened a little as she listened. "I respect your wanting to protect your friends. Family and friends are very important in my culture. We call it *guanxi*. The circle of people around you, the exchange of favors that is more important than a contract in business. In modern terms, it is the social and business networks of your family and friends. You protect each other. You work together. You support one another."

"That is exactly what we are doing here," Samantha said. Cindy looked at her carefully, but Samantha thought she was softening a bit. "We're talking about a million and a half dollars these crooks stole."

Cindy's eyes widened. "That is substantial." She fiddled with her napkin as the waiters cleared the table. "Singapore does not appreciate foreigners who run here to hide their crimes. We are a law-abiding society here that runs efficiently because of strict rules and social structure."

"I read the notice on your Customs declaration," Perkins said.

"Oh, that is not really correct. If you bring in drugs, you will first be given a fair trial and then be executed," Cindy said. There was no levity in her voice.

Silence at the table. A fresh pot of tea and a plate of fresh fruit and exquisite little Chinese pastries appeared. Samantha glanced around the room and realized that they had been given a prime table. And there was a lot of room around it, so that conversations would remain private. She suddenly wondered who had the clout—the police, or Cindy's family.

"We have been able to locate your two suspects," Cindy suddenly offered. "The artist's sketches proved to be very valuable. Our facial recognition technology got them at the airport and then several times on the street."

Perkins stared at her.

"The man has an apartment in a high-rise on the west side of the city. He's rented it for six years. He comes here—well, we're still working that out. He seems to have more than one identity." She frowned as if he wasn't playing the game fairly. "We are continuing that investigation."

"The woman is currently at the Primrose Hotel. It is an American chain hotel, forty-four storeys tall. It is very… American," she said with a slight shudder. "She is in Suite 3809. It is a one-bedroom suite that is costing her $611 per night. Plus room service, massages, and spa treatments, of course."

She nibbled one of the little pastries as Samantha and the sheriff absorbed the stunning information.

"Shall we go?"

CHAPTER 53

THE SMALL BAR at the Wainwright Hotel seemed to meet with Cindy's approval. The three had adjourned there after the fabulous dinner.

"This is quite comfortable, isn't it?"

"Yes, we like the hotel," replied Samantha. "Quiet. Staff is very accommodating. The room is lovely."

"You made a fine choice." They all sipped their drinks—cognac for the inspector, bourbon with water back for the sheriff, and a Drambuie with one ice cube for Samantha.

"The bathroom is wonderful," Samantha said with a slight note of awe. "It has a glass shower stall with a view of the harbor. It has three different faucets, a steamer, and a bunch of jets that hit you from different angles. And two sinks."

"Ah. Wonderful. Yes, that is wonderful."

Perkins sat listening. Yeah, the bathroom had a shower and a sink. And a toilet. What more did you need? Why would they possibly need two sinks?

Women.

The Inspector seemed to be thawing a bit, thought Samantha. Holmes popped a cashew from the nut bowl and sat back.

"We realize that this is not a normal sort of case for you," Samantha began. "And we realize that confronting the two of them would not be effective. Perk has no jurisdiction here. What we are most interested in is getting the money back to our friends. And then shooting them," she concluded under her breath.

From Cindy's startled look it may not have been quite as quiet a comment as she'd thought. Perkins just shook his head, grinned, and sipped his bourbon.

"Now that I understand the problem," the Inspector began, "I have a much greater appreciation for what you are trying to achieve." Her faint British accent lingered. Samantha assumed she'd gone to school in England for a few years as a child.

"I wonder," Cindy finally offered, "if I might make a suggestion?"

"Yes, please. We would welcome your help. Ideas."

"You will appreciate, Sheriff, that this is just two colleagues chatting informally. Nothing official, of course. Certainly nothing on paper."

Perkins agreed with a wave.

"It seems to me now that you need to focus on the return of the money, rather than on retribution or punishment."

Again Perkins agreed.

"Well, then, might I suggest that you consider ways to extract the money from the woman and man who stole from your friends?"

It took them both a moment. Then both Samantha and Perkins burst out almost simultaneously. "We've got to con the con artists! That's brilliant!" A moment passed. "How do we do that?"

Obviously another drink was required. The elderly waiter served the fresh round, changed the nut bowl and straightened the vase of flowers that had somehow gotten tilted.

"If they are living apart, are they still partners, do you think?" Holmes looked at the two of them for direction.

"I'm waiting for US law enforcement to identify them for real," Perkins told her. "Should get the results tomorrow. I hope. So I don't know if they are just business partners, or have some kind of personal relationship, or what."

"I don't think they are together in any kind of sexual way," Samantha announced. "I've only met them a couple of times, but from her body language I don't think she can stand him personally. I'd bet on their being partners in these scams, but not together otherwise."

The Inspector and the sheriff contemplated this.

"Okay, let's accept that as most probable," Perkins said. "I trust Samantha's judgment on those things. So then we've got a couple of problems. Why are they both still here in Singapore? And how do we get the two of them together so we can get the money back?" He thought for another moment. "And then the third question obviously becomes, how much longer will the two of them be here? Once one of them leaves, any chance to get the money back pretty much disappears."

"Then we've got to act quickly." Samantha reached for her glass and continued. "What are their weak spots? Where are they vulnerable? If we got one of them, would the other come to their rescue?" She drank. "And then the biggie—how do we get back the money from their greedy, grasping, dirty little hands?"

Silence around the table.

Drinks were drunk. Their waiter floated by on arthritic knees.

Finally Cindy spoke. "I haven't met either one. So I trust your observations. Tell me, Samantha, the man. Massey Ferguson. What are your thoughts?"

"Not his real name," Perkins offered quickly. Holmes nodded, looked faintly annoyed at someone trying to act illegally in Singapore.

"I didn't like him," said Samantha. "Always felt I wanted to go and wash my hands after meeting him. Smarmy. Just my reaction as a woman. I guess he was smooth with his con, but I didn't find him charming in any way. A phony."

"And the woman?"

"I think men are drawn to her. She is cute, really curvy, short, gave off a sort of 'protect me' vibe that men would find very appealing. I think women saw her as the little sister they had to look after so nobody would take advantage of her. Huh," she added bitterly. "Like that kept her on the straight and narrow."

"Good, good. Now tell me, what do you recall about her personal demeanor, her patterns, and her sense of style? Where might she be vulnerable?" Holmes prompted.

Samantha deliberated for a moment. "She dressed okay. I think when men were around she pushed her boobs out and enjoyed the attention. I suspect she was the closer in the con with men. Probably older men. Likely older, lonely, single men. Yeah, that makes sense to me. They would adore her."

The Inspector and the sheriff were watching her intently. They both nodded encouragement. Samantha reflected some more.

"She liked to flaunt her body but I think she was a tease. I never saw her with anybody but the toad. Wait. Hang on. Here's something. She wore a lot of jewelry. I'm certainly not an expert, but it all looked real to me. A gorgeous emerald ring, a sapphire blue pendant that was stunning, a couple of bracelets with rubies in them, some turquoise that was exquisite. Yeah, she liked expensive jewels a lot. I don't know if men bought them for her or if she does it by herself, but she's got a lot of money tied up in her jewelry. Wait! Jewelry!"

It only took a moment for the three of them to connect the dots.

"That's it! That's the weakness!" cried Perkins and Holmes.

The elderly waiter looked askance. *Shouting in his bar? And a Singapore Police inspector? One might expect that from Americans, but really!*

They lowered their voices and leaned in toward one another.

"Do you know a jewelry store that might be able to, uh, help us out?"

"Oh yes. Part of my *guanxi*. My grandmother's first cousin's second son runs the family jewelry store. He's terrified of my grandmother. If she asks him, he'll do anything."

Wait. The *family's* jewelry store? Samantha thought to herself.

"We need to get a plan together," Perkins announced as he swallowed the dregs of his drink. "But not tonight. We are exhausted, and with the time change…"

Holmes nodded sympathetically. "I understand. Why don't you let me do some prep work in the morning. You sleep in, get settled, and then go to the Long Bar at Raffles. I'll meet you there at around three."

Samantha realized suddenly how exhausted she was. They got up, and, to her surprise, Cindy leaned in for a little hug. She was thawing a little more as time went on.

She shook hands with Perkins and strode out to her waiting car and driver. Samantha and Perk took the elevator to their suite and soon collapsed into bed.

They slept for ten hours.

Chapter 54

"THIS IS WONDERFUL! What a great history this place has!" Samantha was enthusiastic as she and Perkins settled onto stools at the famous Long Bar on the second floor of the Raffles Hotel. The bar was dark polished wood. Tables and chairs were packed around the room. Tall green plants provided relief. But the bar was the focus.

"What may I get you?" asked the barman.

"It is my first visit, so of course I'm here for your Singapore Sling," said Samantha gaily. She watched as the bartender expertly assembled gin, Cointreau, grenadine, cherry brandy, Angostura Bitters, Benedictine, and lemon and pineapple juice.

"This was invented more than a hundred years ago by a former head bartender here," said the bartender as he poured her drink over ice cubes into a large glass. "The ladies were not allowed to drink in a public bar at that time. But being clever ladies, they got together with the bartender and he invented this. It is pinkish. The women told their idiot husbands it was pink lemonade. Everybody was happy. Some of the women reportedly got very happy," he grinned.

"And for you, sir?"

"Ah. I'm not much of a pink drink guy," Perkins commented drily.

"How about a Tiger Beer? Cold, on draft. It is a crisp lager."

"Perfect. How did it get named Tiger Beer?"

"Another great story," the bartender began as he grabbed a chilled, tapered glass. "Many decades ago, a tiger somehow got into the hotel downstairs. Somebody called the headmaster of the school across the street. He marched here in his pyjamas carrying his rifle and shot the tiger." He pulled the tap, tilted the glass, and filled it to the brim with just a small head. He placed it with a flourish in front of Perkins.

"And some smart local entrepreneur got the idea and started brewing Tiger beer. To this day, the label on the bottle is a tiger's head, presumably up in tiger heaven. It is our most popular beer."

Perkins took a large draught. "Ah. That's good. And what a great story."

The bartender nodded and went down to serve other customers along the jammed bar.

Samantha swivelled and looked around. "This is amazing. What a grand experience. Imagine all the famous people—writers, sportsmen, artists, political leaders, businesspeople—who have visited this famous bar. And now they can add our names to their list," she giggled.

Perkins swallowed appreciatively. He looked around for the bartender and motioned for a refill. A moment later another cold Tiger lager was at his place.

Samantha glanced at her watch.

"Are you meeting anyone?" enquired the bartender courteously.

"Yes. Inspector Holmes from the Singapore Police."

"She is coming here?" The bartender's face shone. He promptly went over to the headwaiter and whispered something. The manager straightened up instinctively, brushed back his hair, and looked out at the growing lineup.

The bartender returned. "You must be very important guests," he said respectfully.

"No. Don't think so. She's just helping us on a little matter, here," Perkins said. The surprise in his voice was obvious.

"The Holmes family is one of Singapore's richest, best known and most respected. Her family has donated millions of dollars to help build this city. They are in shipping, exporting, own a couple of blocks of downtown, something about jewelry, telecommunications, I don't know what else."

Samantha and Perkins looked at each other in amazement. Samantha thought back to the clothes and jewelry Cindy had been wearing. That should have been a tipoff.

And suddenly there she was. The head waiter was practically bowing her in as she strode toward the corner of the bar where Samantha and the Sheriff waited.

She briskly shook hands with both. A bar stool magically appeared for her where none had been a moment before.

Several people were watching, Samantha noted. Okay, the entire bar. Cindy settled on her stool and ordered a soda water with lime. The sure-fingered bartender nearly dropped the glass as he prepared her drink.

She was dressed in a red business suit. The skirt came just above her knee and confirmed Samantha's previous estimation of great legs. The black blouse under the red jacket swelled appropriately. Her hair was pulled back into a ponytail. She was wearing simple gold accessories today.

Samantha was scared to estimate their value.

"You look stunning." Cindy's comment stopped Samantha cold. She was wearing an ecru linen dress. Her gold-red hair was long over her shoulders. She wore an elaborate twisted wire necklace that she'd bought at a flea market in New York a couple of years before. If she recalled correctly, it had cost her eighteen dollars.

"I'd love to have your sense of style. And your hair."

"Th-thank you. But you are so gorgeous. I love that suit. And your jewelry."

Perkins watched the female bonding going on. Not something that men went through. He tried to imagine his going up to Captain Williams and gushing over his shirt. The veteran cop would probably pop him one.

He was still grinning over the image of himself going ass over teakettle when he became aware of Inspector Holmes addressing him.

"Sorry. A distracting thought. What was that?"

"I asked, did you get confirmation of their identities?"

"Oh. Yes. I did. Well, his identity, at least."

Cindy nodded, waiting.

"Our team found a fingerprint on the last place people think to clean up when they're wiping down their home. The flusher on the toilet. People almost always go to the bathroom the last thing before they leave on a trip. They always forget to wipe off the handle. My people got a print and we got a hit."

He finished the last of his beer and shook his head at the bartender's unspoken question.

"The guy's real name is Dale Avery. He had a couple of minor raps as a young guy; that's how he got in the system. He's had a couple of complaints against him for scams in recent years, but no convictions. He's got a string of aliases. Born in Indiana. Not a clue how he finally settled on Singapore as his escape route."

Cindy listened intently. "That is helpful. I have assigned a loose surveillance team on him. Since he apparently has broken no laws in Singapore so far, that's about all we can do. I am having the Immigration Division pursue his passport records. That may be a violation that we can nail him with. That is also a path to extradition."

Perkins absorbed that, nodded and continued. "The woman is a little different. We can't get one hundred percent positive ID, but we are pretty sure she is Donna Mulvaney. Grew up in Minnesota. Smart. Got into banking for a while. We think that's where she met Avery. They hooked up, and the scamming spree began. We think they've been working together for three years."

Silence at the bar as they thought through the latest intelligence.

Finally Cindy clapped her hands once. "Okay. Let's think up a plan to fleece the fleecers."

Perkins paid the bartender a staggering amount of Singaporean dollars for the drinks and they hustled down the stairs. The chase was on.

CHAPTER 55

"Now," CINDY CAUTIONED, "you understand that the Singapore Police cannot be part of anything that is remotely illegal." Perkins nodded. "I have spoken with Superintendent Keong, and he agrees that we don't want these two in Singapore. He is willing to give me some, oh, let's say, latitude, in handling this situation."

"And we are grateful for your help."

Cindy nodded her head at the sheriff. She went on. "It seems to me that Samantha hit on the best solution last night. I think we should focus on Ashley. I know she has a new name, or an old name or whatever, but we're all used to referring to her as Ashley and to him as Ferguson."

Samantha and Perkins nodded agreement.

"Fine. Now, how do we get to her?"

"I've been thinking about that," Samantha offered. "What if we could get her interested in some rare jewel or something that is being sold at a big discount for some reason? A family crisis or emergency or something. She's finely attuned to vulnerability, to taking advantage of such people. Maybe she'd see that as an opportunity for her to get a great deal on something of value."

A brief silence as Cindy and Perkins thought about that.

"I like it," she ventured finally. Perkins nodded. "The thing is, how do we create the scam? How do we get the money back without offering her something of value? She's no dummy."

That took more thought. Geez, Samantha mused, this criminal stuff is hard work.

"What if we got some big ruby or emerald or something that she could get at a big discount? But what frustrates me is I can't figure out how to switch it or get it back or something," Samantha said.

"There's an idea in there," Perkins said. "What if we got a fake and—no, I suppose she'd know enough about jewelry or she'd want to have it appraised or something."

More silence.

Deep thinking.

Samantha finally spoke again. "Take Perk's idea. And mine. Put 'em together. Could we offer her a real jewel and then pull a switch? Replace the real with a fake? But I don't know how to do that!"

Cindy finally looked up. "I think I have it," she said and took a deep breath. The other two looked at her expectantly. She drew another deep breath. "But to pull it off, we have to go and see Grandmama." She paused. There was an unspoken warning in her voice. "She is…formidable."

(HAPTER 56

"I HAVE NOTHING TO wear," snapped Samantha as she angrily pushed around hangers in the hotel closet.

Perkins observed what he guessed were at least eight or nine dresses and suits and outfits in the closet. He declined to respond. That was a no-win path for any man.

I guess I'm getting smarter about relationships, he thought to himself.

"Nothing!"

No comment.

Perkins thought about his own extensive wardrobe. He had his dark blue suit that Samantha had made him pack. He had one nice light blue dress shirt. He had one red and blue striped tie. Whew. Off the hook.

"Uh, honey?" He tip-toed onto the battlefield. "Why don't you go and buy a new dress?"

"Because then I don't have the right shoes or accessories to go with it!"

Perkins retreated behind a bottle of Tiger beer.

The phone in the hotel room rang. Samantha grabbed it savagely. "Yes!"

Her voice softened a moment later. "Yes. Thank you. I would love to do that." She hung up. "Cindy is coming to take me shopping." She began bustling around figuring out what clothes to wear to go shopping for clothes.

Completely mystified by the female species, Perkins flipped on the satellite TV service. A bunch of guys in white flannels with big bats standing around a field. No. Horses running in the wrong direction. No. Twenty-two men wearing really ugly uniforms chasing a round ball. No. A bunch of muscular, mean-looking dudes doing violent things to each other while pursuing an oval ball? Australian Rules Football? Great. He watched for a few minutes. He could discern no actual rules of play, perhaps other than when an arm was ripped off it had to be returned to the other team.

Samantha left a few minutes later. Perkins congratulated himself on escaping with only a few minor scars. He popped another Tiger to celebrate.

Two hours later, Samantha returned with a couple of long garment bags. She ordered him to clean up and get dressed so she could have the bathroom.

Perkins obeyed. It was still an hour and a half before they had to leave for dinner with the old lady. What could possibly take so much time?

He and the tiger on the label mulled that conundrum after he had taken five and a half minutes to get dressed. And that included tying his shoes, he noted to the tiger. And his tie.

The tiger seemed to approve.

There was a lot of spraying and water running and zipping and grunting and stuff from inside the bathroom. Perkins and his tiger buddy ignored it all.

He was looking at his watch when the bathroom door finally opened. He looked up. And a vision appeared before him.

Samantha was wearing a black *cheongsam* dress. It was embroidered with intricate gold thread in a dragon design. Red beads were sewn throughout the dress. It was high-necked, tight at the waist, and had a long, long slit edged in gold down her elegant naked right leg. Shiny black heels accentuated the leg. Her hair was piled up in an intricate hair style. She was wearing gold earrings and bracelets. There was a faint aroma of jasmine coming from her.

Perkins stood up. He stared at her. "Holy crap! Where did you come up with that? You look absolutely…stunning!"

She smiled happily at the heart-felt compliment. She pivoted to give him a look at the entire outfit. She felt him come close and grab her around her waist. She felt him rubbing against her jutting behind. They both savored the sensations for a long moment.

Reluctantly she pulled away. "We have to go. The driver will be waiting." He sighed. "But remember where you left off," she smiled at him as she got a small black clasp purse.

She took one more look in the full-length mirror. "They insisted on taking in the waist half an inch," she told him. "I won't be able to eat tonight or some seams will be popping."

"They're going to be popping when I get you back here after dinner," he told her in a throaty voice. She felt little frissons go through her body.

Reluctantly he gathered his hotel key, wallet, and business cards. Samantha had taught him the proper way to present his business card: with two hands, the printing extended to the recipient, and a small bow.

He couldn't resist one solid butt pat as they left the room. She smiled.

They were escorted to the back seat of a vintage 1984 Rolls Royce that Grandmama had sent for them. Cindy would meet them at the residence.

"You look very nice," Samantha assured him.

"Tell me again why we are doing this dress-up act for granny?"

Samantha glared at him. "From what I've figured out, she is the 'grande dame' of Singapore society. Long family history here. Wealthy. Community leader. She's seen all the goods and bads of the city's history. As a child she survived the Japanese occupation. She raised her family in Singapore. I think she has been the dominant force in arts and culture here for many years. I hear she's a fearsome dragon. She doesn't suffer fools gladly—she doesn't suffer them at all."

Samantha stopped. She shrugged. "She's rich. She's old. She's smart. She can do any damn thing she wants."

Great, thought Perkins. Say a wrong word and the dragon eats you. Or breathes fire on you, or whatever dragons do. Didn't much matter, he concluded—it was going to end badly for you.

The car drove through the sultry Singapore night. Lights were dazzling from a hundred different high-rise buildings. The streets were well lit and clean. The ride in the Rolls was very comfortable.

Finally they pulled up in front of two gates. The security people on duty immediately opened them and they entered the estate. They both gasped.

The house was incredible. The driveway and exterior were beautifully lit up to display the mansion's design features and landscaping. The grounds were a spectacle of colorful oriental flowers and shrubs.

The grand staircase leading inside the house was just that— spectacular. Ornamental lions were posed at the top of the staircase. Huge urns displayed potted flowers in a riot of color.

The large, intricately carved teak doors were opened by two smiling servants, who ushered them into the foyer.

The curved carved staircase dominated the entrance and led to the upper floor. The marble floors gleamed. There was an astonishing array of precious oriental art on walls, pedestals and tables. It all combined into a breathtaking display of taste, culture, and sophistication.

Cindy paraded down the grand staircase. Like Samantha, she was wearing the traditional formal dress. Hers was a deep blue with intricate patterns throughout the fabric. Her dark hair shone. Her jewelry tonight was a large sapphire necklace, earrings and a series of gold bracelets down her left arm.

"Welcome," she said, hugging and kissing Samantha and giving Perkins a warm hug.

She took a deep breath. "Come. It is time to meet Grandmama."

Chapter 57

THE CHAIR COULD have been a small throne for some lesser Asian country, Samantha thought. It was tall, intricately inlaid with jewels, and had a filigreed design that accentuated the beauty of the carving. It had a regal purple seat cushion.

And seated on that cushion was a woman in her eighties. Her back was straight, her posture impeccable. Her ankles were crossed demurely. Her hair was silver.

She was still beautiful, Samantha thought to herself, but she must have been absolutely exquisite in her youth.

She too was dressed in a *cheongsam*. Hers was primarily silver with scarlet accents and designs. Her jewels were rubies. Her slippers were also scarlet. It was an audacious, breath-taking outfit for anyone to wear. For someone of her age to pull it off was astonishing.

Cindy pulled them closer to the regal chair. "Grandmama, may I present two friends from North America. They have come all the way here from Florida in the United States. This is Samantha Summers. This is LeRoy Perkins. He is the sheriff of his city and county, a very important man." The aristocratic neck bowed slightly as she acknowledged the visitors. "This is my beloved grandmother, Mei-Ling Holmes."

Samantha was briefly paralysed by the protocol. It was almost like meeting royalty. One didn't speak before they did. One didn't shake hands unless they initiated it. One didn't—oh shit.

"Howdy, Ma'am. It is a pleasure to meet you." Perkins stepped forward to the chair, hand outstretched. Grandmama flinched for a second, but then extended her own hand. They shook. "Say, that's a great dress you've got on. I really like the color."

Samantha searched for a hole to swallow her. Cindy looked as if she was about to faint.

"Hey, that's some chair you've got," Perkins continued. He finally released her hand and circled around the chair. "What is that trim, bone of some kind?"

"Ah. Yes. Ivory. Carved a century ago. Before the ban on importing tusks."

"Wow. That's really something. And you look great sitting on it." He patted her shoulder as he returned to Samantha, who looked as if she'd just eaten a bad eel.

"This here's Samantha," he continued as he prodded her forward. "She's wearing a dress just like yours."

Samantha went pale. Please, Lord, a nice heart attack. Now.

Mei-Ling almost cracked the wisp of a smile at that sentence. She beckoned Samantha forward. She took a few tentative steps and stopped before the chair. Mei-Ling studied her from head to toe.

"You are very beautiful," she finally declared after a long moment. "Very few American women can wear the *cheongsam* properly." She nodded approval and then made a little hand gesture. Samantha retreated.

Cindy came up and kissed her grandmama on the cheek. They murmured in Chinese for a moment.

"Grandmama is very happy you have joined us," she said. "Would you like a drink before dinner?"

A tuxedoed butler appeared from some side door. Samantha was barely able to speak. "A sherry," she croaked. Grandmama nodded approval.

"I'll have one too," Cindy amended. The butler glanced at a servant who had appeared at the corner bar. He quickly poured two small glasses of thirty-four-year-old Portuguese sherry and served it to the women.

"Ah, heck, I'm not much of a drinker like that," Perkins said loudly." Any chance I could get a cold beer? I've grown quite fond of that Tiger stuff you've got over here."

Both Cindy and Samantha sucked in their breath. The butler nodded and began to move toward the bar when Mei-Ling spoke softly.

"You know, I haven't had a Tiger beer in many, many years. I believe I will join you in one tonight, Sheriff."

Cindy's glass hit the marble floor.

CHAPTER 58

THE DINNER HAD been exquisite. Ten courses. A magnificent poached fish. Spicy prawns. A pork dish in an utterly delicious dark brown sauce. Tiny dumplings stuffed with shrimp and chives.

Samantha lost count after a while. She sampled everything but was terrified of the seams at her waist exploding.

Cindy spent most of the meal eating and staring at the sheriff and her grandmama. Inexplicably, they had bonded. Grandmama was sipping her second Tiger beer. Cindy had never seen that before.

Perkins was trying hard to use his chopsticks. Samantha had taught him but he was still a Southern boy at heart. She'd have to give him a special reward tonight for persevering, she thought. That brought a smile to her lips. Perhaps it would start with her asking him to help remove her long dress.

Another course was served. Small bowls of rice. A spicy Malaysian curry. It was all delicious.

At one point, Samantha asked the regal lady about her marriage.

"That is a very difficult question," she responded after a pause. "It was a very different society then. I was much younger than he was. My family did not approve but we were deeply in love. For many years we were not...accepted...by society here. It simply drove us to work harder and to give more back to the community." She sipped the last of her beer. "It is lovely of you to ask. We learned to treasure each other and our family. We survived," she concluded simply. "I hope you find the happiness that we did in your own lives."

Samantha wiped away a small tear. She could only imagine what the lovely lady had been through.

The Sheriff was having a great time. He had funny comments about Southern food in the US, his impressions of Singapore, and some of the bizarre cases he'd had in his career. His description of deputies trying to catch a pet alligator that had grown up in the bathtub of a high-rise condo and then one day escaped, and the naked old woman jumping in terror onto her bed as the alligator eyed her, had Mei-Ling wiping tears of laughter from her eyes.

"Took four deputies to settle the scene," he concluded with a grin. "Two to catch the 'gator, and two to catch the old lady." He paused. "I think those guys are still in therapy!"

Mei-Ling bent her head as she laughed. Cindy stared across the table at Samantha, who looked back at her helplessly. She shrugged her shoulders. Cindy shrugged hers back. Who could have predicted this?

"Shall we move to more comfortable chairs," said Mei-Ling. It was not a question. She waited for a servant to pull out her chair. Perkins moved quickly to her side.

"May I have the honor?" he asked gallantly as he extended an arm. He had noticed the walking stick with a gold handle that was placed discreetly in the corner.

Mei-Ling nodded thanks as she put her hand on his strong left arm and they walked into a quiet den with large, comfortable leather chairs. Perkins got her seated before taking the chair next to hers. Cindy and Samantha sat in the two opposite chairs.

The round coffee table between them was set with chocolates, petit fours, decanters of port, cognac, and liqueurs. Pots of tea and coffee sat on the sideboard.

Once everyone had chosen and settled back, Mei-Ling looked at Cindy. "This evening has been delightful. Your new friends are lovely." She sipped a tiny bit of cognac. "But I was under the impression that you had some urgent problem..."

Cindy didn't hesitate. "Yes, Grandmama." She then explained in detail the fraud that had happened in Florida to friends of Samantha, the way the two fraudsters had fled North America, and the discovery of the two of them now in Singapore.

Samantha described the two people who had conned her friends.

Then Cindy took a deep breath and explained to her grandmama the idea they'd come up with to con the con artists and get the money back. That took several minutes.

Mei-Ling was silent for a long moment after her granddaughter had finished.

"So neither one of you really has legal jurisdiction," she commented shrewdly. "One of you has a crime but no authority here, the other has the authority but no crime."

Perkins and Cindy both grimaced. The elegant lady had just very neatly summed up their conundrum.

"Well, then," she continued, unperturbed. "Samantha is quite correct. You need to do a jewelry switch to get the money back from the—uh," she enunciated carefully, "big-breasted bitch. Is that the correct term?"

It took several minutes for the laughter to stop and decorum to return. Mei-Ling continued. "I believe I may have something that could be useful to you." She waved over another servant and spoke quietly to him. He nodded and departed.

"More drinks?" Mei-Ling enquired brightly.

There was silence around the room as everyone waited, three of them not knowing for what.

Finally the servant returned with two beautiful jewelry cases. He placed them on the table in front of Mei-Ling and then stood back. She leaned forward and selected the turquoise box. She opened it and gazed at it with great pleasure. Finally she sighed and looked up.

"You need a piece of jewelry that would interest this nasty woman. It is imperative that she thinks she's getting a fabulous piece of jewelry at a huge discount. I wonder if this little bauble would be helpful to you?"

With that she put the opened box on the table and spun it toward Samantha and Cindy.

Samantha gasped.

In the box was a gorgeous diamond pendant necklace. The facets in the very large rock sparkled even in the dim light. The platinum necklace was designed plainly so it would not detract from the star of the show. As if anything could diminish that diamond.

Cindy reacted the same way. Then she looked at her grandmother. "I haven't seen this in twenty years."

"No, it has been a long time since you have seen it. Or I have worn it. It is one of my most favorite pieces. My late husband gave it to me after I gave birth to your father. I am willing it to you, of course. So if you want to take an advance on your inheritance, you have my permission."

She paused and then slid in the stiletto. "And perhaps it will add to your dowry so you can finally find a husband and give me great-grandchildren."

Cindy rolled her eyes. Samantha chortled inside. Some family issues cross all generations and all cultures.

Mei-Ling stared at her granddaughter, who promptly stopped the eye-rolls and bowed her head. Grandmama's house, Grandmama's rules.

Samantha saw the steel that had to be part of Mei-Ling's makeup. You didn't get to be a billionaire without hard work and making tough decisions. It was obvious that she and her late husband had worked together to build their empire. She didn't hesitate to show tough. No wonder most people were in terror of her.

"The diamond is absolutely exquisite," Samantha said to break the tension. "But," she added, "how do we switch it out? It is such a unique, magnificent design."

"Ah. You are correct. That is why I thought this might be useful to you. Sheriff, would you open the other box for us?"

Perkins obligingly leaned forward, took the purple box and opened it. A perplexed look instantly crossed his face. Without a word he left it open and offered it to the two women opposite him.

There sat a second, identical diamond necklace.

No one breathed.

Mei-Ling sat back with a satisfied smile on her face. Finally her granddaughter looked up at her.

"You have two of these?"

"Of course not. But when Singapore was going through turmoil, trying to sort out its independence, our insurance company insisted that we lock away all of my jewelry in London. We had a duplicate of this necklace made by one of our family's most trusted gem designers. I kept it here and wore it. Only after the political unrest settled did I bring my real jewels back."

She sipped a final drop of cognac. "It did occur to me that this might be perfect for your bait and switch. Oh yes," she smiled at Cindy's astonishment, "I try to keep up on the current jargon."

Perkins finally leaned over to her. "You know, ma'am, this is just about the nicest thing anyone has ever done for me in all my years in law enforcement. Thank you."

Eyes twinkling, he added, "And you know, if I was just ten years older, I'd be chasing you for myself."

Without missing a beat, her own eyes twinkly with delight, she replied, "And if I were just ten years younger, I'd let myself be caught!"

They laughed together. She patted his arm. Then she rose stiffly. "It is time for me to depart. Forgive me. Sheriff, you have brightened my evening in a way that hasn't happened for years. Now you go with your beautiful lady," she ordered Perkins, "and you look after her." He bowed respectfully.

She eyed Samantha. "You have a very special man. You look after him."

Samantha blushed and bowed her head in respect.

"And you look after those necklaces," she told Cindy acerbically.

Cindy nodded. Perkins nodded. Samantha nodded.

And with that, two servants magically appeared to assist Mei-Ling out of the room.

The three sagged back into their chairs.

"She is just a…a…force of nature!"

Cindy smiled at Samantha's comment. "Always has been. Scared the heck out of us as kids. She was unrelenting in teaching us manners, respect for the family, work ethic. Now I realize what a dynamo she was. Is. And what she's contributed to this city. I love her a lot."

"Agreed. She is a very special lady."

Perkins closed the two jewel boxes and gave them to Cindy. "Now we need to get the cheese to the mouse."

<h1 style="text-align:center">CHAPTER 59</h1>

ASHLEY WAS GETTING bored. She'd been in Singapore for two weeks. It was a very nice city and she was in a very nice suite in a very nice hotel.

That was the problem. She craved some rough edges in her life. Some excitement. The thrill of the chase. The risk. Dodging cops. Conning old farts. Buying new jewelry. Taking a kinky lover. Dumping a kinky lover. Exploring a new city or country. Ashley always had to be moving on, searching for she knew not what.

She flicked a shiny red fingernail at the bartender. He nodded and fixed her another Tom Collins.

She checked her nails. It had been ten days since her last mani-pedi at the spa.

She looked around the bar. Not much action. It was almost one p.m., but still, you'd think there'd be some couple ready for a fight, or a tight-pantsed Lothario looking for an afternoon quickie, or some other action to amuse and entertain her.

Maybe it was time to move on. She'd solidified her banking here for the moment. It would be accessible by her secret codes to be transferred wherever she wanted. Her accounts were pleasantly stuffed.

Bali? She'd never been to Bali.

New Zealand? She'd heard really nice things about New Zealand. A lot of sheep, apparently. Well, she liked roast lamb and mint jelly.

Two middle-aged Chinese men came in the bar. They found a table a couple away from hers. Each ordered a Tiger. They immediately hunched together and began talking vigorously. Soon their voices were raised.

Ashley was intrigued. At least this was something to amuse her.

"But she doesn't want this made public!"

"How does she expect to sell it without…?"

"No! The jewel is too precious. Too many people here would talk. They would know she's in financial trouble!"

"But the necklace is so valuable! She's getting desperate. Is this her only way out?"

The second man gulped his beer. "I guess so. I don't know. Don't care. I just know there's a great commission for us if we can find the right buyer. If we have to offer a big discount, tough for her."

The other man cocked an eyebrow. "Yeah, I guess. Whoever buys it is getting the steal of the century."

They both sat back and finished their beers.

Ashley sat back, thinking. She motioned for the bartender to bring the two men another round. She looked around the bar. The other guests had left for lunch.

The two men were surprised at the two Tigers delivered to their table. The bartender simply pointed at Ashley and left. They swivelled around. She smiled at them. They tipped their glasses in salute. They hunched together, speaking quickly in Mandarin.

Ashley crossed her legs and waited. It didn't take long. The two men rose and approached her table. "Thank you for the beer. May we join you?"

She smiled and nodded. She leaned forward, glad she was wearing a low-cut blouse. Although when she thought about it, almost all of her dresses and blouses were low-cut.

Attracting men for Ashley was about as tough as handing out free tequila shots during Spring Break on the beaches of Florida.

They chatted. She ordered another round. It turned out they were in the jewelry business. One managed a big store, apparently.

It took them one more round before blurting out their dilemma.

"We have this magnificent diamond necklace from one of the grand old families in Singapore," one of the men confided. "It is the greatest diamond I have ever seen. Over five carats. Pink. Beautifully cut. Old-school workmanship. Absolutely stunning."

Ashley licked her lips. "What is the necklace worth? Golly, it sounds really nice." She leaned forward again.

"Oh, expensive. Very expensive. Not for you, pretty missy."

That got her dander up.

"Listen, asshole, just tell me the price. Let me worry about the money."

That straightened up both of them. They whispered in Mandarin again.

"The owner has it appraised and insured for $3.1 million."

"Yeah, right."

"No, no. For real. The necklace is from the—." His partner grabbed his arm. Hard. He stopped abruptly. "It…well, whatever." He glanced at his watch. "I must go."

He stood and fled the table. The other man remained, shaking his head.

Ashley sat back. Was there a steal of a deal here or not?

"So sorry," the man said as he stared into his nearly empty glass. "This is such a terrible story. The family is desperate for money and this is their most valuable asset. It has been in their family for many years. They would lose great face if the sale was public."

She thought some more. "Do you have a picture of it?"

He pulled out his phone, hit some keys and suddenly thrust it at her. She gasped. The diamond was unbelievable. She could feel its warmth and love through the ionosphere. The pit of her stomach clenched with desire. Of all the jewels she'd ever bought for herself, this is what the journey had been leading her toward.

She fought to keep emotion out of her eyes or voice. "Yeah, nice piece." She handed the phone back. "What's it worth again?"

"Insured at 3.1. Probably worth more now. The market for diamonds is heating up again. Hong Kong is hot. Shanghai is— well, there's so much new money there they can't coin it fast enough. Then there's all the money from the oligarchs in the 'Stans and in Russia. I don't like them, though." He shuddered theatrically. "Coarse people."

"I, uh, have a friend who sometimes buys jewelry. He's very discreet. If he was interested, what would your best price be?"

He thought. "Just because of the circumstances and the timing, I think she'd go for 2.6."

"Nonsense. This is what we call in America a distress sale. You need a lot bigger discount than that to attract fast money."

He grimaced. Thought. "Maybe 2.3"

She shook her head. "Way, way off base. You're not getting the picture yet. This woman needs the money. Now. Badly. Just how many people do you think would be interested in dropping a couple of mil for a bauble?"

"This is no mere bauble," he protested. "This is a once in a lifetime opportunity to get a great bargain on an heirloom piece of jewelry."

"Oh, stop reading the brochure," she snapped. She thought. She looked at him. "I think we need to talk about this some more." She leaned over the table. "Why don't you come up to my suite?"

CHAPTER 60

"OF COURSE I'M going to get it appraised!" she snapped. "You think I trust these people? Lordie!"

Ferguson held his telephone away from his ear. Ashley got loud when she got revved up.

"Just sayin'. Can't be too careful. I hear there are lots of con men out there," he chortled.

She didn't.

She was beginning to regret even bringing her erstwhile partner in on this deal. The trust level between the two of them was hovering around the freezing mark.

"I'm doing this," she declared. "You want a piece, fine. You don't, no problem."

"So we each put up $800,000?"

"Yeah, that's the price we settled on. Basically half its value. I saw the appraisal certificate."

"And then what happens?"

"We keep it for a couple of years. Wait for the market to rise some more. Then sell it. It'll be a nice retirement fund bump."

"And you get to keep it, of course?"

"Of course. I don't think you wear a diamond necklace that often, you twisted pervert."

Ferguson grinned into the phone. They were back to normal.

"And just how am I protected if something happens to you?"

"Oh hell, Fergie. Let's not do this. It just isn't worth it if we're going to bicker over these little things."

He paused. He was surprised by her tone. "Well, I…"

The dial tone cut him off.

The bitch had hung up on him. His hand shook as he punched his cellphone.

CHAPTER 61

"SHE WANTS AN independent appraisal," Songdai reported back.

"Of course. Anyone would. Can we direct her to Mr. Chow's Jewelry Emporium?"

"Yes. But she might want her own second choice. She's a pretty tough little thing." He grinned to himself. "We had to negotiate for hours."

The sex with her had been the most exciting thing to happen to the jewelry store manager for years. He was now very glad that his great-aunt Mei-Ling had demanded he get involved in this plot. Not that he'd had any choice. When Mei-Ling decided something or ordered someone to do something, it was done. There was very little negotiating with the matriarch of the family.

Still, he doubted she had anticipated the vigorous romping in Ashley's big hotel bed.

He made a note to send flowers to his great-aunt.

"You couldn't get her down to 1.5? That's all we wanted."

"God no. I had to practically tie her up to get that price." He had tied her up, but not over the price of the necklace. She liked silk scarves and bedposts and…

"Well, we'll give the extra money to charity or something," Cindy announced. "Grandmama supports the local symphony."

And art gallery. And theatre. And museum. No, it wouldn't be difficult to give away the excess. They would do it to honor Grandmama.

Samantha and Perkins nodded agreement. Cindy turned back to them.

"Do you have the bank account set up?"

"Yes. Radar did it last night. One here in Singapore for the initial deposit, then one in Panama where we'll transfer the money just to get it out of this jurisdiction. That will make you invisible in this matter, in case it ever comes up."

Cindy nodded her thanks. This entire thing was getting more complicated than ever imagined. She had briefed the superintendent on the broad—okay, very broad—details. He had looked dubious. Then she'd dropped her grandmother's assistance. That ended any opposition.

Songdai continued. "We are doing the independent appraisal at four p.m. at Mr. Chow's, and then she is coming to my store at five p.m. If she is satisfied, we will do the exchange at noon tomorrow. I don't know where. She won't do it at the store. So doing the switch with the second necklace is getting, uh, challenging."

The brain trust thought that through. They had hoped for a clean switch of the necklaces at Songdai's family's jewelry store, once the money had been paid. They would be able to control the environment. That strategy was breaking down.

"Go do the appraisals with her," Cindy finally ordered. "Call us after. Get the details on the payment, and the transfer."

Songdai nodded and fled before he could get further trapped in this plot.

On the subway back to his store, he did remember to send flowers to Mei-Ling. His memories of romping with the big-busted blonde would linger for a long time.

CHAPTER 62

CINDY, SAMANTHA, AND the sheriff were watching on CCTV from the back of the jewelry store.

"Yeah, that's her! The bitch!" Samantha glared at the monitor.

Songdai disappeared into the back of the store to fetch the turquoise jewelry box that his assistants had just brought back. He returned and escorted Ashley into the private viewing room. The door was closed. The CCTV remained on, the camera hidden in the corner of the ceiling.

Songdai reverently opened the box. He pushed it gently across the table toward Ashley. She took a long, slow breath. It was as if she was trying to inhale the essence of the diamond.

She had to hood her eyes to shield the look of avarice. She had a physical reaction to the stunning jewel. She tightened her crossed thighs. This was an extraordinary piece of art.

Slowly she reached out to lift the necklace from its velvet casket. She held it in her hands for a long moment. Finally she moved her right hand down to cup the diamond itself. She stopped herself from squirming. It was magnificent.

She rubbed her thumb over the surface of the diamond. The rose color was so unique. The diamond had been magnificently cut. The facets glittered with joy at being exposed to the light once again.

Slowly she raised the necklace and dipped her head to fasten it. She looked down at the necklace and knew it was home. She looked in the mirror that Songdai produced.

The necklace clung to her slender neck beautifully. The diamond nestled at the top of her cleavage as if it had been designed for that specific purpose.

She sighed in pure joy. This made up for all the times she had had to rub her boobs against sweaty old men to get them to write checks.

Reluctantly Ashley reached around to unclasp the necklace and return it to the table. She knew it was real. She knew because it spoke to her.

"The other jeweler appraised it at 3.4 million," she announced. "The workmanship is lovely. The diamond is flawless."

"There must be no publicity about this sale," cautioned Songdai. "It is all secret for two years until the family has restructured its financial affairs. You cannot show it in public or tell people about the purchase. Because of that there will be no formal bill of sale. And you will have to sign a Non-Disclosure Agreement."

Ashley agreed.

"That was a brilliant move," Perkins said to the two women in the back room. Samantha nodded her thanks. She could still manage to contribute a few things to this case.

"It will keep her quiet about this whole transaction," Cindy confirmed. "And keep the fake necklace off the market." She chuckled. "In some ways, this is the perfect con: pay the money, take the fake merchandise, and then you can't tell anybody about it!"

In the private showroom, Songdai continued to play his part. "Now, after you have made the payment, where do you want to take possession of the necklace?"

This had turned out to be contentious. Ashley didn't want to be seen walking out of the jewelry store with the necklace because of fears that US Customs would eventually find out, or Singapore gangs would steal it.

She reached into her big purse and pulled out a distinctive black velvet bag.

"This is what you put it in," she instructed." Not one of your store bags. This one. The necklace goes inside with its case. Once I verify, the money gets transferred electronically to the account you gave me. Once you've confirmed the transfer, you give me the bag and we never see each other again."

On the one hand, Songdai was sort of hoping for another vigorous celebration in her bed. On the other hand, the dangers of his wife finding out about his dalliance would grow. That would not be good.

"If that is how you want it. And where do we make this exchange?"

She was ready. "On the Singapore cable car that leaves Sentosa Station at 1:04 p.m."

He was shocked but he agreed. He had no choice.

In the back room, Cindy turned pale. "That is going to be a problem," she told her two compatriots.

"Why?"

"It is a cable car that goes over the city. It has several stops. Sentosa Resort is this enormous amusement park and vacation destination and casino and hotels. It is an amazing island just off Singapore's mainland. It was built in three years using 9,000 men and women working every day. It is enormous. It is where President Trump and North Korean leader Kim Jong-un met for the Singapore Summit in 2018. The cable cars only handle six or eight people at a time. There's no way any of us can be on that car. Once she gets off at whatever stop, she can disappear into the crowds. There would be no way to follow her."

"Damn. That's really smart," Perkins said bitterly.

In the little room, Ashley gathered her purse and stood up. She had been making secret travel arrangements for two days now. It was time to get out of town. She could feel that. Ferguson could do what he wanted. She was done with him.

"I'll call you at eleven a.m. tomorrow to confirm everything," she told him.

Chapter 63

"We've got the airport police all briefed," Cindy reported. "They'll be waiting for her. They'll do a passport check, find irregularities, and that will give them the excuse to pull her out of the queue and then check her luggage. Then they find the necklace, and that will open up the other charges. She won't have a bill of sale. It is quite clever, this trap we have designed. Once we've got her on the diamond necklace, then the US fraud charges get introduced—along with you two." She chuckled. "That should shake her up."

Perkins nodded. They were trying to devise answers to questions they didn't know and to make contingency plans that would stop this clever woman. It was hard playing from behind. And certainly when the rules of the game were so fluid.

Samantha was still voting for deep dungeons and nasty snakes.

"We've also alerted the security division at Sentosa," Cindy continued. "They will help us watch her, but they also have the casino and the entire amusement park to worry about. Their facial recognition software could be useful, though."

She blew out her breath in frustration. "We just don't know how this is going to go down."

Perkins nodded. He understood. Often police actions were reactions. It made planning very difficult.

Samantha glanced at her watch: 10:03 a.m. The wait continued.

Chapter 64

THE PHONE RANG in Songdai's private office at 10:58.

"I've changed my mind," Ashley told him. "Bring the necklace to my hotel room. We'll do the money transfer there. And then you can just leave the necklace with me." She paused. "If you're lucky, maybe I'll model it for you."

At that image his mind leapt, along with another part of his body.

"Maybe I'll teach you some new games," she teased.

"On my way," he said hoarsely.

He immediately called his cousin Cindy and told her of the change of plans. He could hear her muttering under her breath. She told him to go ahead, take the two necklaces to Ashley's room in his briefcase, get the money paid, do the switch, and then get out.

He was on his way within minutes. He had bought an identical bag to the one Ashley had left him. One of his female staff members had recognized it from an exclusive gift shop near Ashley's hotel. He had carefully planned out the way he packed the two necklaces.

He was still worried about making the switch. It would have to come after she had confirmed the real necklace and then transferred the funds to the account the Americans had established, but before he left her room.

He was nervous. His hands were sweating just a bit as he stepped into the taxi. If he screwed up the transfer, Cindy would be very angry. But if he lost the real necklace, Mei-Ling would be beyond furious.

Frankly he was more scared of his formidable great-aunt than police bullets.

Ashley was wearing a short mauve dress when she answered the door to her hotel suite. No shoes. He saw a couple of large suitcases standing in one corner.

She locked and bolted the door. She sat down on the couch in her living area. Her skirt rose high on a creamy thigh as she pointed at the briefcase. "Show me."

He sat opposite her and slowly opened the lid. He reached in to take out the black bag she had given him for the transport. He handed it to her.

She took it reverently. She took a deep breath as she slid the jewelry box out of the black velvet bag and opened the case. A slow smile spread across her face as she stared at the magnificent rose diamond.

Ashley gently ran her fingers over the stone as she lifted it from the box. "You're finally home," she whispered to the necklace. She fondled the necklace for a long time.

Songdai sat entranced as he watched her. He was getting aroused just seeing her be so intimate with an object.

She suddenly seemed to feel the same way. "Go in the bedroom," she ordered. "Take off your clothes. Lie on the bed."

"But the payment," he stuttered.

"Later," she snapped. "Now go. Strip."

He stumbled to obey. It didn't take long. She appeared a moment later sliding four red silk scarves through her fingers. "I'm going to take control," she told him throatily, "and it will be the time of your life."

Swiftly she tied his hands and feet to the bedposts. He grinned at her. She smiled back. "Now I'm going to model the necklace for you, just like I promised." She licked her lips and turned back into the other room. He could hear clothes rustling.

She reappeared a moment later. She wore nothing but the diamond necklace. It was a magnificent piece of jewelry, he noted proudly. And dangling between her breasts was a luxurious setting for the very special diamond.

Then his eyes reluctantly left that vision. In her left hand, Ashley was holding the second necklace. She bounced it gently as she looked at it, then at him.

"Uh, what's this?"

He was paralysed.

"You weren't planning on the ol' switcheroo on me, were you?" She looked at him sternly.

He looked at her nipples. They were getting hard. So was he.

"Uh, no, no," he finally choked out. "We had this other necklace in the store and I thought you might like it as a gift. They are kind of a pair," he gasped out. "It was going to be a surprise for you."

"Uh huh."

He tugged at his bindings. The silk was strong and unforgiving. Sort of sexy, though. He shook his head. If he got out of this mess, he'd never be unfaithful to his wife again.

Except with his mistress, of course, but that didn't really count.

She dropped the second necklace on his stomach. He twitched. She patted him. The real necklace gleamed from its home on her chest.

"I think, sweetie, that that bucket just doesn't hold a lot of water."

He thought that through. It made no sense to him.

She rose. "I'm just going to finish packing and mosey on outta here," she said. She patted him intimately. "You just relax here. Comfy?"

She leaned over him to plump a pillow behind his neck. He groaned at the sight.

"Anything else you want to tell me, honey?" He shook his head. "No? Well, OK. You just lie there in comfort and we'll talk in a minute or two."

She got off the bed, took the second necklace and walked into the living room. Ten minutes later she reappeared, clothed in her purple dress and now wearing black heels. She disappeared into the bathroom and he could hear toiletry items being packed and bottles being capped. She came out holding a couple of make-up bags and hurried into the living room.

A moment later the suitcases clicked shut. She reappeared, ready for travel.

"I'll just let you rest here and think about things," she told him sweetly. "I've got to run to the airport. Sorry we didn't get a chance to finalize that bank transfer but I'm sure you'll figure something out." She patted her hair and came over to the bed to soothe his forehead as he struggled against the scarves. "It's been a blast."

"Wait! You can't leave me here like this!"

"Well, that's sorta where you're wrong. Again." Her voice hardened. "Nobody cons me. Nobody."

With that she spun and walked out.

"Oh, I'm putting the DO NOT DISTURB sign on the door so you can relax for as long as you want," she shouted as she rolled her two suitcases out the door. "Enjoy."

He groaned and again tugged at his bindings.

The maid was in for a very rude shock when she finally appeared.`

Chapter 65

"WHERE THE HELL HAVE YOU BEEN?" Songdai tried to remain calm as his cousin Cindy practically climbed through the phone line.

Hotel security had finally come to the room after he had banged the headboard against the wall enough times to irritate the poor clown in the room next door. When the knock on the hotel suite door finally came, he had screamed loud enough to scare the sea gulls flying by.

It had been rather awkward when the security guard burst into the bedroom. Naturally it was a female. The added humiliation pretty much summed up his day.

Ah, well. Songdai suspected this was going to make an awfully good story at the next hotel staff party.

"She's heading to the airport was all she told me. I don't know what flight."

"Did you at least get the necklace back?!!?"

Well now. That was a rather awkward question.

"Uh, well, there's a story there. You see…"

"YOU IDIOT!! You lost my necklace!! I'll kill—no, wait, I'll tell Mei-Ling. What she will do to you will make my shooting you seem like a blessing!"

Songdai swallowed hard. He was scared of his cousin and her gun and her karate skills, but he was terrified of his great-aunt.

"AT LEAST TELL ME YOU GOT THE MONEY TRANS—wait. You didn't, did you???"

"Yeah, well, you see, that's another story that is pretty complicated. You see…"

"YOU ARE DEAD MEAT! I'm going to…" Cindy spluttered as Perk and Samantha listened in dismay. Cindy finally took three deep breaths.

"So. Let me sum this up. You didn't get the money. You don't have the necklace. Oh, wait. Tell me you also lost the second necklace!"

"Uh, funny story about that…"

"OH MY GOD! It is the perfect fuck-up! You lost the real necklace, you never switched it with the fake necklace, and you never got paid! Three little things you had to do! That was all! And you got nothing! You are so finished! I am going to…" She spluttered in anguish at the triple play of incompetence.

Perkins finally took the phone receiver from her. "Sheriff Perkins here. Just so we all understand. You did not complete the money transfer?"

"Uh, no."

"You no longer have the original diamond necklace?"

"Well, no."

"And the ersatz necklace is no longer in your possession either?"

Songdai wasn't sure what ersatz meant, but it seemed to be an easy guess on his part. He sighed regretfully. "Sadly, no. She got it, too."

There was a long silence. Songdai looked around the hotel room for an exit because his cousin would be coming for him in about eight seconds.

It was only a thirty-eight-storey drop off the balcony. There was a remote chance he would survive that fall. If he did, his cousin would rip him apart bone by painfully broken bone.

No, the better solution was to disappear for a while. Say for the next millennium.

"Listen, Sheriff, sorry about all this. I've got to run."

"Yes. I bet you do. By the way, why didn't you call Cindy earlier with this disaster?"

"Oh, I just couldn't. I was tied up."

Chapter 66

SAMANTHA SAT BY herself in a chair by one of the windows in a ninth-floor conference room in the Singapore Police Headquarters. The digital clock on the wall ticked 3:38.

She was staring out the window at the harbor as a whole lot of senior Singapore police officials sat or stood around the conference table. Their anger was palpable. Most of it was directed at Cindy.

There was a mixture of Mandarin, English, Malaysian, and Australian being spoken—Australian not necessarily being the same as the Queen's English.

Samantha was just sick. She felt that this entire mess was all her fault.

She was the one who had pushed Perkins into travelling halfway around the world in this futile attempt to get her friends' money back. He was now being embarrassed in front of his peers as the complete failure.

"Samantha's fault," kept ringing in her head.

She was the one who had entangled Cindy in this whole debacle. Cindy was now also being subjected to professional humiliation and her career seemed to be cratering abruptly.

"Samantha's fault," the refrain continued.

There were angry shouts from the senior staff about the loss of face for the department; the loss of not one but two necklaces from Singapore's most-revered philanthropic and cultural icon, Mei-Ling; and the loss and disappearance of the money stolen from American residents.

"Samantha's fault," the chorus sang again.

Perkins sat at the conference table but said nothing. He had nothing to add at the moment.

3:43.

Samantha felt ashamed for promising her friends at Sapphire Blue that she would recover their money. Who was she to make such an idiotic commitment? Now all their money was gone. Ashley had disappeared. Ferguson was at his apartment but apparently clean on the jewelry heist.

"Still no report from the airport?" demanded a burly inspector.

"No, sir," replied a sergeant who was in constant communication with the security team at Changi Airport.

"But that's impossible!" Superintendent Keong was stirring this stew-pot of disaster. "She told that idiot Songdai that she was heading there. She had her luggage with her. The hotel desk clerk heard her order a taxi for the airport. WHERE IS SHE?"

The clock ticked over to 3:46. Its inexorable electronic tick was beginning to really annoy Samantha.

No one had an answer for the superintendent.

Finally Perkins asked, "Are there other routes out of Singapore?"

"A road to Malaysia but a very long ride to Kuala Lumpur. A short hop to Indonesia by boat or plane. I don't think this Ashley would be welcome in either country. Her dress and... immodest...behavior would not be tolerated. They are both predominantly Muslim nations."

Samantha continued to stare out the window. There was a lot of action in the harbor. Little boats darted by larger crafts. Tugboats blew their horns importantly as they guided larger ships out.

The clock clicked over again. 3:48. Samantha was beginning to hate that damn—

"Cindy." She spoke softly. To no avail. She tried again. "CINDY!"

That got the attention of the group. They all stopped and stared at her as Samantha surged to her feet. She was pointing out the window. "Look! In the harbor! The cruise ship! What if she is escaping on—"

There was a rush to the windows. Docked there was a large white cruise ship. About twelve storeys. The sun sparkled off the brightwork on the deck railings. A steady stream of new passengers was embarking as they climbed the gangway into the middle of the ship.

The police officers all looked a little abashed. Cruise ships were such a ubiquitous part of life in Singapore that no one ever thought much about them. Besides, what criminal would be stupid enough to escape on a slow boat to wherever?

"It's the *Duchess of Singapore*," reported a staff sergeant who had grabbed the binoculars that were on the side table.

"I know her. Her captain is a stickler for departing exactly on time."

All eyes went to the digital clock. Delighted to be the centre of attention, it clicked to 3:49.

"What time does the ship sail?"

"They all leave at five p.m., sir."

Superintendent Keong stared icily at Cindy. "What are you waiting for?"

Chapter 67

THE UNMISTAKEABLE SOUND of a champagne cork popping was music to Ashley's ears.

Her private butler carefully poured it into a chilled flute and handed her the glass. "Welcome on board the *Duchess of Singapore*," he said. "It will be my pleasure to look after you on the cruise."

The handsome young Indian man bowed and put the bottle into an ice bucket. Ashley kicked off her shoes and stepped onto her private balcony. She sank into one of the soft chairs with a contented sigh.

"Thank you." She swallowed deeply. "Ah. Lovely. Yes, perhaps a drop more," as her butler offered the bottle again.

"May I get you anything else right now?"

"No, no thanks. Just leave the bottle in the ice bucket."

"Of course, Madam. And I will have a maid come to unpack for you once we have the other passengers settled on board. And I shall return with a tray of canapés for you to enjoy before dinner." He bowed his way out of the stateroom.

Ashley could feel the stress oozing out of her body. It had been a frantic few days. Her inspired idea to leave on a cruise ship instead of flying out had worked perfectly. The immigration checks at the port were cursory. She had negotiated a really good deal with the cruise line for what would have been an empty Penthouse Suite. They were happy to get a last-minute deal for $24,000 for the three-week cruise.

She glanced at the itinerary. Malaysia. Thailand. Myanmar. India. Oman. Abu Dhabi. Dubai. Lovely. She would be in international waters whenever the poop hit the fan in Singapore.

She gazed out on the harbor scene. Her stateroom was on the port side, so it was in shade right now, away from the noise and confusion on the dock.

Her watch said 4:11. She sighed happily. Just a few more minutes until the ship embarked and she left Singapore.

She lifted the dripping bottle and refilled her glass. Life was good. Very good.

CHAPTER 68

IT TOOK CINDY three minutes to assemble a team. A detective. Three two-person police units. She told Samantha to stay put, and told Perkins he couldn't come because of jurisdiction problems. She had an assistant call the ship to warn them of her imminent arrival and to not leave the dock without her approval.

The third officer who answered the call had just laughed at that. "Captain van Hoeven leaves on schedule. On the dot. It doesn't matter if passengers are missing or late. If crew are AWOL. He is rigid. Be warned." He hung up.

The police officers ran down the stairs to the parking lot. Cindy's unmarked car was flanked by the three police vehicles, which promptly roared out of the parking garage, sirens blaring and lights flashing.

4:14, according to the clock on her dashboard.

It took nine minutes to scream into the port district. Two more minutes to talk to the guard at the gate. Another minute to rush to the gangplank into the ship. There were still many people completing their boarding.

Cindy and her police colleagues hit the first step of the gangplank at 4:28 p.m. She pushed through the lineup. Apologizing and hoisting her police badge in front of her, she led her team up the gangway. A group of ship's officers and staff were at the top, checking in new passengers, taking their passports, and escorting them to their staterooms. It was well-organized chaos.

4:29.

It took another couple of minutes to try to explain to the officers why a squad of Singapore Police had suddenly arrived on board in the middle of the confusion of passenger embarkation.

In frustration, Cindy finally looked for the youngest male officer there. He was a fresh-faced one-striper. She grabbed him. She held out the picture of Ashley. She described her in plain terms that the young man would grasp very quickly.

"American. Big boobs. Big. Single."

She could see comprehension dawn on his boyish face. "Oh. Oh! Miss Ashley. Yes. Uh, Penthouse Suite 1113. On the eleventh floor." He smiled. He licked his lips.

Cindy would have shot him if it weren't for all the paperwork that would ensue.

4:34. Shit.

They sprinted past the amazed officers and staff. "Elevator!" she hollered. One of them pointed.

Naturally it was on the third floor. And it turned out to be the slowest elevator in the history of elevators. Compounded by the new passengers getting on and off to explore each deck of the ship.

She gave up in frustration. "Stairs?" she shouted.

The young officer pointed to the corner exit. She led her team up the five flights. Two of them were puffing pretty good by the time they arrived.

4:39. She could hear the engines running and felt the gentle vibration of the big generators. She imagined the deck crew beginning to take off the huge hawsers that anchored the ship to the deck.

"1113?" she snapped at a passing steward. He almost dropped his tray of canapés. "Duh, uh, down there," he stuttered. "Port side."

They charged down the narrow hallway. Cindy screeched to a halt in front of 1113. She looked at her watch as she stood at the door. 4:41. What if Ashley was wandering around the ship? They would never find her in time.

On the other hand, if Cindy remained on board and stowed away on the ship, maybe some time at sea would ease the problems she was facing at the police department.

She raised her hand and knocked firmly on the door.

Chapter 69

AH, MUST BE her butler with the canapés, thought Ashley. Lovely. She took a last swallow of the champagne, padded barefoot to the door and opened it.

It was not her butler. It was some really pretty, very fit dark-haired woman who was shoving a police badge at her. What the hell?

"Are you Ashley Monroe? Or shall we call you Donna Mulvaney? Or are you using some other name now?"

The woman was very pushy. Somehow Ashley found herself in the middle of her little living room as six burly police officers surrounded her. The detective was circling her stateroom.

"You are being charged with grand theft, fraud, immigration identity fraud, and no doubt a few more things that our very competent lawyers will think up. Please put your hands behind your back. You are under arrest. We are transporting you to police headquarters. Your luggage will be brought. Cuff her." She gestured to one of the officers.

"WAIT! What the hell? Who are you? You don't have any jurisdiction over me! I am an American on a Dutch cruise ship."

"Your crimes were committed in Singapore," was the imperturbable reply. "Or at least some of them. And this ship is docked in Singapore. We retain jurisdiction until it is in international waters. That is something you are unlikely to ever experience," Cindy said snippily.

She looked at her watch. Oh shit. 4:48.

"Go and hold an elevator for us," she snapped at a junior uniform. He fled the stateroom. "Bring her suitcases. Check the safe. Make sure we have everything. You have four minutes," she ordered. "Everything!"

Semi-organized chaos. It took two officers to get Ashley's shoes on and rustle her into the corridor. She resisted with vigor while shouting imprecations.

Her luggage followed. It didn't say anything.

The rest of the officers opened drawers, checked under the mattress, reached into closets, and ran hands over furniture.

"That's it! We're out of time! Let's go! Hustle, people!"

4:55.

They fled down the corridor. Interested but terrified passengers lined their stateroom doorways, peering out at the spectacle. None of their travel agents had promised them a live show quite this fascinating.

The young cop was valiantly holding the doors, despite the elevator buzzing impatiently and guests above and below saying nasty things. Some of them were quite mean.

They barely fit in the elevator car. Ashley was white-faced and still protesting. No one listened to her.

The elevator was going down. Surely gravity would make it work faster, thought Cindy. She was afraid to look at her watch.

4:57.

The elevator finally arrived on six. They burst out and rushed to the departure door.

"We're going!" Cindy shouted as they dragged Ashley and her luggage down the steep gangway.

"But. But. But she hasn't checked out! And her passport!" shouted an anguished crew member responsible for passenger security.

"She won't be back. And she won't need a passport for the next twenty-five years," Cindy shot back as they stumbled down the plank. The last policeman grabbed the passport and fled down the gangplank, three steps at a time.

Crew were finishing pulling the hawsers. A tugboat was poised and tooting.

Cindy glanced up to see an angry, full-bearded captain glaring at her. Her feet hit the dock. She checked her watch: 4:59… and there it was, 5:00 p.m.

She waved at the captain. She could hear him shout something but the wind took his comment away. No doubt suggesting she should get a citation for her great work, she laughed to herself as they trekked down the dock.

The gangplank was raised, the hawsers brought on board and the big ship began to edge away from the dock. The captain looked down at her one more time. She thought she saw him give her half a peace sign. Aw, how thoughtful.

CHAPTER 70

"WE GOT HER," reported Cindy on her radio to the conference room. She couldn't hear the cheer, but she was sure it was happening.

"Had a solid eight or ten seconds to spare getting her and her luggage off the ship," she confessed with a little chuckle.

"Yes," Superintendent Keong told her. "I just got off a rather testy phone conversation with a Captain van Hoeven." He paused. "He had a somewhat different view of your actions," he told her coolly.

Oh, great. Just when she was starting to climb out of the deepest hole she'd ever been in…

"I told him you would apologize in person the next time his ship is docked here," he went on. "I would also suggest a bottle of twenty-four-year-old scotch."

"Sir. Yes sir."

"How is the prisoner?"

"She keeps protesting that she's innocent. She says she doesn't know anything about a stolen diamond necklace. Or anything else. Just keeps whining that she's an American citizen and has rights. That she's innocent of everything."

"Well, we've certainly never heard protests of innocence from a prisoner before," Keong said drily.

"Yessir. We'll be arriving at HQ in a few minutes. I'll get her processed and we can start interrogating her. Or," she added thoughtfully, "we could let her sit overnight in the cells. I don't think she's ever experienced jail before. It might soften her up."

Keong grunted. "I'll talk to the team. We'll let you know when you report back here." He hung up.

"Yes, sir," she replied to the dial tone.

An hour later it was decided to let Ashley think about her situation for the night. It would also give the forensic people time to recover the necklaces from her luggage, along with any other contraband she was carrying.

Samantha was the most enthusiastic about keeping her in jail. Or, as she continued to suggest, "In the deepest, nastiest cell in the dungeon." Her suggestions of spiders and snakes amused the officers.

They thought she was joking.

Perkins finally took her out for dinner. They invited Cindy, but she needed to process all kinds of paperwork from today's events.

"Now that we have her, we can get the money back, right?" Samantha questioned Perkins.

"I don't see why not." He paused. "But from a legal standpoint, it is very complicated. One hang-up is if some court wanted to put the entire amount in escrow until a final resolution. Another is if she fights extradition. That could get long and ugly. And I don't know where the final case on the fraud might be heard—here? The US? Canada?"

That wasn't what Samantha wanted to hear. She picked through her dinner, steaming inside about how Ashley had screwed so many people out of so much.

She remained out of kilter for the rest of the evening. They went to bed angry, neither sure exactly why or with whom.

CHAPTER 71

SAMANTHA PRACTICALLY HAD to buy a ticket to get a spot in the small observation room that looked through the one-way mirror into interrogation room #4 in the Singapore police headquarters.

"We put her in with The Screamer for the night," Cindy had confided to Samantha that morning. "She's a regular who screams half the night. She has some social problems. I wouldn't think Ashley'd get much sleep." A small grin. "Ashley's still shouting about her innocence and police brutality. Huh. I'd like to show her some real—well, anyway. And of course Ashley went through a strip search to ensure there was no contraband." Cindy flashed an evil grin. "Breakfast was cold cereal and bad coffee."

Samantha gave a satisfied nod. Now they just needed to get the money returned and the necklace found, and she and Perk could head home.

Cindy told her there had been a double-homicide the night before so the Forensics investigation of Ashley's luggage and personal belongings had been delayed slightly. The results were expected later this morning.

Cindy couldn't wait to get her necklace back. She had had a sleepless night over what her grandmama would think of her losing this precious family heirloom.

Ashley looked tired and rather wan when she was brought in to the politely-named interview room. She had not been allowed any of her own makeup or toiletries while in jail.

It was a police interrogation. The room had that cop shop smell of sweat, fear, urine, and stale coffee. Ashtrays no longer were a feature of the little room. A digital camera was.

A handsome, middle-aged Chinese lieutenant skilled in interrogations would lead the interview. Marcus Lee was dressed in a sharp black suit with a striped tie. Cindy would be in the room as backup.

They let Ashley marinate in her fear for several long moments before they entered the room. Lee took the lead.

"I am Lieutenant Lee," he introduced himself. "You met Inspector Holmes yesterday."

Ashley glared at the two of them.

"I demand a lawyer. I demand to see someone from the American embassy. I demand to be set free immediately. I Have Done Nothing!" she said slowly, emphasizing each word. "I will be suing you and you and the entire damn police force!"

The lieutenant was not shaken by these threats. It was not his first prisoner interview.

"Would you care for a cup of coffee? Tea? Water?"

"Not if the coffee is the same as that cup of warm piss you served me in the cell this morning! I thought Singapore was a civilized nation! How can you serve coffee that bad?"

Lee looked a little shaken by that charge. He was strictly a tea drinker.

Cindy smirked a bit. She had given special orders to…well, perhaps now wasn't the time to…better to just move on.

Lee shuffled papers for a moment. He pulled out her passport. "Let's begin by figuring out just who you are. Your passport says Ashley Monroe. But US law enforcement has identified you to us as Donna Mulvaney. So just who are you?"

Ashley shrugged. "I was born Mulvaney. Hated the name. Changed it. Somebody got me a new passport. No biggie." Somehow Ashley had acquired a soft Southern drawl overnight.

"Was your new passport obtained from the US government?"

She shrugged again. "I assume so. A friend of mine arranged for it." She paused to look at Lieutenant Lee. "I would never do anything against the law." She offered a tentative smile. She leaned back. The fabric of her orange jail uniform stretched across her chest.

Cindy could see it coming. Ashley just had this way of appealing to men. The little-girl pout combined with her full-bodied sex appeal was irresistible to a lot of men between fourteen and seventy-four.

Cindy banged the table hard. "Where is the necklace you stole?" she demanded.

"Goodness gracious, whatever are you talking about? And why are you so angry? You are scaring me." She batted her eyes at Lee. Cindy's temper went up two more degrees.

"The diamond necklace that you stole from Songdai the Jeweler."

"Oh. You mean the man who sexually assaulted me? That man?" She looked appealingly at the lieutenant, who straightened up in his chair at that accusation.

"What!" Cindy snapped back. "If he assaulted you, how did he end up tied to the bed in your hotel suite?"

"He asked me to do that. Goodness, I had to do what he wanted. He was such a big strong man."

It was all Samantha could do to stop from smashing the glass and charging into the interview room. Perkins pressed on her shoulder as a precaution. He knew what she was thinking.

"The necklace! Where is the diamond necklace??!"

"What necklace would that be, Inspector? I have a couple of little gold chains that men have given me as gifts." She side-eyed Lee. "You know, for special things I've done for them." He sighed.

"And I've got a couple more in my luggage that are beads and stuff. You can look. But a diamond necklace? Golly, I wish I could afford one of those!"

Ashley deftly fended off more questions for half an hour when suddenly a sharp knock at the door stopped all conversation.

Lee opened it to find a wide-eyed forensic assistant standing outside.

"We need to talk," he said softly. Lee nodded and shut the door.

"Let's take a break," he suggested. "You may go to the bathroom if you need to. There will be water and other beverages available. I will have a female security guard escort you."

With that he and Cindy abruptly left the room. Ashley sat back in the hard chair. She looked directly into the tinted mirror. She gave a tiny smile.

Samantha felt as if Ashley could see directly into her heart and brain. She swallowed hard. There was something wrong here. Why wasn't she cracking? They had her cold on the theft of the necklace as well as the fraud at Sapphire Blue.

Samantha stared back through the mirror. Something wasn't right.

Chapter 72

"WHAT DO YOU MEAN, THERE IS NO NECKLACE?" Cindy was shouting at the little forensics guy who had drawn the short straw to report that finding to the brass.

He looked as if he was contemplating an immediate switch to a safer career. Dental work on sharks, perhaps.

"There was no diamond necklace in her luggage. We searched twice. Very carefully. We slit open the liners. We checked the wheels. We X-rayed both of them. We did the same for her purse and carry-on. Nothing."

The young tech swallowed hard and wouldn't meet Cindy's eyes.

"Did you X-ray her?"

"She could not have swallowed a necklace that size," he told her.

"With that big a mouth, she could have swallowed—"

The superintendent interrupted her. "That means we missed something. It may be hidden in her hotel room. She may have passed it to someone else. It may be hidden in her stateroom on the ship. She may have…I don't know, sent it somewhere?" He looked around the room. "Any other ideas?"

"Maybe a pawn shop? Or another jeweler for some kind of private sale?"

The superintendent grimaced but nodded. "No pawnshop in Singapore would touch this. It is too well-known. A private sale? Yes, possibly." He grimaced. "If that's it, we're in deep trouble."

Cindy sagged in her chair. The nightmare had just gotten worse. How was that even possible?

That was what Samantha thought when Cindy briefed her a few minutes later. "I know she did it. I know she's got it," she said to her new friend.

Cindy nodded agreement. "So do I. The problem is without the damn necklace, we've got nothing. We're going to have to cut her loose if we can't find something soon."

Samantha shook her head in despair. "No, no, no. You can't let her out. She'll flee the country immediately and we might never find her again! Or your grandmama's necklace!"

Cindy waved her hands in frustration and returned to the interview room. Lieutenant Lee was waiting for her. A guard brought in Ashley. She seemed to sense a different tone in the room.

"Now, about my lawyers," she began. "And how are you going to fly me to re-connect with my cruise? And who will compensate me for the missed days on board?"

The change in tactics surprised both interrogators. Ashley had to know that they would search her luggage and personal belongings very thoroughly. The only logical conclusion was that the necklaces had never made it on board the Duchess of Singapore. And Ashley knew that.

The interview went on for the rest of the morning, but there was no more passion in it for Cindy. Lieutenant Lee obviously sensed that as well. Ashley grew ever more smug as the morning went on.

Even challenges about her alleged scam in Florida drew denials. "A private business investment plan for some lovely ladies," was how Ashley described it.

When Cindy pointed out that the WYRT was a fabrication and did not exist, Ashley just batted her eyes and repeated that Asian E-currencies were just emerging and that she knew stuff that Cindy didn't about global finance and foreign currency speculation.

Cindy could have slugged her.

Lee seemed dazzled.

The interview ended in the mid-afternoon. Lee promised she could talk to an attorney. He was almost apologetic that she'd have to spend another night in jail. Ashley smiled warmly at him.

Cindy walked out in disgust. She slammed the door. Hard.

CHAPTER 73

"WE'RE LOSING." THE bleak analysis from Cindy at dinner with Samantha and the sheriff was at least honest. Her two hosts agreed with her.

They were eating a spicy Madras seafood curry, the best Naan bread Samantha had ever had, and wonderful mango chutney at a small, family-run Indian restaurant. They were all drinking cold Tiger beer.

The silence stretched for a long time. Finally Perkins spoke up.

"What if we shake the whole thing up? We must be missing something. What I'm wondering is, we've let this Massey Ferguson character off the hook because we've been so focused on BBB."

The nickname drew smiles from the two women. Ever since Mei-Ling had collapsed them in laughter after calling Ashley "the big-breasted bitch," that had become their official nickname for her.

"What if we brought him in for questioning, at the request of a branch of American law enforcement?"

Cindy half-shrugged. "Sure. Might work."

Perkins continued. "Then, what I'm thinking is maybe I get to confront him along with you when you're interviewing him. Might shake him up a little."

Cindy looked more attentive at that. "You would be the American law enforcement requesting the information." Perkins grinned at her. "Well. That's a little different. For sure there's the passport fraud stuff. I think he's been very careful about staying clean here in Singapore, but you never know." She thought some more. "I know a friendly judge who would probably give us a search warrant for his apartment." She absently dabbed a piece of the Naan into her curry bowl. "Yeah, I like it. Let's go."

Perkins scrambled to pay the bill and joined the two women at the door.

CHAPTER 74

FERGUSON WAS ENJOYING the girlfriend experience when his doorbell rang.

The girlfriend experience cost him 800 Singapore dollars each time. He figured it was still a lot cheaper than the real girlfriend experience.

The cops kicked out the hooker and waved the search warrant in his face as he dressed and collected himself. Cindy was leading the raid.

She disliked Ferguson upon meeting him. Her police instincts immediately told her that he was slimy. Crooked. Dishonest. Mean-spirited. Unfaithful.

All of which he was.

Then there was his moustache. She couldn't tell if he was trying to grow a new one or he'd just done a really bad job of shaving the old one. It was some kind of ugly.

After the usual huffing and puffing from a surprised resident relaxing when a bunch of cops show up to search their home, Ferguson was ordered to sit down and shut up. He sat down. Apparently nothing could make him shut up.

The search team fanned out throughout the attractive two-bedroom apartment. It was furnished in Danish modern. Some really lousy art on the wall, Cindy noted in passing. About what she'd expect from a single man with money and bad taste.

"Inspector?" A young female officer poked her head out of the master bedroom and waved.

Cindy went over to the bedroom. The smell of sex lingered in the crumpled sheets. She tried not to gag but it—

"Are you kidding me! Where did you find it?"

The kid was holding the diamond necklace.

"In a drawer right there. You mentioned the black bags and the jewelry in a bulletin a couple of days ago. I remembered. I looked. Here it is."

She handed over the black bag, the royal purple jewelry box and the diamond necklace. Cindy took them and made a mental note of the young officer's name. She'd keep an eye on her career.

She looked at the necklace carefully. She was not an expert. She didn't covet jewels the way Ashley did. But it was her family's heritage and it was important to Grandmama that it stayed in the family.

Now, was this the real one or the copy? She couldn't tell. Where was Songdai when you needed him? Oh yeah, he was running far, far away from her. Wait. Dinner. Two boxes from Mei-Ling. Was purple the real one or the...

"I don't think it is real," the young officer said after a respectful moment. "My father is in the jewelry business," she explained. "I learned a few things. But it is a very beautiful copy."

Rats. That would have been too easy, thought Cindy. Still. It was progress. It gave them a legitimate reason to drag Ferguson through the toughest interrogation in the SPD's history.

Just a damn shame about the rubber hose technique that some namby-pamby court had ruled was—

"Inspector?"

She looked up. Another young officer was waving to her. She handed the necklace back to the young woman. "Good job. I'll remember you. Make sure this gets to my office once it has been logged-in as evidence."

"We found some financial records in the second bedroom," reported the other officer. "He uses it as an office. Do you want his computer as well?"

"Absolutely. Our nerds will have a field day tracking whatever's on it. And any mobile devices as well."

She looked at Ferguson. He was sitting on the couch staring at the necklace in the jewelry box as it was carried out.

Cindy rubbed her hands together. This was turning out to be a very productive raid. Good call by the sheriff. And it would be great fun to watch Ferguson react when Perkins walked in during the middle of their interrogation.

"Arrest him," she ordered. Two officers grabbed Ferguson, cuffed him and hustled him out the front door.

He protested. Loudly. No one listened.

Chapter 75

I T WAS ANOTHER SRO event in the viewing room. Samantha was given a chair at the end of the front row. She sucked in her breath as she watched Ferguson be escorted into the interview room. He looked as repulsive to her as he had in Florida.

"That's him," she said to the assembled officers.

"What's that thing on his upper lip? Some kind of skin condition?"

Samantha snorted. "He thinks it's a moustache. Horrid little thing." She paused. Timing is everything in comedy. "So is his moustache."

She got a nice laugh.

Cindy strode into the interview room, accompanied again by Lieutenant Lee. She was the lead on this one and wasted no time.

"Do you prefer being jailed in Singapore or the United States?" She stared him down hard.

As an opening line in an interrogation, Samantha thought, it was really good.

"What...what...who...why am...what the hell is going on?" he sputtered.

"We've had a complaint filed from a US law enforcement agency. Our Immigration people want to have a serious chat about your passport. We don't even care about the hooker last night, although you might want to talk to a doctor about STDs."

Ferguson twitched violently at that.

Cindy smiled inside. She had absolutely no evidence the prostitute was carrying any STD, but it certainly had made Ferguson squirm.

Anything that kept a suspect off-balance was fair game.

"Apparently there is a string of fraud charges waiting for you in the US. Like, a bunch." Lieutenant Lee shuffled a pile of papers, studying them intently. He sucked in his breath and shook his head several times. Samantha could see from her vantage point that the papers were just yesterday's cricket scores, but obviously Ferguson wouldn't know that.

Cindy continued relentlessly. "But for now, let's focus on the stolen necklace. The one we found in your possession in your home."

She turned to Lee. "What is the appraisal, Lieutenant?"

He didn't hesitate. "3.4 million Singapore dollars."

Ferguson's eyes widened.

"Yes, 3.4 million. A lot of money for a lovely necklace. Perhaps it was something for one of your, uh, lady friends? It would have to be a rather special friend, but…"

"Not mine! Never saw it before! I'm just holding on to it for a friend while she's out of town!" began his denials.

"And who would that be?"

"Ashley. Ashley Monroe. She's just an acquaintance. She didn't want to leave it while she went travelling. I don't know how she got it. Don't care. Not mine."

He sat back, arms crossed, a petulant look on his face. It had taken him about nine seconds to give up his one-time partner.

"So let me get this straight. A casual acquaintance hands you a three-million dollar diamond necklace to look after for her while she is away? Does that make any sense to you, Mr. Ferguson?"

He had the grace to look a tiny bit embarrassed but he stubbornly stuck to his story. "Not mine. Don't know how she got it. She likes jewelry. Probably got a good deal from some jeweler."

"Okay, Mr. Avery, if that's what you say."

He barely flinched at her use of his real name. He was a professional con man. "Who?"

"Let's go on to your fraud and theft in Florida recently. A number of women have filed complaints with local law enforcement there. There are warrants out for your arrest."

"Nonsense. I've received no such information. I'm an investment counsellor. I sell financial opportunities to clients all over the world. Sometimes they take time to develop and pay off. Sometimes they don't work out. There are no guarantees in the investment world. Surely you know that, Inspector."

"But you were selling something called WYRTs," Cindy said with a note of incredulity in her voice. "Here's the problem. WYRTs do not exist!"

"It's a new E-currency being developed," Ferguson fought back. "I am simply ahead of the curve on this. That's where you make the biggest money—anticipating financial markets correctly. I told the women that."

"Don't know if local law enforcement there would believe that."

Ferguson sat back comfortably, or as comfortably as the metal chair secured to the floor would allow. The hick sheriff from Dumbsville, Florida, was 10,000 miles away. What could this pretty but tough Singapore police officer do to him?

They didn't have anything on him. No way could they break into his encrypted password-protected e-files.

He didn't think they had anything on him.

A self-satisfied smile touched his lips.

Then there was a loud knock on the door. Lee opened it wide. And Ferguson's jaw dropped five feet.

Standing there in a well-cut blue suit and a red tie was the freakin' sheriff of Hicksville.

No way! No way could he be here!

At least his damn dog was nowhere in sight.

Ferguson smoothed his moustache. This whole thing had just gotten a lot more serious.

CHAPTER 76

"AH, MR. FERGUSON. IT has been a while. Or do you prefer Avery?" Perkins boomed as he stepped into the room.

Lee slipped into the back corner of the small interview space so Perkins could sit down and stare Ferguson in the eyes.

"Inspector Holmes has been kind enough to invite me to ask a few questions. Just to help out her investigation." He rubbed his hands together. "There is so much of interest to talk to you about. Where to begin?"

He glanced over at Cindy who was trying very hard to keep a smile off her face at his performance so far. Good interrogators played many roles when talking to suspects or witnesses.

"Why not here?" Perkins finally said. He bent forward over the table to get even closer to Ferguson, who involuntarily leaned back. Perkins leaned in even closer.

"You just conned those nice ladies at Sapphire Blue out of all that money. You and that woman. Ashley. You betrayed their friendship. You stole money they need for their retirement. You came into my territory and flim-flammed my people. I'm taking you down and I am going to enjoy it," he announced flatly. He slapped the table.

Red-faced, Ferguson flinched at the sound.

"I hear you flew over here First Class on some fancy airline," Perkins continued aggressively. "Well, when I drag you back it'll be tied to a rope out the back of the plane on Cheapo Airlines."

The collected officers in the sound-proofed viewing room burst into laughter at that image. Someone patted Samantha on her left shoulder. "He's a dynamo, that sheriff of yours." She nodded. "I've never seen an interview quite like this one," he continued, still chuckling.

Perkins pushed a little closer. Ferguson was practically recoiling in an effort to get some breathing room.

"Let's try to sort out this mess. First, the passport stuff, that's between you and Singapore Immigration. And the US government. I can't imagine they are very happy about you using false names and documents and everything...right, Inspector?"

"Very serious," she confirmed.

"Then second, this necklace thing I've heard about. Suspect that's a really big problem down here," he continued as he again looked at Cindy.

"Huge," she agreed. "Huge. The necklace was stolen from an old, highly respected family here that goes back generations. They are outraged. They are demanding justice. We at the Singapore Police are committed to returning the necklace to its rightful home. And ensuring the culprits are punished." She glared across the table. "Fully punished," she concluded slowly. "Long and thoroughly punished."

The image of keelhauling and public floggings hung in the fetid air of the interrogation room.

Samantha felt cheered by the mental pictures. Finally someone was listening to her.

Perkins waited a long moment for Ferguson to contemplate his woeful future.

"Then third, we've got this whole can of scummy, scammy worms you tried to pull off in Port Manatee. My home. My territory. The county I've sworn to protect." He glowered at Ferguson. "You picked the wrong community to try your slimy little games, buster." He leaned forward a little more. "Besides, my dog didn't like you. That was good enough for me."

Ferguson nervously stroked his little stub of a moustache. That fucking dog.

Lieutenant Lee stared at him. Inspector Holmes stared at him. Sheriff Perkins stared at him. The unrelenting camera lens in the corner stared at him.

Ferguson looked around. There was no hope of escape from this horrid little room.

"Look," he began finally while attempting a sordid little smile, "let's figure this out. I think this is all just a big misunderstanding. I was simply trying to let those nice ladies gain some financial independence. There are new financial instruments being developed all the time. Look how many people mocked Bitcoin when it first came out. And then look at how many millionaires it made!"

He coughed and took a sip of water. He could feel himself confidently sliding back into con mode. Talking was what he did. Getting the confidence of victims. Why should these dumb cops be any different?

"If the ladies don't want to wait for their investment to pay off, then of course I'd be happy to refund their money in full. No problem."

He sat back. Smooth, he thought to himself. Convincing.

"Inspector Holmes, in your long career as a distinguished member of the fine Singapore Police Department, have you ever heard of a bigger load of barnyard deposit in your entire life?"

"No, Sheriff Perkins, I don't believe I have. Lieutenant?"

"No, Ma'am. Never. Need big boots to walk in the stuff this guy is spreading."

Perkins smiled at the imagery. He turned back to Ferguson. "Well. The vote is three to zero. You lose."

He stared Ferguson down again. The minutes stretched. Ferguson tried to not squirm on the hard chair, but his body language betrayed him.

"Here's what I'm thinking," Perkins finally said. "Yes you're going to repay all of the ladies in full. And immediately. The entire 1.5 million dollars. Then we're going to—"

"Wait! What? It was only $50,000 from each of the ten women. Er, the investments they made. Voluntarily. What is this 1.5 million?"

Perkins sat back. Then he slapped his thigh and started to laugh. "Inspector. Lieutenant. Make a note of this moment." They both looked at him, puzzled. Perkins laughed some more. He pointed at Ferguson who was red-faced and struggling to understand.

"The...the con man got conned!" Perkins finally spluttered out, laughing. "She never told you about the million she got from Dr. Al-Saadi, did she?"

Ferguson stared at him in disbelief.

"Yeah," Perkins continued, "she got Samira to invest a million bucks of her family's money into this phony currency scam you cooked up. And then she never shared it with you! Nice partner!"

The others in the room caught on immediately and started grinning at the enraged man in the witness chair in the small interrogation cell.

Behind the window, Samantha gasped as it hit her. The other officers were buzzing amongst themselves. This was turning out to be a stunning case. The intrigue. The lies. The back-stabbing and betrayals. Looking at the bitter expression on Ferguson's face she thought, "The double-cross could be our big break!"

Ferguson finally shook his head. "Don't know anything about that." *The bitch. After all he'd taught her. Nice.* Then he thought some more. He looked up at Perkins. A crafty look came to his eyes.

"How about we make a little deal, Sheriff?"

Chapter 77

THE DIAMOND NECKLACE shone warmly on the scratched and filthy table in the interview room at the police station. It was a table that had seen so many tears fall and so much fear exuded and so much sweat poured out. Not to mention the lies.

It had never seen a piece of jewelry like this.

Ashley knew in an instant that it was the real necklace. It spoke to her soul. She reached out to take it. She held it and caressed it. It was so beautiful. It was the most gorgeous thing she had ever owned.

Tears glinted in the corner of her eyes as she turned to Cindy. "How...how did you get it?"

"Our forensics team went over your belongings again. They found a receipt from the post office hidden in an inside pocket of your handbag. Our detectives got to wondering why you would have sent yourself a package through the mail. We got a court order, picked up the parcel, and just look what we found inside."

Cindy paused. "Pretty smart of you, actually. Got rid of the evidence. Got the majesty of our postal service to keep it safe and secure until you returned with the receipt to claim it," she admitted grudgingly.

She shook her head. "The rest of our investigation was pretty simple, actually. We had a nice chat with Massey Ferguson about a similar necklace we found in his apartment. You know him? No? Really. Well, he seems to know you. He got really vocal once he understood how serious the charges against him were going to be. Shared lots with us."

Ashley flushed.

The door to the interview room opened. Perkins stepped in. Ashley's face dropped in shock.

"How lovely to see you again, Ashley," he began as he settled himself.

"Believe the last time was at Sapphire Blue. Samantha's floor. Where you conned some nice ladies out of a bunch of money. Including one particular friend of ours. Samira. A million and a half bucks! For shame, Ashley."

She didn't even try to justify the whole scam. They had her cold. And apparently Ferguson had ratted her out. The bastard.

Still, you never knew. She cleared her throat and headed for the nearest lifeboat.

"Sheriff," she drawled softly. Her southern accent was back. "I was jus' a li'l pawn in Ferguson's con game. I didn't know what was going on. He was the one who thought it all up. I jus' acted as his girlfriend. That can't be against the law?"

"Law of good taste," he grunted. Cindy smiled.

"And this necklace? I was just holding it for a friend. Keeping it safe. He's a jeweler in town. Songdai? Maybe you know him?"

"Interesting story about that," Cindy broke in. "He's my cousin. Just how do you explain his being tied up naked on the bed in your hotel room?"

"He's into kinky sex," Ashley responded innocently. This was a game she could play all day. She batted her eyes at the sheriff. "Sometimes so am I."

Strong hands kept Samantha from plunging into the interview room and clawing the bitch's eyes out.

"So you just happened to mail it to yourself before you left on the cruise?"

"He told me it was a fake. I didn't ever know there was another necklace. I thought it would be safer to mail it to myself and have the post office hold it until I returned, rather than bring it on board a ship. You know, I hear sometimes crooks go on those cruises." She dipped her eyes and thrust her shoulders back.

Samantha fumed. Perkins looked amused. Cindy was getting steamed.

"Yes, that second necklace," she cut in. "Just how did you know there were two necklaces? Identical."

It only took Ashley a second to reply, but both veteran interrogators noticed the hesitation.

"I didn't. I just did what Songdai told me to do. I was kind of scared of him," she confessed in her little-girl voice as she looked appealingly at Perkins. "He could be mean to me."

"What about scamming Dr. Al-Saadi out of a million dollars of her family's investment fund? Ferguson claims he knew nothing about that."

"Ferguson's lying to you. I just did whatever he ordered me to do."

Perkins turned to Cindy. "Isn't it amazing, just amazing, how nothing is Ashley's fault? How men always take advantage of her? What a poor little girl. All alone and helpless in this ocean of mean men."

Cindy grimaced. "Astonishing," she agreed flatly. "Almost unbelievable."

Ashley's hair swirled as she swung her head.

"I don't think it's going to fly, Ashley," continued Perkins relentlessly. "Ferguson says he knew nothing about the million dollars from Samira. He was really upset when we told him." Perkins swivelled to look at Cindy. "Upset. Is that a good word, Inspector?"

"Upset. Royally pissed. Either works."

"Yes. That's when he told us about your scheme with the two necklaces. How you were going to travel to the south of France and sell it to a Russian oligarch for one of his model girlfriends, and then switch it with the fake one when it was being delivered." He paused. "I'd be real careful dealing with those men. They don't have a lot of appreciation for being scammed. They tend to react rather...violently."

Ashley sat back. This wasn't going well. Time to save her own very cute butt.

She looked at Perkins and smiled warmly.

"How about we make a little deal, Sheriff?"

Chapter 78

"Honor among these thieves, my grandmother's army boots!"

Samantha was aflame. She paced around their hotel suite as Perkins and Holmes looked on with awe. And trepidation.

"But honey," Perkins tried.

"Don't 'but honey' me! Making a deal first with that sleazy, slimy little worm Ferguson! And then next with that phony bitch with her batting her eyes at you and sticking her boobs in your face! What were you two thinking?"

Perkins sipped his Tiger as Holmes buried her nose in a large glass of Pinot.

Sometimes the wise move was to hide in the basement until the typhoon passed by.

Samantha ranted for another minute and then finally flung herself onto the sofa, still steaming.

Perkins peeked up at her. After a wait, he finally ventured out of his cave, one paw waving in the air to carefully check on the meteorological conditions.

"What we're trying to accomplish is to get the money back to all of the ladies. Right? Including Samira's family. Right? And to get the necklaces back to Mei-Ling and her family. Right?"

Samantha glared at him but finally gave a curt nod. "So these con artists, these thieves, these liars, these people who invaded our home—they just walk?"

"Nope; no; not at all. Uh-unh."

"Right."

"What we're thinking is this. We get the $1.5 million deposited into that escrow account that Radar set up. It then goes to Panama or wherever, for reasons I don't pretend to understand, and then gets transferred from there into another escrow account at our sheriff's department. From there we can make immediate restitution to the ten women as well as Samira."

"But..."

"Yes, there is a but. If we don't do it this way, they can both fight extradition and tie up all the assets for years. Extradition can be a very long and uncertain process. This is a white-collar crime. No violence, which is often a factor for a judge. There is no guarantee the courts here would concur with an extradition request."

"There will be some violence when I get my hands on that scheming little hussy," said Samantha softly. Perkins blinked. Cindy drank more wine.

"A trial in the US is also problematic," the sheriff continued, "because of, well, some unusual procedures that Cindy and I took here. And each of their lawyers would argue I have a conflict of interest. And no authority here. That is certainly true."

"How does your grandmother feel?" demanded Samantha as she stared at Cindy.

"Much like you, frankly. She is not happy about how her jewelry was taken and abused, and how close we came to losing it for our family and our nation. She seeks…retribution."

Cindy shuddered. Having Mei-Ling seeking retribution for something you had done was not pleasant. Nor a path toward a long, happy and comfortable life.

Fortunately, her grandmama's wrath seemed to be primarily focused on Songdai. With some clever side-stepping, Cindy figured she could escape with only minor flesh wounds.

Then there was Songdai's wife. That was going to be a whole different story for Songdai when Mei-Ling was finished with him. Cindy almost felt sorry for her horny little cousin. Not.

"Immigration here doesn't want anything to do with them. They just want them kicked out of the country. For good."

"So they walk." Samantha's voice was flat and angry.

Perkins cleared his throat. "Well, it's complicated. Once Ashley told us about the scam in Michigan that Ferguson was running, I phoned James Robertson at the FBI. They are now very interested in the two of them."

"And?"

"Well, here's where it all gets a little murky. She wants to give up Ferguson in return for immunity in the Michigan scam and the Florida situation. But then Ferguson has promised to squeal on Ashley and give up the fake ID place in Chicago in return for his immunity in Florida and Michigan. That's a big win for the FBI. They are really interested in shutting down that fake document factory."

Samantha was practically chewing her wine glass. "So is that the end? Is that the highlight of this whole sordid little adventure? People get their money back, fine; Cindy's family gets their necklaces back, good. And these two con men…persons… whatever…win a GET OUT OF JAIL FREE card?"

Cindy cleared her throat. "We talked to the crown attorney about all of this. Frankly, nobody wants to touch it. They are not sure a crime has been committed on Singaporean soil because of Songdai's involvement. No money was ever paid for the necklace. No bill of sale exchanged. No clear evidence. And the necklaces are now returned. Superintendent Keong, my boss, is also onside. He just wants this whole pile of burning crap out of Singapore."

She drank deeply and banged her glass down. "Look, Samantha, I'm not happy either. But sometimes in police work, you've got to play the hand that is dealt. The whole messy situation…it has gotten too big, too ugly and too complicated. It could tie up lawyers and the courts and police here in Singapore for years. The expense would be huge. The end result would be…uncertain. My bosses see this as an elegant solution. It gets these two out of the country and closes a bunch of books."

"Besides," Perkins added, "James at the FBI is willing to avoid an extradition and just escort them back to the US. He figures once his interrogators get their hands on them, there'll be other crimes and misdemeanors that will result in real jail time."

Samantha sat fuming. The logic was irrefutable. The result was horrific. She believed that people who broke the law should be punished. Particularly when they had hurt her friends.

Silence in the suite.

Finally she shrugged her shoulders in dismay and looked at the two police veterans.

"I hate this. I always will. But if you both think this is the way to go, then I'll have to accept that. You are the professionals. I trust you both. But I won't like it. Ever. It is a lousy, lousy ending."

She poured another round of wine and Perkins popped another Tiger.

It was very quiet in the room.

CHAPTER 79

SAMANTHA WAS CHECKING out the makeup counters at the huge duty-free store in the Schiphol Airport in Amsterdam. Perkins was many counters away, looking at boxes of Cuban cigars. Sometimes he enjoyed a nice cigar after a special dinner.

Their long flight back to Florida was routed through the capital of the Netherlands for a change of planes.

She and Perkins were both tired after the long flight from Singapore. There was also the unhappy—and, to Samantha, the repulsive and unsatisfactory—conclusion to the entire affair involving the disgusting little twerp Ferguson, and the scheming shrew Ashley, who kept trying to seduce the big lug of a sheriff with whom she happened to be in lust and probably also in love.

She sighed. There was still some unresolved tension between her and Perkins.

At least, she thought to herself, she had been able to sneer at the two con men—she still couldn't decide if con woman was a word—on their way back to the US and what she hoped would be a very uncertain future.

James Robertson at the FBI had sent a junior agent to escort the two back to American soil. They happened to be on the same flight as Samantha and the sheriff, although many rows and several cabin classes behind them.

Still, it had given her considerable *schadenfreude* to have the flight attendant fill a glass with champagne so she could stroll back and scowl at Ashley and Ferguson. They were in A, B and C in row 38.

Naturally Ashley had sweet-talked her way into the window seat. Samantha sniffed. The FBI agent assigned to bring them back had introduced himself to Perkins before the flight. Steve somebody. He was in the aisle seat. He looked as if he'd just graduated from Quantico the week before.

Samantha checked out the lipstick displays. A couple of interesting shades. She glanced at Perkins at the opposite wall. He was still salivating over the walk-in cigar humidor.

She watched a woman in very high heels and a rather short skirt teeter through duty-free. Her husband trailed, dragging two big roller suitcases, two carry-ons, and what looked like a pet carrier. As a veteran traveller, Samantha was wearing comfortable slacks and flat shoes.

She moved on to the moisturizing creams. A lady of a certain age— well, any age—could never have too many moisturizers. Maybe she should get some for Perkins. Like most men, he didn't pay enough attention to skin care. She rubbed one of them on her finger. A little too—

Samantha startled the clerk as she suddenly whirled around from the make-up counter. That scent! That disgusting cloying lily-of-the-valley perfume that only Ashley wore! Samantha would recognize it anywhere.

But Ashley was supposed to be under FBI escort as they changed planes for the US. Samantha quickly surveyed the crowded duty-free. No one looked like—wait! That woman in the rose pink raincoat. It was way too long for the person wearing it. No woman would buy something that badly fitting. And the hat was inexcusable.

She moved away from the counter and began to trail the woman. She could still smell the distinctive aroma. She speeded up. Suddenly the woman looked back. Samantha finally saw her face. It was Ashley! She started running.

Samantha hollered to Perkins as she began chasing after Ashley. He dropped the cigar box and started pushing his way toward Samantha, but he was a long way behind.

Ashley tried to swerve through the tight aisles in the store. She pushed two women out of the way. They were outraged. They hollered at her in Slovenian. Ashley didn't pause to apologize.

Samantha gained a few feet. Ashley looked back again, and then redoubled her effort. She grabbed a rack of clothes and threw it on the floor.

Samantha had run track in high school and her first two years of college. Her long legs had made her a natural for the hurdles. Those old instincts came back in a flash. She adjusted her steps, leapt up and over the rack sprawled on the floor, and kept chasing Ashley.

People were screaming now. Perkins was running hard but he was still several aisles back. The FBI agent was nowhere in sight. Ashley broke left around the handbag counter and headed for the booze. Samantha gained a few more precious steps. Ashley was not built for sprinting.

Samantha glanced up. Ashley appeared to be heading for the adjacent train station. Damn. If she got on a train she could disappear anywhere in Europe. Samantha closed the gap a little more. Ashley broke through the gin display and tossed a bottle of Tanqueray at Samantha. She deflected it and heard it smash onto the floor as she darted ahead.

Ashley was tiring. People were pointing and shouting. Samantha closed a little more. Just as Ashley was nearing the turnstiles for the trains, Samantha launched herself forward. It was a diving tackle that any middle linebacker for the Chicago Bears would have been proud to execute.

She crashed into Ashley's back. They both went down in a heap. Samantha could hear the WHOOSH as the air went out of her captive.

They lay there, Samantha on top. She was focused on sitting on Ashley to keep her still. They were both panting. Samantha finally looked up.

Four armor-clad, dark grey uniformed anti-terrorist police surrounded her. They were all wearing helmets. They were all holding short, black, lethal-looking automatic machine guns. Those were all pointed at her.

CHAPTER 80

NOBODY MOVED FOR a long moment. Samantha was terrified of blinking. Ashley was still trying to catch her breath, so blessedly she had nothing to say at that moment. That was a rare and pleasant interlude, thought Samantha in one part of her brain. The rest of her brain was too paralysed by fear to contribute to the conversation.

Perkins arrived a moment later, with Stevie the FBI dweeb in tow.

He held up his badge for the security officers to see. He nudged Steverino to do the same.

"American law enforcement officers," he introduced himself. "This woman," he said pointing at Samantha, "is working closely with us to apprehend this criminal," he said pointing at Ashley.

The guards lived in Amsterdam. They all spoke English and three other languages. The guns were slowly lifted and their safeties relocked.

Samantha let a long breath exhale. She hadn't even realized she had been holding her breath. She had been too scared by the guns to move.

Perkins continued to quietly take charge. He gestured to the senior corporal, who nodded. He then reached down and helped Samantha up. Steve rolled Ashley onto her back. The four security men gasped when they realized that she was already wearing handcuffs.

The crowd around was buzzing at the excitement. Cellphones were turned on to record this—whatever it was—public spectacle.

Perkins grabbed Samantha firmly by the arm. "This one's mine," he grinned at Steve. "You figure out the rest. I suggest you say the FBI will pay for any damage in the duty-free." He stopped and then added, "Oh yeah. There's a box of Cuban cigars that is going to be damaged in the mayhem. That goes on your tab as well."

He looked again at the senior corporal. "Let us know if you need a statement. Our plane leaves in, ah, an hour and fifty-eight minutes. We'll be in the first class lounge if you need us."

He guided Samantha out of the little circle and pushed through the crowd. Now that the danger was gone, the crowd was intensely interested in the next act in this very dramatic play.

Steve gaped at Perkins as he and Samantha retreated. He finally hauled Ashley to her feet. He kept a firm grip on her manacled hands. The four security guards waited. "Well," he stuttered, "first of all, there's a man down that aisle with one hand cuffed to a chair..."

The guards looked at each other in wonderment. Americans.

Chapter 81

"HERE'S WHAT HAPPENED," Perkins began as he leaned closer to Samantha. They were seated in the first class cabin for the final leg of their long journey back to Florida.

They each had one hand filled with a glass, and their other hand filled with the other's hand. Samantha's sprint to stop Ashley's escape had broken through the wall that had developed at the end of their Singapore adventure because of Samantha's dissatisfaction at the end result.

"After I got you settled in the lounge, the security people wanted a statement. Naturally. Police always want a statement. I gave them a much-edited version. Stevie, however, spilled his guts." Perkins sighed at the youngster's naiveté.

"Naturally it was vintage Ashley. She did her usual poor little girl act with Steve. He fell for it. She said she had to go to the bathroom. He cuffed her hands in front and sent her in. She goes in wearing her dark blue coat. It's a big bathroom of course, and she starts conning some nice women in there that she was being abducted into a white slavery ring. She shows them her handcuffs. The women rally around. They give her that pink raincoat and a floppy hat to help disguise her. Some money for the train to go to Rotterdam; they give her somebody's aunt's name who will keep her safe there. Then they all go out the door of the bathroom together, with Ashley hidden in the middle of the pack. Stevie never saw 'em. He was looking for Ashley wearing her navy coat. Kid got scammed big time." He sipped his Tiger beer. "Kid'll have some explaining to do to James Robertson," he said gleefully.

Samantha smiled at that image. She sipped her own glass of champagne. It just seemed to be fitting to enjoy her own celebration.

"Anyway, after a few minutes she doesn't appear. Stevie starts to panic. He handcuffs Ferguson to a chair, goes looking for a female security officer to help him. That's about when you discovered Ashley sneaking off to board a train to Rotterdam." He paused. "How did you see through the disguise?"

"Her scent. It is very distinctive. I always disliked it. I recognized it immediately when she waltzed into the duty-free to hide in the crowd there."

"Huh. Well, you're certainly the hero of the day. What a great tackle! I'm very proud of you."

She tightened her grip on his hand. They clinked glasses. The flight attendant was happy to bring them more.

"Instinct or something, I guess," Samantha said, eyes shining at the memory. "The air went out of her like a popped balloon when she hit the floor. Oh, thank you," she nodded to the flight attendant as she poured. "I have to confess," she whispered to Perkins who leaned in closer, "that it was very satisfying."

He erupted in laughter.

"Anyway, she will be charged with escaping custody and resisting arrest and who know what else the FBI will slap her with. She'll end up doing some hard time," Perkins promised her.

Samantha smiled in satisfaction. Justice. Finally.

Meal service began. Samantha chose the fish, naturally. Perkins chose the steak, naturally. They napped for a bit. The flight attendant tossed an extra blanket over their hands after they awoke and started to fool around rather ambitiously, just so the other passengers wouldn't complain.

They broke it up to devour warm cookies and ice cream sundaes.

Samantha stretched and looked at her watch. They would be landing in about forty-five minutes.

"They aren't even on this plane, are they?"

"No. Robertson got 'em locked up for the night with Dutch authorities. They'll ship 'em back tomorrow. The Dutch wanted a really full statement about the entire episode. The kid needed help with that, so James sent another agent to get them all out of trouble. The Dutch are pretty edgy about terrorism at airports and on trains. Can't blame them. They've had some bad incidents."

They both drank more water. "There was talk of giving you a citation or something for your actions at the airport. You might hear from the Dutch ambassador or somebody sometime. They were pretty impressed with what you did."

Samantha blushed prettily. "I'm glad that Cindy got it all worked out in Singapore," she said to change the subject. "Mei-Ling was very gracious about forgiving her. Then she gave her the necklaces to keep. Cindy says she will treasure them."

"And the police cleaned up everything very efficiently," Perkins added with respect. "Very professional." He paused. "I think we're probably welcome back in either country."

Samantha laughed lightly as the plane began its descent. She could hear the landing gear lock down.

The lights of the Tampa International Airport appeared in the distance. Dawn had just broken. The colors were gorgeous as the sun reflected off the Gulf Coast.

Chapter 82

ROSIE WENT CRAZY greeting her mommy and daddy. She danced around them, bestowing doggie kisses with enthusiasm. Her tail-wagging could have powered ten homes for a month.

When Samantha finally came up for air, she asked Kim how Rosie had been. "Fine. But I took her over to check your mail one day. The mailman had just arrived and had that parcel you get from Mama Jones at Starwind Construction. You know, the smoked brisket that she does. Man, that's good. We ate it all, by the way. Well, Rosie went nuts for it, of course. She practically set up a tent and camped out there waiting for the mailman each day."

The two women linked arms as they dragged suitcases, travel bags, packages of gifts and Rosie's leash through the condo's lobby. Perkins just looked at them. His one suitcase sat in lonely splendor in the taxi's trunk.

"Er," he began.

Samantha stopped short. She turned around and then laughed. "Oops. Sorry. Rosie, go to daddy. You can come over tomorrow."

Rosie smelled the air to make sure there was no stray brisket hiding in the lobby, and then trotted over to Perkins.

"Let's go home," he told her. She wagged her tail and led him to the taxi. He turned and waved at the ladies. "I'll call you tomorrow," he promised. "Thanks for everything, Samantha." He grinned. "It was an adventure." Kim looked at him. "She'll tell you all about it," he said as he followed Rosie out the door.

The taxi driver had been waiting. The meter was running. He didn't care. He did complain about the dog.

"Service dog," Perkins snapped. "For my fear of rogue taxi drivers." The driver shut up and drove. The meter kept running.

By the time Samantha had unpacked, it was time for lunch with Kim. Then they wandered down to the pool to relax in the sun and catch up.

The Wives were ensconced in their regal corner. Several of them rushed up to greet Samantha. There was anxiety in their eyes.

"It is all good," she confided. "I can't say anything official yet, but tomorrow the sheriff will meet with all of you." She smiled at them. "You should all relax and enjoy tonight. I think you'll be very happy."

There were pats and hugs and words of thanks. Kim had grabbed three lounge chairs near their corner. As Samantha settled onto her towel, she could hear the husbands nattering.

"Geez, George. You remember Christie Brinkley?"

"Oh yeah. God she's good looking. Better now than as a teen model."

"Right. Hot. Well, now look at that hot tub over there, the one you usually go in at night. What I'm telling you is that there is a better chance of Christie Brinkley joining you in that hot tub tonight than there is of your wife saying YES to your going to Las Vegas by yourself for your birthday."

Samantha couldn't help but laugh out loud. "I see little has changed," she confided to Kim.

"He's had a tough week," another of the men said, talking about a state politician.

"He's had a tough decade," replied another.

Kim and Samantha eavesdropped shamelessly as the conversations zipped around.

"He is an idiot. Can't do anything. Useless. He's such a klutz that he kills the artificial plants in his condo."

"How do you get a sweet little old lady to use the F-word? You get another sweet little old lady to yell 'BINGO!'"

"The guy is from a different era. He's Archie Bunker in the twenty-first century. It's not a good fit."

More beers were popped open. The conversation continued. Kim and Samantha remained fascinated.

"He won't offer an opinion until his wife tells him what it is."

"Hey, did you hear that some drunk driver crashed his stolen truck through a wooden fence around a farm pasture? The cows got angry— they surrounded him and kept him from running away until the deputies arrived and arrested the man. There's talk now about a good-citizen certificate for the herd."

Laughing, Samantha and Kim slipped into the sparkling blue water of the pool. Samantha sank gratefully up to her neck and let the warm water ease some of the travel aches. This was definitely a hot tub day.

Two women from Wisconsin stepped into the pool. They were having an intense conversation. "My teenage daughter says I'm nosy. At least that's what she wrote in her secret diary."

"Ah," Samantha said with a soft smile. "It's good to be home." Then she told Kim all about her trip.

CHAPTER 83

THE TEN WIVES were assembled in the conference room of the Sheriff's Department. It had taken three SUVs, two vans, and one sedan to ferry them all. Cliques.

They were nervous and feisty. Samantha was tucked into the corner of the big room. The women were greeted by Mary, the sheriff's assistant, Deputy Chad, and a public information officer. There were no cameras.

Perkins arrived quickly. The ladies had swooped down on the coffee and donuts—it was a police station, after all—and were seated at the table.

"Welcome. I am happy to have you here this morning. And not to prolong the suspense, I am happy to tell you that you will all be receiving full restitution of the money you 'invested' with those two con artists, Ashley Monroe and Massey Ferguson."

He paused for the applause and thanks from the ladies. It was very genuine.

"It will not surprise you to learn that those were not their real names," he continued. "They are—were—professional con men. Women. Whatever. It was their business to scam smart people out of money. You should not feel any embarrassment at what happened to you."

There were looks of relief around the table. Mixed with some abashed feelings, despite the sheriff's kind words.

"Besides, this is Florida. Historically the home of scammers and con artists galore. This is where Charles Ponzi ended up after his notorious schemes. Where Bernie Madoff took billions from nice people like you. There will be no publicity about any of this, or your inadvertent involvement in it, from our office."

That drew relieved looks around the table. The Wives had maintained complete secrecy from their husbands over this whole sordid incident. Now it seemed they were actually going to get away with it. There were happy grins from the ten women.

"I can tell you that the FBI has taken over the case and has the two scoundrels in custody," Perkins continued. He paused and grinned. "You may thank Samantha for that."

The ladies turned to look at Samantha. Questions were bubbling up, as yet unspoken.

Perkins continued. "The FBI may pursue further charges. I think both of them will face long jail sentences. They both have, ah, lengthy backgrounds in the con game. We suspect other instances of their activities will come out in the investigation."

He sipped some coffee. "In Singapore, I was just there to carry the suitcases. Of which there were many," he added with a glare toward the corner. "It was Samantha who drove the entire process to get us to Asia and every crazy thing that happened over there…and who made the flying tackle that stopped Ashley," he concluded with a chuckle. "She may or may not choose to tell you about that, but she's the real hero here."

Applause and smiles from the women around the table. Two of them even put down their donuts to clap. Powdered sugar flew.

"Now," he concluded, "I know you are all busy. Deputy Chad has a check for each of you, and a receipt to be signed. And with that, I think we are done."

There was an uncomfortable pause as the sheriff gathered his papers and prepared to leave.

"No. We are not done." It came from the quietest of the Wives. Everybody froze. "We first of all owe you our thanks. And Samantha. But you and your staff resolved this in the best possible way for us." Luanne took a deep breath. "I for one want to give something back. We weren't real smart about this whole thing. None of us," she glared around the table. Nobody argued with her.

"My church believes in tithing. So do I. So I want to donate $5,000 to a charity of your choice, Sheriff."

The other women immediately sat up and joined in the chorus. "Yes. Good idea, Luanne. Right. Let's all do it."

A moment later there were pledges totalling $50,000 on the table. Perkins was stunned. Samantha was flabbergasted. These were The Mean Wives who terrorized Sapphire Blue and their husbands?

It took the sheriff a long moment to speak. "That is…most generous of you. Not needed. We just did our job. But thank you." He turned his hat around in his hands a couple of times.

"We have no special charity here. Our department supports several causes and our staff volunteer with a number of charities and community groups. But there's one that has always had a special place in my heart. And that's the groups that come together to feed kids breakfast in the morning. It just breaks my heart to think of children going to school hungry. So if it is all right with all of you, I'd like to give your very generous donation to that feed-the-kids program."

The women spontaneously stood and applauded him. They came forward to shake his hand and thank him.

Samantha sat in her corner fighting back tears. No wonder she loved the big galoot.

Checks were handed out. Receipts were signed. Promises to get the donation checks to Mary were made. Donuts were finished.

Perkins escaped out the side door to go back to work. Samantha continued to sit quietly in her corner as the Wives departed. They were in a jovial mood. Samantha expected it would be very celebratory at the pool that afternoon—and their husbands would never understand why.

Mary came over to her after tidying up the room. She sat down and looked at Samantha.

"This is a good day. We don't have all that many good days in our business. Too often it is death and mayhem and sadness. The sheriff told me a little about what you did over there. Good job."

She rose and headed back to her own office. She stopped and looked back at Samantha with a grin. "Oh. And great tackle!"

Chapter 84

SAMANTHA REPORTED FOR work at the Delvecchio Bridge development project the next morning. She met with Starwind Construction CEO Elliott Webster.

"You can really see the foundations taking shape," he explained as they toured the site wearing safety boots and hard hats. He'd presented Samantha with her own hat with her name inscribed on it. She was touched.

They stopped to chat with some of the neighborhood leaders. They were excited about the layout of the children's playground and the community park that Samantha had designed as part of her contribution to the multi-million dollar project.

Neighborhood liaison was also part of her new responsibilities. Samantha spent an hour listening to the women as Webster conferred with the construction foremen. She made notes about a couple of suggestions. It felt good to be back working in her city, she thought.

"How was Singapore?" Webster asked her at lunch.

"A really interesting city. I liked it a lot. And it turned out to be more, uh, exciting than I'd expected."

He waited, obviously expecting to hear more. Samantha kept eating her salad. She'd decided not to talk about the frantic chase and the scams and back-stabbing. If Perkins decided to keep it quiet when he could have revealed it all to the media and gotten a lot of favorable publicity, she thought she could honor it the same way.

Their talk turned to Port Manatee city hall. Webster had become a keen observer of what went on there. After all, he now had a huge investment in the city.

"The manager, Roy Crawford. Smart guy. Good to do business with. Gets things done," he told her approvingly.

He worked on his cheeseburger and fries for a moment. "And Mayor Rodriguez is really developing a good touch. I think she's going to be a great mayor for this city."

Samantha couldn't resist. "And the new councillor for Ward 3?"

"Well, there's a problem there."

Her heart sank. This is what she'd feared—getting put in the middle of a situation between her boss and her dear friend whom she had gotten elected to city council.

Webster paused. He poked some fries into the ketchup. Samantha squirmed, waiting for the onslaught. He chewed some more fries, enjoying the crisp salty flavor.

Finally he stopped chewing, put down his burger and looked at her. "The problem is…" he paused dramatically. "She's working too damn hard."

He grinned at the expression on Samantha's face. "HA! I finally got you back! Took me months, but I did it!"

He picked up the final two bites of his burger and chewed happily. Samantha sagged back. What the hell was—Oh. "I get it. For my telling you I didn't eat meat when I visited your company last year. The look on your face that day…"

She grinned at him. "Okay, now we're even. You got me good."

Just to punctuate his triumph, he stuck her with the check.

CHAPTER 85

"I'M TAKING YOU to La Casa Adrianna," Samantha told Samira and Kim.

"Never heard of it."

"No, it is pretty exclusive. It's a good thing you'll be with me, because they wouldn't let either of you badly dressed bums in."

Samira was in a stunning scarlet Givenchy dress. Kim was wearing a peacock-blue dress down to her ankles that swirled and sparkled.

Samantha wore a black sheath from a young designer in New York. It looked simple, but to a knowledgeable eye it was the elegant cut that allowed it to subtly cling to her. She loved the way it moved on her body.

The limo driver had a bit of trouble finding the out-of-the-way boutique hotel where PJ Hozworm had taken Samantha for tea. It seemed a long time ago.

It had been tea then. Tonight it would be wine, and lots of it, so the driver was necessary. Besides, it made the evening that much more special.

Samantha's two closest friends were enchanted with the small hotel. "It was converted from a wealthy family's hacienda," she explained as they walked slowly through the lobby with its polished wood and lovely art. "Very private. Very exclusive. We'll be the bottom of the social ladder here tonight."

Rosita greeted them at the front of the small, perfect restaurant. "Senorita Samantha! It is so nice to have you back with us. Welcome."

She escorted them to a beautifully set table for three in the corner of the room. The lighting was modest and flattering. Candles flickered on the tables and along the wall sconces.

A waiter helped to get them seated. "This is Mateo. He will be looking after you tonight. This is Señorita Stevens, Councillor Sharpe, and Dr. Al-Saadi," said Rosita.

Samantha was blown away. She had only used the first names of her friends to make the reservation. Somebody had done their homework.

Kim and Samira were captivated.

"I never knew this existed," Kim exclaimed.

Samira shook her head. She turned to survey the room. "Fabulous. Do I have to have an invitation from you every time I want to come here, or can I come on my own?"

Samantha shook her head. "Only with me. You wouldn't rank high enough."

The three friends giggled. Mateo approached discreetly.

"May I bring you a drink? Perhaps a glass of sherry to begin?"

"That's a lovely idea. What do you suggest?"

"We have a very drinkable Oloroso variety that has been in our cellar for a few years. It is ready now for drinking. Perhaps with a bit of Manchego to sharpen the taste buds for dinner? It is a Spanish sheep's milk cheese that provides a beautiful contrast on the tongue."

The gala evening began. The aged sherry and the cheese were a wonderful match. Mateo carefully guided them through each course. He paired small glasses of different wines with the plates of tapas that included the famed Spanish potato omelette; then fried squid; croquettes; and finally garlic shrimp.

Mateo suggested the paella for the main course. He assured them that the chef was from Valencia and made it in the traditional manner. He then daringly paired the spicy rice, chicken, and seafood dish with a cinsaut-grenache grape blend. The chilled light red wine was a perfect counterpoint to the deeply flavorful main course.

An elegant vanilla flan concluded their memorable dinner.

Rosita came over a couple of times to check on their meal. The three ladies all gushed over the food, the service and the ambience. Rosita smiled approvingly and went to check on the other tables. An NBA star enjoying a night off was at one. A US senator sat at another. A retired astronaut dined with her husband.

After a moment to settle the wonderful meal and allow Mateo to serve them coffee, Samantha tapped a well-manicured nail on the tablecloth.

"Did you enjoy dinner?"

"Fabulous. One of the great meals of my life," Kim said promptly.

"I agree. A marvellous discovery. I loved it," said Samira. "But it was odd…did you notice there were no prices on the menu?"

Samantha grinned at her. "No, they are very tactful here. I guess if you have to ask, you can't afford to be here. They just bring the bill at the end. But that doesn't matter to Kim or me, because we're sticking you with the tab."

Samira looked bemused. Kim grinned.

"But," Samantha continued, "to help you out of your poverty-stricken state, here's a little contribution."

With that she reached into her purse and extracted a sealed envelope. She passed it to Samira who took it, puzzled. Samantha nodded at her. Samira quietly tore it open and took out two papers.

Then she gasped. There was a check for one million dollars made out to her. It was on the Sheriff's escrow account. The second paper was the formal receipt for her signature.

After a long silence she exclaimed, "Oh my lord, I never thought I'd see that money again. When you said you and the sheriff had made some progress, well, I…"

She broke off to wipe away a tear. "This was my family's money. For our global investment account. Losing it would have been embarrassing. Now I won't have to 'fess up about my stupidity. My father and brother would never let me hear the end of that!"

She swallowed hard. "Do I get to hear how you did this? How did you recover the full amount?"

Samantha gave her a shortened version of the Asian adventure. She made a point of how much she disliked Ashley. And Massey. And his moustache.

Kim was laughing as she listened to the story that Samantha had told her in the pool a few days earlier. When Samantha got to the duty-free store, Kim interrupted her.

"No. Let me." She turned to Samira. "Sammy long-legs here starts chasing the bimbo through the duty-free store. Gin bottles are flying, clothes are getting thrown about, and she hurdles a clothing rack and just keeps chasing the bitch. Ashley is heading for escape on the train, but Samantha keeps chasing her and leaping over everything in sight. Then just before she gets to the train turnstiles, Samantha launches herself, hits the rotten little babe square in the back with a tackle, flattens her on the floor, knocks the breath out of her, squishes her boobs on the floor, and is sitting on her back in triumph when she's surrounded by half the Dutch army pointing guns at her!"

Samira was laughing and gasping at the graphic images.

"Anyway, Perkins finally shows up, flashes his badge and somehow talks their way out of the situation. He leaves some little FBI kid to clean up the mess and pay for the damages. And then, Perkins sneaked back into the duty-free, got a box of really expensive cigars, dropped it on the floor so the corner got damaged, and then told the clerk to charge it to the FBI along with all the other damage in the store!"

It took a few minutes for the three of them to compose themselves and finish the story. Samira was entranced. She was particularly interested in the diamond necklace. "It is my mother's birthday soon," she mused. "Do you think they'd sell it?"

Samantha and Kim had known her family was mega-rich, but this idea was way beyond their pay grade. Samantha shook her head. "Never. Family heirloom." Samira nodded. She respected that.

Mateo offered liqueurs and more coffee. He brought tiny, handmade chocolate truffles on a delicate china plate.

"Last topic of the night," Samantha announced. She pointed at Kim. "Her."

Kim blinked. "Hey. What did I do?"

"You're doing too good, that's what. A political talent scout or mastermind or whatever he is has spotted you. He thinks you're headed for bigger things politically. 'Higher office' are the words he used. He suggested that you may not be quite the idiot that Samira and I know you to be."

Kim snorted derisively. Samira looked amused.

"Anyway. This clever little man suggested that we should start doing some fundraising for you. Now. Get out there in front of the next election before everybody else does. Start building a broader base of support for you. I like the idea."

Kim was nodding thoughtfully. "Makes sense. I never thought of that."

"No, I hadn't either. As your campaign manager, I thought I was done, but apparently I have to keep running your life. Nobody warned me about that."

More snorts.

"He specifically suggested we go after professional women. Not enough of them are engaged in the political process. Lots of them have lots of money. And smarts. So how do we tap into that revenue for you, and get them in your corner?"

Dead silence at the table. Nobody looked at the other.

Finally Samira looked at Kim. "I guess the first question is: Do you want a career in politics? Do you want to continue in public life?"

Kim played with the spoon still at her place setting. "I guess the short answer is, yes. I am really enjoying the city council work. I love working with people. And in a few ways, I'm having an impact. That is really rewarding." She waggled her head. "Higher office? I have no idea what that would look like or how it would be. But eventually? I wouldn't say no."

"Okay, so we start building a war chest for you. See what develops. There's nothing wrong with having some money in the bank in political life, just in case something comes along," Samantha said.

Kim kept playing with her cutlery. "But what do women want out there in fundraising land? How do we appeal to them? There are so many fundraisers for so many good causes. It is hard to have something new, unique..."

More silence. The senator and his guests got up to leave.

"Kim asks a good question," Samira observed. "What do women want? How do we cut through that clutter in the fund-raising world?"

They batted ideas around. Clothes. Shoes. Business contacts. Days at the spa. Wine. Male strippers. Wine. Trips. Male strippers.

Nothing was connecting.

"Look," Samantha said with frustration. "We need to really focus." The NBA power forward looked over at the three women as he stood up. It took a long time for him to stand up to his full height. He was dressed in a custom-tailored suit. His entourage was not quite as sharp.

Rosita checked her dining room. There was only one other table still full: An older man with what might be his niece. His quite young niece.

"Let's think about a party of some kind. Get the ladies to an interesting venue. Somewhere they probably haven't been." Samantha looked around. "This place would be fabulous, but I don't think they would allow it."

"Good," said Samira. "We take them to a great new spot. Then what do we do with them? What's the attraction?"

Samantha kicked her tiring brain into gear. It was about nine in the morning in Singapore, and her body was still somewhere over the Atlantic Ocean.

"Well, we've got to feed 'em. Canapés, whatever. Easy. And a special drink. What are women drinking these days?"

Kim snapped her fingers. "Mixed drinks are really coming back. Cocktails. Old-fashioneds. Cosmos. Rob Roys. All of those."

"Great. That's a start. What about, 'Krazy Kim's Cocktails'? No, that sounds like a cheap bar. 'Kim's Krazy Kocktail party'? Doesn't sound right yet," Samira shrugged.

Samantha tapped her nail on the table again. She looked down at hand.

"Hey! That's it! That's it! What else do women love? Spa treatments! Manicures. Pedis."

Kim and Samira looked at her strangely.

"No, you don't get it! That's the party theme. That's the attraction for these women. Something completely different. We can have it at my condo at Sapphire Blue. We'll hire some girls from a beauty school. We get a bartender. We get a caterer to do great tapas. And we invite this exclusive list of leading women in business, society, whatever. We'll charge them, I don't know, five hundred, maybe a thousand bucks apiece for Kim's Political Action Committee."

Kim and Samira were nodding now. "Yeah, I like it."

Samantha drummed her fingernails on the tablecloth. "A name. The hook. We'll call it...something special, something different to attract them...a party...'Kim's Private Mixer,' playing on the mixed drinks? 'Exclusive Mixer'? We need to put on a special event that they have to attend and they'll love and where Kim can talk to them and—wait! I've got it!"

Samantha paused to build the suspense. Samira and Kim were staring at her. Samantha smiled like a shark before lunch.

"And this is the event that will start Kim on her rocketing political path:

Ladies, I am happy to announce the title theme for our first private and exclusive Kim Sharpe fundraising party: MARTINIS & MANICURES."

— — —

About the Author

GORD HUME IS the author and creator of the popular "Samantha and the Sheriff" adventures.

He is also the author of seven non-fiction books on building better cities and improving local governments. He has enjoyed an award-winning career in broadcasting, newspapers, and business.

Gord was elected to city council four times. He is a sought-after public speaker who has appeared at major conferences in the United States, Canada, Europe, Asia, and New Zealand.

Gord loves exploring the culture, cuisine, and history of people and nations around the world.

Enjoy all the "Samantha and the Sheriff" adventures:

Sapphire Blue
Alligator Alley
Singapore Bling
Martinis & Manicures
Torches & Trouble
www.gordhume.com